CHLOË WALFORD

Catching the Nightjar

Brass Loupe
Publishing

First published by Brass Loupe Publishing 2021

Second edition

ISBN: 978-1-7399089-2-8

Illustration by Rachel O'Callaghan

This novel is dedicated to all those who roam the world's periphery.

Preface

As a child, I spent many summers amid the sun-soaked fields of rural Provence. I could describe every inch of that old farmhouse from memory—the dried corn hanging from the ceiling beams, Mr Chauvin's cherry tree creaking in the heat, and the eternal metronome of the cicada.

It was there that I made two important discoveries: firstly, that my love of France ran deeper than a fondness of its language, later guiding me from a Bachelor's degree to calling Paris home for many years; the second was a chapel perched on a mountain ridge that my siblings and I came across once during a hike.

Judging by its exterior, the stone had undergone centuries of sun, snow, and wind. Its location, however—a fifty-minute climb from the village—indicated that this secluded place of worship was no longer the locals' choice for Sunday Mass. With barely room for nine chairs inside, it was difficult to imagine a service ever having taken place there, but the pot of wilting flowers on the altar swiftly ended our assumption that we had been the first group to venture this far. So, too, did the tea-coloured letter hanging on the wall.

A series of enquiries to our neighbours would reveal that the origin of this document remained something of a mystery. Legend told that it had washed up in a bottle on a beach over a hundred years ago. Its author? Unknown. If a signature had ever existed, it had long been destroyed by the sea on its journey from wherever the bottle was thrown.

In time, a combination of curiosity and my acquisition of more reliable linguistic skills brought me back to the chapel. What I found when I translated the letter has stayed with me since, and it is this message that I wish to share with you now:

My dear friend,

Michel de Montaigne once wrote that 'the greatest thing in the world is to know how to belong to oneself'. Today, these words fill me with meaning, for I have finally come to realise that the more I see of the people in this world, the more I am able to understand them.

I, like everyone, am part of an expanding tapestry, held together by thousands of interconnected threads. Beauty, strength, fear, loneliness; these are not qualities of which one can either be in possession or wanting—they are the strands of humanity itself, upon which each of us is placed differently, from one end to another.

This is, I believe, the essence of what unites us, along with one simple but ever-neglected truth: that wherever we may fall on these threads, we are lucky to have been part of the tapestry at all.

* * *

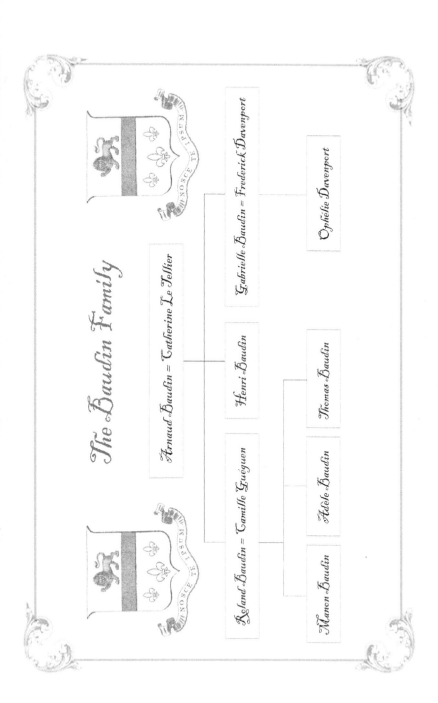

The Baudin Family

Arnaud Baudin = Catherine Le Tellier

Roland Baudin = Camille Guéguen   Henri Baudin   Gabrielle Baudin = Frederick Davenport

Manon Baudin   Adèle Baudin   Thomas Baudin   Ophélie Davenport

I

Summer

1

The Body

22 October 1871, The Moreau Institute of Botany and Horticulture, Aixelles, France.

Murky clouds were swallowing the sky as Isabelle entered the gardens of the Institute. While Mr and Mrs Moreau attended a function across the lake, their daughter's nurse escorted her down the path towards the greenhouses, where it would be safe for Isabelle to play.

It was a bleak autumn evening—the air heavy and agitated. Early signs of fog had relieved the groundskeepers of their duties for the afternoon. But beneath the blanket of silence formed by their departure, nature's stirrings warned of something more sinister than a storm.

The wind encircled Isabelle as she sat humming to herself. Even the trees from the orchards seemed to be stretching their limbs towards her with every murmur of the breeze.

At five o'clock, Isabelle's nurse left to return her medicine bottle to the house. The dropping temperature hastened her steps, but by the time she had re-emerged to bring Isabelle back indoors, the child was nowhere to be seen. Across the dirt lay only the scattered shards of what was once a porcelain doll; beside them, a single set of footprints led the nurse to the fence separating the gardens from the woods. And there—fluttering from a nail in the loose planks—hung the powder blue sash from Isabelle's dress.

A hoax, a childish game; the elapsing minutes saw theories surge among Isabelle's search party. With each cry of her name, the expectation of finding the girl in a favourite comfort spot or hiding place felt more remote to them. How their expressions would drain when distant screams finally led them to the crime scene.

From the woods behind her body, demands for answers were met forthwith in the form of Kacper Smolak—a notorious local trader—stumbling towards the group. In his coat pocket, the ransom note to Mr and Mrs Moreau offered a motive for the abduction; across his face and torso, child-size scratches confirmed their suspicions that the gentleman had not accounted for Isabelle fighting back.

Appalled by the suspect's laconism, justice would be swift by the powers that be. Kacper Smolak's execution took place on 15 November 1871 and was attended by an audience so large, in fact, that spectators all but mounted each other's shoulders to witness it.

And yet, absent from the heckling crowds were the voices that had summoned them—the men and women of Isabelle's village. Their faces would not fill the pews of church that Sunday either. No, for this community, retribution would apparently take another form.

Adorned with candles, they would assemble by the lakeside every November thereafter, greeting nightfall with a curse for 'the wicked Polack' who had ended an infant's life for money.

Twilight's descent on this tradition induced a collective ache for morning, but as uneasy heads lay to rest each year, another ritual would only be beginning for one individual among them.

From the top floor of the Institute, the gentleman typically commenced by wiping his glasses while he waited for the corridors below to fall silent. Next, he would remove a white handkerchief from his pocket and sketch his pseudonym above a new entry in his notebook.

'The Watcher'; it was a name he had come to adopt in recent years, but not one for which he could claim ownership—the term had been thrown at him in childhood after a family friend lost his nerve, demanding to know why the boy was staring at him so fixedly.

The gentleman liked to revisit this memory often in his writings. On these hallowed November nights, however, he found that he could manage only the words:

Another anniversary has gone by, Ortus, and still she is not here.

From the threadbare handkerchief in his hands to the shelves on the far wall, his gaze, like the muscles in his neck, would then stiffen, until once again they swarmed his ears—those faithful whispers reminding their listener that his reward for the killing of Isabelle Moreau drew nearer.

2

Pandora's Box

4 June 1881, Baudières Estate, Aixelles, France.

With a final heave, Arnaud Baudin cleared his lungs of another layer of mucus, then relaxed in his armchair and tossed the blood-spattered tissue onto the growing pile atop the bin. As the pain subdued, he glanced at his pocket watch again to gauge how much longer he would have to wait until morning.

21:13; incredulous, given the amber sunlight attempting to penetrate his library from the crack between the curtains. Over the haze of recent weeks, spring must have turned into the first tedious days of summer, Arnaud concluded. And there, surrounded by his closest companions—the great philosophers in whose works he had spent a lifetime seeking refuge—the old man prepared himself for a long night ahead.

Shifting his weight onto his feet, the sensation of being upright without assistance felt as unstable as it had the first time he had learnt to walk. Step by step, Arnaud pushed through the shakiness and approached the glass cabinet behind the door. The object of his mobilisation? A particular key he had refrained from using for a decade.

While there was no shortage of locked rooms in Baudières, Arnaud's estate, the item he wished to access was a small wooden chest by the fireplace, on which the gentleman's housekeeper had resorted to stacking his post. Evidently, she had ceased subjecting herself to this daily balancing act ten months ago; the most recent addition to the pile was a flyer dated August 1880, promoting the first in a series of region-wide cavalcades to commemorate twenty years since Savoie voted to become French.

Glaring down at the red and white cross at its centre, Arnaud rolled his eyes.

Ever since the Capetian dynasty, the Baudin family's own coat of arms had been tied to a small castle in Burgundy. Despite its foundations having survived the early days of the Revolution unscathed, Arnaud had been happy to forego his claim to the land as its sole remaining heritor. Being a doctor and a self-professed 'citizen of his own microcosm', the ten-mile span of Lake Annecy, instead, would put a convenient distance between the gentleman and the din of French politics, he had reasoned. As such, watching Napoleon III's ship laud before his window in the summer of 1860 had proven exacting.

Shrugging off the flashback, Arnaud ripped the flyer in half and swept the remaining letters onto the floor. He was in no doubt about what the tumbling envelopes contained; messages from budding medics, desperate to learn from the man who—according to an interview of Europe's most revered practitioners in their heyday—had surpassed all feats in life. Decluttered of these 'insufferable accolades', their recipient creaked open the chest and peered inside.

Toys, doodles, trinkets the size of a thumb coming alive in the candlelight; such mementoes could never have belonged to the doctor himself, nor to his children for that matter. Where the former was concerned, Arnaud's infant souvenirs were limited to the image of his parents fading into estrangement with the successive deaths of his seven siblings. As regards the latter, his disappointment ran somewhat deeper.

In hindsight, it was only the beauty of youthful idealism that had allowed the doctor to contemplate building a family of his own when a tolerable enough woman came along. His wife's premature passing had caused him minimal grief, and on the odd occasion that Arnaud had set aside time for his sons or daughter, he had been decidedly unimpressed by Roland, Henri, and Gabrielle—the three supposed protegés destined to follow in his footsteps. No, the shrivelled daisy chains and papier-mâché globes staring up at him had been put together by a very different set of hands.

Upon his next breath, the doctor dropped to his knees and extended his fingers towards the crumpled letter nearest the top. It was a statement addressed to Arnaud himself, written by a teacher at the local school:

Dear Dr Baudin,

As well you know, your granddaughter continues to be regarded as our most valued pupil in both her courteous interactions with others and her advanced faculty for learning. However, I feel I must inform you of a worrisome account of Miss Ophélie Davenport that was reported to have occurred yesterday in front of the school.

The incident pertains to a Mr Louis Fabron—the older brother of another pupil—whose parents claim that he returned home from collecting his sister in a most distressing state.

8

From witnesses, I have pieced together this narrative: that Mr Fabron exited his family's carriage after our last class was dismissed, whereupon he proceeded to tease Miss Davenport about her use of a walking stick. His gibes then extended to others in the vicinity, I am told, until your granddaughter beckoned Mr Fabron over and whispered something in his ear that rendered the boy frightfully taciturn. Despite repeated calls to procure the words that she told him, both parties have been unwilling to divulge this information.

While I remain sympathetic to your granddaughter's tragic handicap and condemn any attempts to make light of it, I trust you will encourage Miss Davenport to confess to whatever hurtful rebuke she employed, and ensure that such retaliation is not resorted to again. This act was extremely out of character for Ophélie.

Yours sincerely,

Mrs Anne Chevrette.

Prompted by this recollection, Arnaud gripped the side of the chest for composure, before reaching back in to unearth other keepsakes from the four years that his granddaughter had lived with him.

For better or worse, it was all there—a collection of memories that was at once complete and utterly wanting; the puzzles that the pair had constructed, the pieces of clothing she had left behind, and hardest of all to confront again, a scrap of paper hosting the message *I love you,* that Ophélie had given him 'for the times when he felt her distant'.

This was the trigger that sent the doctor retreating to his armchair with the prostration of a convict. Unable to tear his attention from these words, Arnaud failed to notice his library receding into darkness inch by inch, or dawn's overture commencing beneath the window.

The next time he remembered to check his pocket watch, the time was 6:14 and his lengthy wait had nearly come to an end. In under an hour, his solicitor would be arriving to see to his final orders. From there, it would no doubt be a matter of days before the jaws of death closed around him. By now, the doctor could only hope that his calculations had been correct and that if nothing else, he would be gone before Ophélie's return.

Commensurate with his reputation for timeliness, Mr Girard knocked on the door at seven o'clock sharp and waited for confirmation to let himself in. Using the dim radius of the desk lamp as his guide, the solicitor followed Arnaud's ensuing request and made his way over to the seat beside his armchair. At this point, his eyes had adjusted to the obscurity enough to remark that the plate of food left out for the doctor's dinner the previous evening had gone untouched. The same could not be said for the bottle of cognac lying next to it.

Eyes unmoving from the floorboards, Arnaud sucked his pipe twice, before delivering the instruction: "Let us cut to the chase. I need you to send three letters, Julien".

"Certainly, Dr Baudin". Nodding solemnly, the solicitor retrieved a pen and a suitable piece of paper from his briefcase and continued: "Who is to be the first recipient?"

"Whichever pillock runs the Residents' Council these days", Arnaud muttered.

"That would be Mr Eduard de Corbiac, sir", Mr Girard replied awkwardly. "And the subsequent two?"

"My sons".

Mr Girard fell silent. Shifting uncomfortably in his seat, he allowed himself a minute to clear his throat, before responding: "And what is the message?"

3

The Letter

The hamlet of Petit Pin sat atop a quiet, narrow valley, thirty miles from the city of Nantes. Comprising only a farm, a flour mill, and six cottages scattered around a stone well, it was the sort of settlement you would have to go out of your way to stumble across. City-dwellers would find that one day there rolled slowly and indistinguishably into the next; those seeking solitude would take comfort in sitting on a wall and listening to the wind whistle through the surrounding wheat fields.

For generations, the people of Petit Pin had been agricultural workers—the kind, honest folk you would expect to find in a place where the postman's wagon pottering up the lane was cause for excitement. Once a fortnight, they might convene in a barn to play music together, or share a drink in somebody's kitchen at the end of a long afternoon. Front doors in Petit Pin remained permanently open throughout the summer months, in fact—all except one.

Separated from the others by half the valley slope, it was inhabited by Arnaud Baudin's elder son, Roland, his wife,

Camille, their three children, and their niece. And in this cottage, nothing—least of all hospitality—could disrupt the bliss of routine.

Having concluded that the job of a clerk did not agree with him, Roland Baudin had been enjoying early retirement in Petit Pin for the last sixteen years. Each morning after breakfast, he would descend to his office armed with a cup of tea and two madeleines. An interlude of reading in his armchair was then common practice, before the gentleman would settle at the desk to resume painting the figurines in his replica of the Battle of Waterloo. Should the notion carry him, Mr Baudin might factor in a turn of the room to neaten his immaculate displays of soldiers, foliage, and weaponry, but this deviation was contingent on his having the energy to do so.

Midway through applying a splash of red to Napoleon's collar that morning, the gentleman was to face two confrontations of a startling nature. An overconfident wasp first dared to break his concentration, forcing him to spend several minutes with a rolled-up newspaper locating and eventually 'slaying the beast'. The second disturbance was the rarer and more unsettling sight of his wife's smile after she thundered down the staircase and into the office, clutching an envelope that she had already taken the liberty of opening.

"Do you have any idea what this means, Roland? We must begin arrangements at once", was the breathless explanation that left Mrs Baudin's lips as she slapped the letter onto his desk.

Now, to the average person, the news of an elderly family member's deteriorating health might be received with some expression of concern—sincere or otherwise. As it happened,

Camille Baudin prided herself on being an equalist. By this, I mean that having grown up on the outskirts of Nantes—'deprived of the privileges' her husband had enjoyed—it was only fitting to Mrs Baudin that this imbalance be redressed later down the line.

You could hardly be surprised, then, that when her eyes scanned the letter warning Roland that his father had been seized by a chest infection and was showing little sign of recovery, Camille would waste no time in orchestrating the family's installation in his estate. On a practical level, her haste merely spared them from having to make the journey to Baudières in winter. Or, at least, Mrs Baudin insisted this was the case when her husband voiced his reluctance to leave Petit Pin until after his father had passed away.

"I cannot believe you would have us trek across the country in blizzards", Camille snapped, striding back and forth as if mirroring a pendulum. "No doubt Thomas will be thrilled to learn that his father wants him to remain unhappy with his tutor here when he has the option to attend a real school elsewhere. And what about the girls, Roland, and your niece? They should be in charge of their *own* households by now, yet you content yourself to delay their chances of marriage by keeping them cooped up in this wasteland for a few more months?"

Her husband rearranged his paintbrushes on the desk and sighed. "You have made your point, Camille. I shall write to Mr Girard informing him that we shall be with them at Baudières before the summer is out".

And like the successful defusing of a bomb, there it was: silence. While Roland sank into his armchair, his wife rushed upstairs to break the news to the next generation of Baudins.

Having never left their hamlet—let alone the province—in twenty-two years, Camille's twin daughters instantly abandoned their card game to speculate about the properties of their new home. That Arnaud Baudin was a 'cantankerous old snob' who had made his fortune as some sort of doctor was the extent of what Manon and Adèle had been told about their grandfather. This detail was of no consequence next to the pressing matters at hand, such as what the gentlemen and fashion might be like further south.

Slumped across his cousin's lap, their brother, in contrast, barely acknowledged Camille as she barked orders to their maid from the doorway. For the most part, Thomas' endeavour to avoid eye contact could be attributed to last week's disobedient episode at dinner, from which he had still not returned to his mother's good graces. Being the youngest of the Baudin children by a considerable interval, though, his opinion was rarely solicited. And then there was Ophélie Davenport.

Suffice to say, it had come as a shock to Mr and Mrs Baudin when they received a letter written by Arnaud a decade prior, detailing the existence of Roland's eleven-year-old niece. The last time Roland had heard from his sister was when Gabrielle had eloped with a Franco-British soldier, aged sixteen. Evidently, this union had been cut short by the loss of Gabrielle's husband, prompting her to return to their father's estate for refuge with her daughter, Ophélie. Gabrielle's own death from tuberculosis had followed shortly after their arrival, and was, as Arnaud reported it, 'a blessing akin to an insomniac being granted sleep'.

His choice of words—coupled with Roland's dwindling memories of his sister—did little to allay suspicions regarding

Ophélie's inherited temperament. Alas, his niece had been living with Arnaud in Baudières for four years now, and as her grandfather insisted in his follow-up letters, she urgently required a 'more nurturing environment in which to grow up'.

And so it was that Mrs Baudin had conceded to raise Ophélie in Petit Pin, alongside her own children. Having a little one around must have become a nuisance for Arnaud, she had reasoned, and for now at least, her father-in-law wielded sufficient power to make these sorts of demands. The imposition was lessened by the size of the annuity settled on Roland to maintain his niece, and where the couple's reputation was concerned, this adoption would serve as a beating stick against accusations of meanness.

Contrary to concern, any abnormality identified in Ophélie upon initial inspection appeared to be entirely physical—namely a crooked tibia in her right leg. That she kept to herself for the first few weeks was probably to be expected, but their niece's aloofness would soon change with the arrival of a tattered envelope in her name.

Whatever its contents, Ophélie had spent the day alone in the garden after receiving it. When she did return to the cottage, stony-faced, she made of her new family one request: that nobody ever enquire about her time in Baudières. Given their general aversion to the subject, Roland and Camille had been only too happy to oblige.

Clearly, there could be no avoiding it now. In the wake of her aunt's announcement, Ophélie's prolonged silence began to attract the attention of the room. Upon Adèle's eventual querying of what was wrong, Ophélie excused herself and slipped upstairs, lifting Mr Girard's letter off the mantelpiece as she passed.

Perched on her bed, she poured over that impeccable penmanship she knew by heart—every stroke of the quill outlined with precision, each word carrying the succinctness of its orator. Hands shaking, Ophélie must have examined the text four times before noticing the faint string of numbers that had been added to the bottom by someone else.

At first glance, it looked as though this might be the same language through which she and her grandfather had left one another cryptic notes around his estate. Substituting each number for the letter in which it appeared in the alphabet, she completed the exercise and found herself staring at a familiar quote by François Rabelais:

Le temps mûrit toutes choses; par le temps toutes choses viennent en évidence, le temps est père de la vérité. (With time, all things come into maturity and become clear; time is the father of truth).

Ophélie rose to pace the room, but lightheadedness drew her to the window. Hugging her knees to her chest, she remained there beneath the sill until the hallway bell rang for lunch. Then, with a heavy sigh, she pushed herself to her feet.

4

Paradise

At the edge of the terrace cradling Eduard de Corbiac's estate, the latest maid to join his house staff rested a hand on the balcony and took in the view before commencing her journey. Perhaps it was the warmth of the breeze compared to last month's outing, or the absence of even the slightest smudge of cloud in the sky, but she would never be more grateful that her name had appeared on the rota to run errands in the city that day.

With a quick pause to adjust the basket under her arm, she continued down the steps and past the gate to the footpath that ran adjacent to the water's edge. Barely wide enough for a carriage, this winding road served to connect the sprawling hub of Annecy with its surrounding communes on all sides of the lake. And for the next half mile or so while she approached the border of her master's village, it would be hers alone to enjoy.

Day may only just have broken, but already the scent of wildflowers from the forests behind was intoxicating. More pleasant still, the maid proceeded to discover, was the array of colours bursting to life around her; spanning the horizon to her right, a verdant blanket of trees covered most of the scree on the mountains. Glistening in the morning light, the surface of the lake reminded her of Mrs de Corbiac's sapphire necklace, and across the waterfront, her vision was drawn to the burgundy tiles of the cottages littered among patchworks of farmland.

Turning her attention back to the footpath, the maid exited the final set of gates separating the village of Aixelles from its immediate neighbours. In that instant, she could not help but recall the windowless flat she had shared with her siblings in Chambéry; could any of them boast to live amid such scenery now, too?

Of course, the resident birds were luckiest of all in that respect, she smiled to herself as a pair of cormorants glided overhead in perfect unison. From their perspective, she envisaged the canvas below to paint a sleepy pastoral haven, yet no sooner had she joined the main road than she was met with a flurry of footfall—cyclists whirring ahead to reach the market, newly-arrived blacksmiths, tailors, and leatherworkers hurrying to set up shop, and parasol-wielding tourists pulled to the charm of Annecy's flower-lined footbridges and cobblestone alleyways.

Their hustle of movement was not limited to the ground, either; by now, a combination of locals going about their daily business by canoe and merchants navigating larger boats meant that the traffic on the water could rival Venice's canals. Every so often, the maid would perceive a Genevan or Sardinian voice among them, and she would feel a strange affinity knowing that whatever their origin, everyone was advancing in the same direction.

After elbowing her way through the fishmongers to pick up that evening's dinner order, she made straight for the dress boutique by Saint-Pierre cathedral, where Mrs de Corbiac's latest gown and bonnet ensemble was awaiting collection. From what the maid could remember, this one had been requested for an upcoming horse race of some kind in Chantilly. Truth be told though, she had lost count of her mistress' social engagements of late.

Then, doubling back at midday, she came to her final stop along the grassy terrain of Le Pâquier, Annecy's famous promenade overlooking the water. It was there—nestled between an old man dozing in a deckchair and a group of youths playing 'that English ball game everyone seems to be talking about'—that she purchased the newspaper.

With ample time before she would be expected home, the maid allowed herself a few minutes to sit and peruse the pictures, gently enough that her master would be none the wiser. Two pages in, an image of a classroom caught her eye, and she jumped to her feet to ask the vendor about its corresponding text.

"Says on 16 June, a law was passed enforcing free primary education", he replied, glancing over her shoulder.

To the gentleman's surprise, his listener had departed by the time he looked up again, but she would clutch that article to her chest all the way back to Aixelles. Only when the village's first gate came into sight did the maid relinquish the newspaper to her basket and straighten her apron, in fact. Before her, an opportunity to prolong her excursion was presenting itself in the form of a dozen out-of-towners craning to peer through the bars.

After spotting the maid, their ringleader beckoned the group towards her. Waving in his right hand was a familiar postcard that depicted a rosy-faced gentleman puffing on a cigar atop a marble terrace.

"Who lives here?" was his ensuing question, though it was not clear what sentiment had inspired it.

"Barons, lawyers, businessmen, and the likes", the maid proceeded to recite in one steady breath.

There was no shortage of elaboration she might have added to this response. Given the thickness of the gentleman's accent and the keen manner of his gawking, she opted for brevity nevertheless. The longer version would have told that the most decorated figures in the entire region owned a primary or secondary home beyond those gates.

Among such names were the Villard family, whose ancestors had struck gold somewhere in the Americas, and the Ponduvals, renowned for their bell-casting mastery. Arnaud Baudin himself had once been the local hero thanks to his contribution to international medicine, his private practice in Baudières catering to a grateful populace of neighbours who shuddered at the prospect of venturing to Annecy's public hospital for treatment.

There were also the Arminjons, recent members of the aristocracy who had been awarded their title by the King of Sardinia before Savoie's annexation to France, and you may have recalled the Ozanams from the shipping company bearing their coat of arms, or the Dupont family who had spearheaded Annecy's booming cotton industry.

With a nod, the gentleman at the head of the group tucked the postcard behind a second image. It was the gated facade of a building twice the size of the others, and the apparent reason that he and his peers had travelled there.

"The entrance?" he pressed.

This time, the maid kicked her heels and fell silent. The Moreau Institute of Botany and Horticulture; barring rumours she had heard that it once accepted visitors, she knew very little about this prodigious establishment in reality. Few outside the village elders did, these days, but its role in shaping local history had been pivotal.

Originally opened to the public as a means of spreading notoriety among the rich, its gardens were founded in the late seventeenth century by Hugues Moreau. Having lost the bid to create the King's Vegetable Garden in the 1670s to lifelong competitor Jean-Baptiste de La Quintinie, Hugues had left Paris indignant and spent the following years beseeching aristocrats for commissions to design new works. Failure turned to fortune when the gentleman inherited his family's estate in Aixelles and he was graced with an ample area in which to give birth to his vision: to create the leading educational centre for young men in the field of botany and horticulture.

The Institute, as he later called it, was divided into his family's living quarters and ground-floor classrooms on one side, and what became commonly known as the Boarding House—home to as many as fifteen students at a time—on the other. Backing from the hallway to the woods behind lay the gardens themselves. Such splendour is rarely seen outside palaces, but picture, if you will, rows of sumptuous vegetation zigzagging through marble fountains, fruit-laden orchards, and exotic flowers imported from all over the world.

Although smaller than Europe's most famous gardens of the time, Hugues' masterpiece became a touchstone for horticulture across the continent. Wealthy parents would pay enormous sums to support the upkeep of the grounds in the hopes that this would secure a place for their sons to study there on their eighteenth birthday, and the students who attended the Institute invariably became leading figures in botany.

As regards its secondary function as a magnet for tourists, Hughes' investment would yield fruit later down the line, as evidenced by the party present that day. By the time Annecy exploded onto the tourist radar in the 1860s, boats carrying as many as a hundred passengers would assemble before Aixelles to see it. But of course, these 'mobs' were a distant memory now, and one that the maid had a difficult time imagining.

"I am afraid the Institute has not run tours for many years", she eventually muttered.

With this, she bid the group adieu and entered the gate, stopping only to collect her master's post en route to his estate. Three postcards in the bundle, two likely invitations, and one envelope marked 'urgent' which she would have to interrupt the gentleman's meeting to hand him—just like that, her fortune seemed to have run out.

At that same moment in the de Corbiacs' entrance hall, you see, a gaggle of feathered hats and pearl-encrusted fans was taking its seat before the lectern. The event in question? The ninth anniversary of their Residents' Council. This independent body met once a month to offer a platform for 'amicable grievances' to be aired, and the opportunity to verify that the community was happy with all that was occurring around Aixelles.

As it happened, the meeting room had never been more packed, or indeed animated. Upcoming elections in the capital threatened a further swing to the left, inciting a heated discussion among the monarchist majority that would dominate the first fifteen minutes.

Aggravated by the sticky weather on top, tensions were rising when Eduard de Corbiac's maid tiptoed over to the podium. His outrage at the disturbance faded to bewilderment as he relayed the letter from Arnaud Baudin's solicitor, detailing the family's plans to settle in Aixelles at the end of the summer.

Within seconds, the audience had erupted into a cacophony of comments. The mysterious Dr Baudin was first discussed, the consensus being that his decade-long absence from the village's sight was most odd. Not since 'The Incident' had the doctor been seen outside his estate, though few dared approach it to check these days.

Some even questioned whether the old man was still alive in there, or if he might have fled the country and taken to the hills of Switzerland long ago. If this was the case, it was inconsiderate that they had not been informed of such news sooner; as the second-closest estate to the Institute, Baudières was one of the best situated in the village. It would be a great shame for the house to fall into ruin from neglect.

The suitability of the gentleman's family was the second issue to be debated. Of Arnaud's sons, the villagers could recall little more than Roland's decision to swap the toils of education for a bucolic existence—inspired by a wheat farmer he had met at the market—and Henri's visits to the police station when he was caught starting fights at the local casino-theatre. On the grounds that 'boys will be boys', these antics were not beyond the realm of forgiveness. Their sister Gabrielle, on the other hand, had been far too erratic for their liking.

While the youngest of Arnaud's children had largely slipped under the radar in her infancy, throughout the nine months during which she moved back to his estate as an adult, Gabrielle had regularly been sighted wading through the shallow waters of the lake in her nightdress or conversing with herself by the window. There were even mutterings of having her arrested after she was reported to have been found roaming the woods behind the Institute one evening during a storm. If perchance Roland and his offspring had inherited whatever madness led to Gabrielle's untimely death, the villagers would be reckless to allow his family to settle among them.

Aixelles' inhabitants were indeed powerful enough to deny residential rights when necessary. Their legal jurisdiction in this respect was limited, but thanks to their close ties with the relevant administrative powers—bolstered by the occasional bribe—the practice of deeds being 'purchased by someone else at the last minute' was more rampant than anyone would admit. It had been demonstrated not three months prior when an Italian writer whose novels were considered too racy had attempted to buy a property there.

Since the villagers remained defenceless against unwanted cases of inheritance—uncommon as they were—it was decided after much deliberation that they would offer Roland's family a chance, but that if the Baudins proved to be troublesome people, their fellow residents would be well within their right to ask them to leave. Should they refuse, the collective resources of the other households would then unite against them, cutting off the Baudins' access to essential industries from textiles to food, until their living conditions became insufferable.

None of this threat was ever actually expressed, of course, but you will find that when every mind in a room has been conditioned to think in the same manner, agreements can be reached through little more than a nod from one row of attendees to another.

Their final talking point was the intriguing Ophélie Davenport, about whom so little was known by her peers, in retrospect, that her name had been something of a mystery even before the girl had vanished from Aixelles. Given the questionable circumstances of her departure, though—days before her grandfather 'went into hiding'—it did not take the group long to conclude that a particularly close eye would need to be kept on Miss Davenport.

By the time Eduard de Corbiac adjourned the meeting and signalled for the catering staff to emerge, all mention of politics had been replaced by this latest development in village affairs. Curiosity clung to the air, such as could only be satisfied if you had glanced out of your front window at exactly 20:01 three weeks later.

5

Strangers in the Village

It was a lethargic evening in August when the Baudin family arrived in Annecy. The lake shimmered like oil beneath the sun's descent. Paddle steamers chugged home after their final crossings of the day, and all along the waterside, groups of children ran to keep up with them. Only the lone vessel gliding towards Aixelles would attract the eyes and ears of the villagers, though.

Engrossed in her thoughts at the back of their boat, Ophélie let her hand traipse in the waves brushing against the wood with each motion of the ores. Had she not known the lake's natural landmarks by heart—from the contour of the Alps to the narrowing water basin ahead—she would have struggled to recognise where she was due to the billowing factories and noisy construction sites surrounding her on all sides.

Miles behind them, the voices of the men unloading cargo at the port of Annecy were still audible. As their destination came further into focus, however, all human activity from the banks was replaced by a looming silence. Only then did Ophélie bring herself to gaze up at the familiar collection of estates lining the horizon.

With the exception of her grandfather's, the buildings looked all but alien to her—not least because they were, to her astonishment, only partially visible behind the heavy iron gates clamped around the village's periphery.

"I believe it's a recent security measure", their ferry captain informed the group after Thomas' third question about this 'cage' before them. "Against animals, of course. You won't find much by way of larceny where you're going".

His attempts at reassurance only fuelled Ophélie's nausea as she fixated on the sight. Holding her head high, she squinted into the distance at Baudières, that exposed, ghost-like edifice by the waterfront that marred the village's armour like a stubborn blemish in a painting.

It was a testament to how well Ophélie knew the man dwelling inside that as expected, nothing in its exterior had yielded to the capriciousness of taste over the years; white stone walls, three floors of forty ever-so-slightly asymmetric windows, and two chairs positioned on the terrace from their last breakfast together—home as best she knew it.

And there, at the end of the walkway leading up to the house from the water, Ophélie could just distinguish the silhouette of a gentleman clutching a parasol and a briefcase in anticipation of their arrival. His formal attire and hunched posture she immediately recognised as those of Julien Girard, her grandfather's lifelong solicitor.

Had they been nearer the land, Ophélie might also have noticed the shadow that appeared in the top-floor window of the Institute at that moment—an individual scanning the water with greater attention than his neighbours. Peering intently through a pair of birding binoculars, the gentleman lingered for several minutes scribbling words in a notebook. Then, as if satisfied with what he had witnessed, he disappeared into the darkness.

Following in his footsteps, the sun had almost vanished by the time the boat disembarked in front of the estate. In the crepuscular glow left behind, Ophélie was surprised to note that Mr Girard had hardly aged a day when his face came into focus. Eyes to the ground, he proceeded to shepherd the group to the door in silence, where Mrs Cadet, Baudières' new housekeeper, awaited to commence their induction.

"Come, you must all get settled. We shall leave a thorough visit of the grounds until morning when you have had some time to rest and the light is on our side", Mrs Cadet insisted, assembling the group beneath the staircase. Turning to the head of the family, her voice became solemn. "I am sure you are keen to learn how your father's health is faring, sir".

Upon realising that he was being addressed Roland gave a perfunctory nod, to which Mr Girard cut in: "I am afraid he does not leave the left wing these days and has requested that no one visit him. Mr Baudin takes all his meals in his room, but I should be happy to answer any questions about the estate on his behalf tonight. I suggest that Mrs Cadet show you up to your bedrooms right away and that we reconvene for supper at nine o'clock sharp in the dining room".

And with a stiff bow of his head, the solicitor all but broke into a sprint to depart from the hallway.

Once a tour of the ground floor was complete, the family was led up the staircase to the right wing, otherwise known as Baudières' main sleeping quarters. Whereas to Manon, Adèle, and Thomas, the fact that this side of the house alone was twice as big as their cottage in Petit Pin was reflected in the dropping of their jaws, Mrs Baudin took to her father-in-law's estate like a beast from captivity discovering grass.

Clutching her husband's arm, her eyes undressed each painting, sculpture, and piece of furniture as Mrs Cadet navigated them through an unfurling network of corridors. There was some significant redecoration to be done throughout—namely removing the portraits of Roland's ancestors from the walls and disposing of them—but rest assured, these were projects for which Mrs Baudin had long been prepared.

Unnervingly for Ophélie, the interior of the estate, too, was exactly as she remembered it. Tossing and turning in bed the previous night, she had presumed that the rooms would seem smaller to her through the eyes of an adult. If anything, taking them in from a greater height only drew her attention to the overwhelming sameness of the place.

It was as if Baudères had been frozen in time—not an object removed or acquired since the day she had left. There was the family tree hanging in the hallway, for example, which began all the way back in the twelfth century. The names and dates were so minute that Ophélie had stacked chairs from the dining room beneath the frame just so she could study it properly. Every now and then, she had used her findings to squeeze snippets of information about various Baudins out of her grandfather, like the discovery that her great-aunt Marianne had liked painting pictures of birds, or that her great, great-grandfather had sported a bushy moustache and spoken with a stutter.

Then there was the front room, with its ceiling-high book-shelves filled with medical records and its oppressive, burgundy wallpaper. Arnaud had treated his patients here, once upon a time, and Ophélie had often waited for him to finish procedures from the clunky wooden chair by the door. She had liked the way the muscles in his forehead relaxed when he worked.

Emerging onto the second floor again would be somewhat more jarring. For some reason, the corridor on this level was so narrow that if you stretched both arms out, you could touch the walls on either side. And there ahead, Gabrielle Davenport's bedroom promised only a haunting reminder of why Ophélie's mother had packed up their belongings overnight and brought her to Baudières in the first place.

Rocking and wailing in bed—or else staring at the ceiling in silence—Gabrielle's cognition had dissipated long before her body did. Arnaud had even restricted Ophélie from going to see her towards the end, but Ophélie had snuck her way in on most nights regardless. To the brass angels above Gabrielle's bed frame, she had repeatedly whispered a plea to grant her mother peace, one way or another.

Ophélie's own bedroom, three doors along, was no cheerier to behold. Even with fresh bedding and the carpet and fireplace polished, it exuded the frigidity of a private space deserted by its occupant with unnatural haste; from Ophélie's drawings on the walls the colour had faded, the books on her desk were unmoved, and the wind chimes her grandfather had bought for her eighth birthday hung motionless from the curtain-post above the bed. Brimming with more nostalgia than any of these objects, though, was Ophélie's thinking spot by the window—the site of so many nightly musings.

A mere ledge beneath the sill it may have appeared to most, but it was this specific feature that had drawn her here the day she arrived at Baudières with her mother. Intrigued to discover why his granddaughter had chosen the smallest bedroom on the right wing, the doctor had later joined Ophélie by the window to query her decision.

"This is the best angle from which to see the water", was her reply. "Did you know that Lake Annecy was formed thousands of years ago when the glaciers of the Alps melted? I would give anything to travel through time and visit the landscape as it was then. How quiet it must have been".

Most cherished in Ophélie's memory was the look that had entered Arnaud's face in response—a parting of the lips so unnatural, she had presumed this was his first attempt to smile. With a pause to clear his throat, he had proceeded to lower himself onto the ledge next to his granddaughter, extending to her a second question, then a third. Before long, the pair had covered every subject from their favourite books to their mutual discomfort around flames. It was sunrise before either of them noticed that they had talked and laughed through the night.

Her grandfather's seat on that wooden stretch beside her might be empty now, but if Ophélie had one thing in common with her seven-year-old self, it was the sentiment that her life was about to change beyond recognition again.

Dinner that night would be abnormally quiet. Roland excused himself straight after pudding to oversee the installation of his Waterloo figurines, Camille unloaded her gripes against the 'blistering alpine climate', and even Manon found herself with few verbal contributions save a handful of flirtatious remarks to Mr Girard.

No comment could have sunk the collective reserve to greater depths, though, than Ophélie's enquiry to the solicitor as to when she might be permitted to see her grandfather. Raising an eyebrow, Mr Girard replied by reiterating Arnaud's instructions on the matter, and an hour later, the family was dismissed for the night.

There was a knock on Ophélie's door after she returned from putting Thomas to bed. It was followed by Adèle's face peering gingerly around the frame. Based on the accompanying noise from the corridor, Manon had discovered by now that her sister's bedroom was marginally larger than the one she had been allocated, Ophélie supposed.

"Sorry if I woke you", Adèle began, inching forward. "I thought you might appreciate some company".

Before her cousin had finished speaking, Ophélie tucked the item she had been holding behind her pillow. Despite giving simultaneous gestures for Adèle to approach, company was perhaps the last thing she wanted. Prior to the younger twin's arrival, the thud of a candle rolling to the floor had forced Ophélie to reach into the dusty void beneath her bed to retrieve it. Thereupon, her fingers had met with an old, familiar diary whose cover she had still not brought herself to open when her cousin leapt onto the mattress beside her.

"I cannot imagine what it must have been like growing up here. It is all so magnificent; the house, the lake, the mountains", Adèle whispered. For a second, she paused to gauge her cousin's reaction, then added: "You barely touched your food at dinner, Ophélie. Last night it was the same. Are you so unhappy to be back?"

Ophélie shook her head and swept Adèle's hair off her face. "I am just a little tired from the journey".

"Well, that is understandable. I had never quite appreciated how big it is, this country of ours", Adèle sighed, before rolling over to launch a prognosis about tomorrow's activities.

When the clock in the hallway struck eleven, she concluded

her monologue and left Ophélie to sleep. Clearly, the younger twin had underestimated her own fatigue, she would tell herself over the ensuing hours, because on both occasions that she tiptoed down the corridor to use the lavatory, Adèle thought she saw a light flickering beneath Ophélie's door.

6

A Childhood Lost

Each of us has behaviour that we adopt away from the prying eyes of others; Mrs Cadet hated it when the corners of a bedsheet came loose from the mattress, for instance. When stressed, Julien Girard found comfort in biting the skin around his thumbnails to chew on the rubbery texture, and Eduard de Corbiac was so frightened of burglars that he trusted himself alone to check that his estate was locked at night.

The summer after Ophélie moved into Baudières as a child, she discovered a compulsion as irresistible to her as any of these examples: listening out for grasshoppers from the top of the garden, then attempting to creep up close enough to glimpse the insect before the chirring noises stopped and it hopped out of sight.

One morning during a busy period in her grandfather's work schedule, she succeeded in stalking a grasshopper from the lavender bushes all the way to the intersection at which the garden joined the woods. By the time she caught up with it, the creature had disappeared into the forest, and Ophélie found herself staring up at the forbidden wilderness.

Now, curiosity is rarely a spur-of-the-moment impulse, but rather a dormant beast that is woken and fed over time. Only the previous month, Arnaud—after considerable persuasion—had agreed to take Ophélie with him to Annecy's Old Town to collect a prescription. In crossing the crowded Bacchus Bridge over the canals, the pair had witnessed a wading fisherman pick an ancient bronze coin out of the riverbed.

Before long, Ophélie had exhausted every book about the Roman occupation of the area in her grandfather's library. Armed with the knowledge that several lime quarries once lay on the mountainside as a result, it occurred to her while she stood there that the masons would have carved paths through the trees ahead to transport the stone. And so, like the grasshopper, Ophélie entered the woods, looking for marks from wagon wheels that had not seen human eyes for a millennium. Every day for the next week, she would do the same.

During her initial excursions, Ophélie scoured the forest floor to the right of the estate, mapping the location and details of everything she came across in a diary that she hid beneath her bed. Satisfied that there was nothing more to be seen there, she then turned her attention to the left section of the woods. In doing so, she was led to the gardens of the Institute.

By a continuous stroke of chance, Ophélie had managed to avoid her neighbours altogether throughout her earlier passages behind their estates. Here, only the thin beams of wood on the fence separated her from a chorus of background voices prattling along the track in front. Still, her grandfather's anger—should she be caught and her venture reported to him—would surely pale in comparison with the regret of abandoning her project now, Ophélie decided.

The following morning, she packed her satchel with suste-
nance and returned to the woods, passing the Institute with
such willingness, in fact, that she failed to notice the white
handkerchief falling out of her pocket behind the fence.

Due to its thickness, the undergrowth on this side would
render Ophélie's search for artefacts more problematic. It
was an hour before she realised she had walked all the way to
the final garden in Aixelles, devoid of any trace of her 'distant
friends'. Rather, from somewhere directly ahead, her ears
began to detect human activity of the living kind.

Keeping her footsteps to a minimum as she approached,
Ophélie was focusing so intently on not drawing attention to
herself that it took her a minute to notice the boy crouched
behind a tree to her right.

Clothes smeared with soil stains, messy, reddish hair, no
shoes on his feet; from first glance, he looked nothing like the
children from her village. Any friends he had been with had
furthermore abandoned whatever game he was playing long
ago; the only voices Ophélie could identify were those of the
two adults he was spying on.

As soon as the boy saw her, he beckoned Ophélie closer and
pointed towards the clearing in front. On the other side, a
dark-haired couple appeared to be shouting at one another in
a language she had never heard.

"Come, quick", the boy began in a lively murmur. "Can you
tell me what they're arguing about?"

Ophélie huddled beside him and strained to listen, before
whispering: "I am afraid not".

The boy nodded. "The name's Étienne, by the way".

"Ophélie", she replied, reaching out to shake his hand.

If the slurred tone of his speech had provided her first suspicion as to why Étienne was requesting this of her, the concentration on his face when he turned back around would serve as her second.

Some years ago, an infection had robbed the boy of his hearing, it would later transpire, although Étienne was quick to insist that this malady had been a gift to improve his eyesight. Alas, despite his 'stellar lip-reading skills' and Ophélie's endeavour to liken the couple's dialect to others she knew, the children could only speculate on the cause of their growing ire.

Finally, having racked her brain for anything that might help to diffuse the altercation, Ophélie peered aside at the crow picking at the forest floor and she formed an idea. Reaching into her satchel, she broke apart one of the biscuits she had taken with her for the journey, then flung the crumbs into the thicket nearest to where the couple was standing. Sure enough, the bird's head shot up and it hopped over to retrieve its meal, generating a series of rustling noises so sudden that both parties ceased yelling and gaped at the bush.

Their reaction was not unfounded; these woods were known to house wolves, boars, and species of deer more than capable of defending themselves if threatened. Gesturing for his partner to stand behind him, the young man armed himself with a branch and inched towards whatever beast was waiting to pounce on them. Then, letting out an almighty groan, he raised the weapon above his head, at which point the crow burst from the leaves and took flight past his face with such speed that the man fell onto his backside with a resounding thud.

For several seconds Ophélie and Étienne held their breath,

until an outburst of laughter erupted from the other side of the clearing. By the time the children emerged from their hiding place the couple had departed, and they, too, were unable to contain their amusement at what they had witnessed. With a dramatic bow to his new accomplice, Étienne proceeded to offer Ophélie a personal tour of his home, and together they continued through the trees to his village.

Astonishingly, it would be four years before Arnaud discovered that his granddaughter was regularly being seen playing in the woods alongside a boy from Mèliez. That day, the corridors of Baudières fell silent. Locked in her bedroom, Ophélie cried until she could no longer produce tears, repeating to herself the doctor's threat that she would be sent to live elsewhere if she left the estate again without him. Only weeks later, his conviction would be put to the test.

Had Arnaud not crossed paths with Charles Moreau on the morning of 'The Incident', he might not have been persuaded to attend Jacques Saunier's dinner party that evening. The doctor's questioning of this decision was already escalating by the time Isabelle's nurse burst into the dining room, screaming that Isabelle had been abducted.

In the accompanying hysteria, the speed at which Arnaud ran to the door spurred others to do the same; Isabelle's parents rushed off to alert the police across the lake, and a search party was rallied within the village. But as the boats set out into the obscurity—led only by the wails of Isabelle's name—Arnaud broke from the group and set a direct course for the village of Mèliez.

Call it naivety if you will, but the innocence of children is a remarkable phenomenon. Unaffected by the known evils of this world, it never occurred to eleven-year-old Ophélie

Davenport and Étienne Sourdois that the small white bundle they spotted by the water's edge at the same moment could have been a body. Only when Ophélie noticed scratch marks on the girl's arms and chest did she realise that something was terribly wrong with this picture; grabbing Étienne's hand, they shuffled forward several paces and froze in confusion before the sight.

Locked in a haunting grimace, Isabelle Moreau's delicate features were all but unrecognisable. Her bloodshot eyes were wide open and watery—black, dilated pupils staring up at the darkening sky. Drifting back and forth in the icy water, her straw-coloured hair had been pulled loose from its bun and the material of her dress was ruched up in parts, as if someone had attempted to remove it.

The internal monologue that took place while Ophélie stood there—transfixed on the girl's face—would have been a poignant one to hear. Like a parasite seeking a host, the image latched itself to the back of her mind with relish. And in one prolonged flash, she felt Isabelle's dying moments as if she were living them herself.

It was not long before the rest of Ophélie and Étienne's group caught up with them at the water's edge. As the children's screams began to attract attention across the lake, Isabelle's search party took an abrupt turn towards Mèliez. No sooner had they brushed the banks than a fleet of lantern-wielding officers descended to evacuate the scene.

The look in Étienne's eyes as Ophélie was grabbed from the crowd—shrieking for her grandfather to let her go—would remain as clear in her memory, now, as a photograph. So, too, would the wallop of the policeman's rifle striking Étienne's head while he ran after Arnaud's boat. But most unshakable of all was the revulsion that had overcome Ophélie the morning his parents replied to her letters in Petit Pin, confirming her fears that their son had been killed on impact.

7

The Rowboat

Awoken by a dream at some point after midnight, Ophélie rose from her bed in a sweat and crossed to the basin under her mirror. With her hands on either side of the porcelain, she spent the next few minutes splashing water on her face and staring at her reflection in the darkness, until satisfied that she had retaken control of herself.

Then, turning to the trunk beneath her bed, Ophélie lit a candle and went to fetch her shawl. As the oldest item in her possession, the cotton was like wool now, blotted by the residuum of a childhood mishap involving an ink pen. At the time, her grandfather's house staff had been keen to wash or replace the section containing the splotch, but Ophélie had declined their offer. She had taken to hiding the shawl ever since.

Relaxing into the coarse fabric, she sat at the window and reunited herself with the view; the moon's beams rippling through the surface of the lake, strips of the mountains illuminated like crinkles in dusky silk, and a vista of stars glinting across infinite blackness. What a shame it is that nature reserves its most marvellous spectacles for the hours during which mankind is blind to them, she found herself remarking once again.

When Ophélie had lived at Baudières as a girl, her grandfather had often stressed the importance of astronomy to her. 'The answers are up there, young one', his post-dinner mantra had gone, after which the pair would turn off all the lamps in the estate, tiptoe up to the attic together, and examine the galaxy through his telescope.

Back then, Ophélie had liked to imagine that the sky was watching over her, somehow. The day after her mother's death, she and Étienne had laid down in his garden and attempted to see her beyond the clouds. His suggestion for Ophélie to whisper to the stars whenever she felt sad—so that they would transfer this message over the lake and he would think of something to make her laugh—was more reassuring to her than any consolation her grandfather had attempted to bestow. These days, Ophélie felt only hollowness when she looked at them.

Dropping her gaze to the world below, she rested her chin on her elbows and cast her eyes to the glimmering concentration of light around Annecy. The city's population must have doubled since she last took it in like that, but memories of its timeless structures resurfaced nonetheless.

From the south-facing angle of her window, Ophélie knew that she was looking at the top of Saint-Maurice Church, for example, even in the darkness. Like the flying buttress around its exterior that she had compared to a fish's gills, she was suddenly reminded of the clang of its bells summoning local Christians—or 'fear-mongers', as Arnaud had labelled them—to worship.

Little did the doctor know that some of his more pious housekeepers had taken his granddaughter to a service there once or twice when he was away at seminars, lest the girl be condemned to spiritual misguidance. For their sake Ophélie had kept these outings a secret, otherwise regarding them as an opportunity to study the congregation.

Children kicking the pew in front, rows of voices chanting declarations of sin alongside demands for forgiveness, the sick and elderly peacefully bowing their heads; did moral obligation bring them there each week, she had often asked herself, or the same stimulus by which the early cave-dwellers she read about had chosen to exist in clans?

From the outline of the city to the port below, Ophélie proceeded to glance away, searching for signs of life. She found this dotted across the water in the form of a surprising number of lanterns bobbing up and down atop boats—presumably transportation vessels for coal, plaster, and other goods passing through the area. What might the men on board be thinking as they gazed up at the sky, she asked herself? Were they lonely? Were they afraid? As night held its beckoning arms out, Ophélie considered her own responses to these questions.

It afforded her some comfort to imagine that she was not the only restless soul awake in Aixelles. In a nearby nursery, a maid rocked a crying baby in her arms, begging him not to rouse his parents. With each breath, she pretended it was Lucien, her own son, whom she was holding again. The boy had been stationed with the French forces in Algiers for longer than she could remember, now. After the bloody defeat of the Trans-Saharan expedition that February, the maid used this hour each night to pray for an injury that would exempt

Lucien from future such campaigns.

On the second floor of another estate, Marie-Charlotte Saunier had just slunk from her husband's bedside to compose a note to her lover. Several houses to their left, the eldest Dupont daughter was lifting the floorboards in her bedroom to remove the first edition of Hubertine Auclert's *La Citoyenne*. She had procured a copy while visiting Paris that February after hearing her father refer to the publication as 'the four horsemen of the feminist apocalypse in print'. On the other side of the Institute, Émile Veaux was taunting himself with visions of a certain solicitor he wished he was sleeping next to, and in the threshold of a final estate, a young gentleman was hoisting a crate into his arms whilst making his way towards the water's edge.

As the only person to be rowing from the direction of Aixelles, his venture instantly caught Ophélie's attention. In the end, the boat crossed all the way to Mèliez until it had faded out of sight, then reappeared some thirty minutes later.

Upon its return trajectory, Ophélie strained without success to make out the silhouette of whoever was rowing. Most deliveries to the village were conducted by carriage during the day, she recalled, so it seemed highly unusual that a member of staff should be out collecting supplies in such a small boat at this hour.

Registering this observation, like its predecessors, at the back of her mind, she eventually slid under her bedsheets again and turned her thoughts to her grandfather—wide awake too, no doubt, on the other side of the estate.

Certain that despite Mr Girard's instructions, Arnaud would not turn her away if she could solicit an audience with him, she awaited dawn pledging to do whatever it took to see the doctor before it was too late. In Ophélie's haste, there was one impediment to this plan that she had failed to take into account, though.

8

An Old Face

Visits by the other villagers began early the next morning. They continued throughout the week, until the hallway of Baudières was glutted with gifts and its wine cellar contained enough bottles to outlast a siege.

The collective procedure tended to be the same; visitors would stay no more than three minutes—just long enough to pass their hamper through the threshold while scanning the figures before them. A comment about the hot spell typically concluded each interaction, after which Manon would wave their neighbours off from the terrace, then implore her cousin for a reason why not one of them had offered the family a subsequent lunch or dinner proposal.

Though reluctant to share her opinion, if Ophélie's intuition was correct, the villagers had agreed not to establish further communication with the newcomers until they had been 'tested' with an inauguration into their community. Her theory would be confirmed the following week when breakfast was interrupted by the outburst of a woman's voice warbling through the letterbox.

With a colossal grin plastered across her face, Mariana Rinaldi's robust frame hovering in the doorway was the next phenomenon to greet them. In one hand she clasped a barrel-bodied terrier sporting a bow named Cornelius, alongside—lo and behold—an invitation for the Baudins to attend their annual ball in the other.

After inspecting each member of the family, Mrs Rinaldi turned back to the marina, crying: "My word, look how charming these girls are, Giulio! Did I not predict they would be?"

Metres behind, her husband had trodden on a flower pot on his way up to the terrace and was hopping around furiously to shake it off his boot.

"Charming indeed Mariana! They shall be the talk of the party", he shouted back with equal jollity.

The sight of the couple was truly remarkable; like a pair of caricatures, Mrs Rinaldi was a good foot taller than her husband, and easily twice his size. Since moving to Aixelles from their home country of Italy—where Mr Rinaldi had made his fortune in textiles—their so-called 'summer extravaganzas' had become a staple in the village calendar.

Each spring, the couple would leave Savoie for the holidays, basing their next event on whichever city they had visited that year. Last summer, a Spanish fiesta had graced their ballroom, featuring a band sent over from Madrid and guests adorning costumes of conquistadors and flamenco dancers. That Easter, Venice had been on the menu, thus the villagers were looking forward to the Rinaldis' masquerade festival with the same zeal.

Having listened to this explanation with growing impatience behind her smile, Camille would waste no time in rounding off their conversation with the response: "We are grateful for your invitation, thank you".

Late for another engagement herself, Mrs Rinaldi proceeded to bid them adieu and waddled away to join her husband, halting at the water's edge to call back: "It is most refreshing to see this old house so full of life!"

They had not been gone thirty seconds before Camille shook her head, muttering: "What a peculiar woman", to which Manon had only to add: "And did you hear her accent, Maman? I could barely understand a word she said".

By the end of that week, the draconian jangle of the hallway bell was enough to make Ophélie wince. Ready to exploit any opportunity to reach the left wing unaccosted, she could hardly conceal her relief when she came downstairs to the sight of Mrs Cadet scurrying towards the door with a shopping list for Arnaud poking out of her basket.

Fortune seemed to be in Ophélie's favour, for this was followed by Camille's announcement that the last of the family's possessions had been unpacked and arranged according to her instruction. In celebration of the milestone, Mrs Baudin ushered the girls to prepare for a trip into the city to peruse the boutiques for ballgowns.

While Manon and Adèle tore upstairs to change outfits, Ophélie picked up her cane and requested that she be excused to rest her legs. From the living room window she waited until her aunt and cousins had set off in the boat, then she hastened her steps in the opposite direction. Now the sole obstacle that stood in the way of her grandfather was Mr Girard.

Chance would be the only threat here; the solicitor had gone out of his way to avoid Ophélie since she was a child. The incident in question had involved her walking in on a heated discussion that Mr Girard was having with their neighbour, Émile Veaux, in his office.

Mr Veaux had only come over to return a book he had borrowed, but the pair appeared to have been arguing about something else, because Mr Girard was wrought with tears when Ophélie peeked through the door to locate the source of the commotion. She had lingered there for no more than a second, but it was long enough to witness Émile seize the solicitor's face and kiss him on the lips. At that instant, Mr Girard had caught sight of their intruder, staring at her with a gape so harrowing that Ophélie almost fell over while turning to run away.

Upon disclosing this account to Étienne later that week, he had raised a finger to his mouth and led Ophélie to a secure location behind his cottage. From there, he explained that they would discuss the matter in detail, then never speak of it again for Mr Girard's sake. As a final provision, the children had scratched their names on a pebble and thrown it into the lake, representing their promise to take the solicitor's secret with them to the grave—a pledge to which Ophélie was more committed now than ever.

Tiptoeing past his office—the first room along the left wing corridor—Ophélie need not have worried. As always, Mr Girard's tireless concentration on his work left him oblivious to her silhouette slinking over to the stairwell. Just as she put her hand on the bannister, though, the mossy aroma of tobacco wafting from somewhere behind indicated that the second-floor master bedroom was not where Ophélie would find her grandfather.

Thrown by its proximity, she paused to take another breath in for confirmation, then doubled back, following the smell until she came to the door of Arnaud's library. If the silence on the other side was anything to go by then her grandfather was either sleeping in his armchair or consuming one of his books. Either way, his choice of setting would make it that much more difficult for Ophélie to work up the nerve to enter.

Whereas the neutral decor of his bedroom would have promised no nostalgic significance vis-a-vis their time to-gether, towering before her was the room that housed an accumulation of memories greater than that of its literature. From the aisles of mahogany bookshelves stacked as high as the ceiling to the glass cabinets displaying Arnaud's geological collection, every inch of that library was connected to a precious childhood souvenir.

Motionless, Ophélie stood with her fingers resting on the handle for so long that the sensation dissolved from them. That her grandfather had selected this hideout fuelled her hope that the threads binding them together had not been wholly sundered, but there would be only one way to find out. The scrape of Mr Girard's chair moving in his office prompted Ophélie to creak the door open and step inside, whereupon her throat gave a stifled gasp.

Despite its enormous size, the library looked more like a cluttered, makeshift bedroom. Blocking the ladder to the balcony where Arnaud kept his favourite volumes was his wardrobe, next to which the embers in his pipe oozed smoke from the ledge above the fireplace. No books laid out or evidence of recent such activity; her grandfather's anthologies had not been touched in years, nor had the telescope collecting dust beneath the window.

And if final proof was needed that this scholarly envi-ronment had become the gentleman's living—or rather, dying—quarters, it was at the centre of the room; his bed, empty, save the curled-up outline of Dante, Arnaud's cat. Of all the tokens of Ophélie's relationship with her grandfather, the feline would leave her the most breathless.

After hearing the cries of a feral kitten from the garden one winter in her childhood, the doctor had reluctantly brought it into his library to keep warm until morning, if only to hush the creature up. When Ophélie spotted it sleeping by the fireplace the following day, however, she had thrown her arms around her grandfather, whispering: "I knew you were a good man". Dante had earned his name and been a permanent resident of Baudières since.

Ready to confront the doctor himself now, Ophélie took another step forward and glanced from left to right. As expected, the moment her gaze fell on her grandfather dozing in his chair by the window—face lit by a sliver of sunlight—the walls began to close in around her.

Even from across the library, she could tell that Arnaud's body was decaying—cotton-like hair and sunken cheeks where his striking features once lay. Visibly weary, his arms traipsed at his sides and his chest twitched in raspy motions, as if his lungs were tired of functioning. It was a sorry sight indeed for anyone who had known the doctor in his prime, and one that only reinforced his granddaughter's interpretation of the many questions with which he had left her—why had she been sent away? And did he regret this decision?

For better or worse, Ophélie had never needed to ask Arnaud for these answers. Standing before him again, it was moreover impossible for her not to love him with all her heart regardless.

Hesitant to stir him, she began retreating towards the door, but a deep, solemn voice took her by surprise.

"Ophélie?"

Rooted to the spot, she slowly turned to face him, and for what seemed like an eternity, neither of them spoke.

"Is it really you?" Arnaud finally asked. Glancing away, he continued as a mumble: "Honestly, what is the point of writing a farewell note when death cannot be relied upon to arrive on time? It makes one lose all credibility".

Ophélie forced a smile and pulled up a chair next to his. "In death's defence, Grand-père, timeliness was never your forte either, added to which you underestimate the power of my aunt's alacrity".

"Well, I suppose I should be relieved that at least one component of that duo is ambitious about something", Arnaud replied, his voice trailing off into a whisper.

Saddened by the old man's sorrow, Ophélie stood up to fetch his pipe from the fireplace, then racked her brain for something to break the mounting tension when she sat back down. "'With time, all things are matured and become clear; time is the father of truth'; was that really to be your final goodbye to me? I am a little disappointed; you know better than anyone that when it comes to philosophy, I am more partial to Montaigne".

"Heavens girl, I am torn between leaping to poor Rabelais' defence and feeling unspeakably glad that my granddaughter did not lose her tenacity in that godforsaken hamlet", Arnaud chortled, pausing to add: "Would you believe it, I did not care for that quote until I was told I had only weeks left. Then, upon reading those words with a visible end in sight, it all became lucid—like an eerie fog lifting. And now you have put me in the impossible position of having to come up with something new to say to you moments before I depart from this world".

"I am confident that you will conjure the right message when the time comes", Ophélie insisted.

There was another minute of silence while Arnaud shook his head and selected his next words. "Let us not stand on ceremony, Ophélie; I owe you a sincere apology and a lifetime of reparations, but we both know that it is not in my nature to admit wrongdoing, nor that anything I might say could make up for what happened".

"Please, I did not come here for a confession, Grand-père, and I do not wish to dwell on the past", Ophélie interjected, pulling his hand into hers. "By the looks of things, you have been doing a sufficient job of punishing yourself as it is. When was the last time you felt the sun on your skin?"

"I am afraid I have seen everything outside this room that I could possibly want to, Ophélie, and none of it interests me—it never has", Arnaud turned to face the window. "Truth be told, I am one of the most difficult individuals that has likely ever existed. I am as aware of that fact as anyone.

"'You are an impossible man to please', your grandmother would whine every time I failed to compliment her on whatever frilly attire she had purchased, or when one of my children attempted to show me an inane new 'skill' they had learnt. She was right; her complaints—however lachrymose—were unable to elicit an inkling of guilt in me. Many decades ago, in fact, a widower told me that loving someone was akin to throwing oneself off a cliff, and do you know what I replied? 'That would explain all the feckless bastards writhing on the proverbial ground'. You see, it never occurred to me that therein lay the sensation of flying, or that the view on the way down could be so much more exciting.

"No, as adults, we are led out into society equipped with endless lessons in science, literature, history, law, and mathematics, but at no point are we taught the fundamentals of how to love. Is that not extraordinary, given the overwhelming stakes involved? Like the blood pumping through our veins, it is a mechanism that is simply expected of us".

The doctor dropped his gaze. "I knew from the moment you stepped through my threshold, Ophélie, that it was only a matter of time before the rest of the world discovered what I had discovered that day. And yet, that time passed more quickly than I could bear. Most perversely of all, I was responsible for its transience.

"How I tortured myself contemplating what that boy could possibly have offered you that my own company did not. I questioned it with such rapacity that you were long gone before those screeching wheels in my mind ceased turning and fell apart. By then, all that remained ahead was a barren, smoke-filled trail, and no means of turning back. Rest assured, not a minute goes by that I do not reprimand myself for this folly".

His granddaughter wiped her eyes with her sleeve. "But surely you must know I am not resentful you sent me away—only frustrated with myself for having so upset you that you could never bring yourself to write to me thereafter, or ask me back to visit you".

Arnaud sighed. "I wanted to, Ophélie, but your company was a source of happiness of which I no longer deemed myself deserving—or so went my initial conviction. Then, with much contemplation, I came to identify the veritable cause of my reticence".

"Grand-père", Ophélie muttered, "can you know me so little as to think I could feel hatred towards you?"

"Hatred?" Her grandfather repeated. "You could never be hateful of anyone, Ophélie. Alas, it is one of your many mystifying features that I remain at a loss to comprehend. Disappointment; that is what I feared. Before 'The Incident', you regarded me with such certitude. It was as if you were convinced that there was some higher purpose in me. I could not bear the thought of you looking at me without that expression, and for ten years, I have been too afraid to stand before you as a result—too afraid to request your forgiveness".

As the reciprocal significance of this moment bore down on her, Ophélie sat back and retreated into her mind's library. Resolved in a course of action, she eventually re-emerged via a deep exhalation. "And if I were to offer you my forgiveness, could I expect you—by way of a compromise—to do everything in your power to postpone death?"

Staring back into his granddaughter's eyes, Arnaud fell speechless. With a shaky hand, he proceeded to lift his glass, promising: "I have let you down once, young one—nothing in the world could persuade me to do so again".

"Well then, there is no more to be said on the matter", Ophélie declared. "You will rest and eat when necessary, take whatever medicine is recommended to you, and we will walk together through the garden on the first day of spring just as we did before. I need not add that my aunt will be hugely disappointed, though".

Her grandfather's laughter coincided with the sound of Mrs Cadet pushing her way through the library door.

"Miss Davenport!" the housekeeper cried, thumping her basket down. "You must leave the room at once".

Between coughs, Arnaud managed to mollify her indignity with the counter-order: "Oh do cease your snivelling, Marie, or you will send me to my grave prematurely. My granddaughter and I have come to an agreement, I believe. From now on, she is to be allowed access to the library whenever she likes, and I will be damned if anyone says otherwise".

With this direction in place, Ophélie kept her grandfather company until dinner, then returned to the right wing displaying a perceptible lightness in her step.

That evening, the sun would set on a village imbued with the symphony of voices whispering. And then there were those taking a more personal interest in the newcomers.

9

The Artist

From beneath the wooden canopy in his garden, Romain Lavarre dunked his hands into a fresh bucket of water and watched the ribbons of paint suffuse the surface until his skin emerged clean again.

Returning to his easel, the gentleman went to complete his canvas by marking the number of hours he had been awake for, but his concentration defied orders; once again, he would regret pinning the impending invitation to his letter board on the wall.

For a humble garden shed, it was a remarkably tidy space, and one whose interior saw more of Romain than his bedroom. By the entrance stood a chest of weights, a shelving unit for his art supplies, and an axe atop a woodpile. On the opposing side, Romain tended to store ice for the aches and pains he incurred from overexertion, as well as a stack of books that the gentleman would read under the stars on nights when he sought a more peaceful enterprise. Yesterday's sundown had proven no such example, though.

Canvas in hand, he proceeded to follow the garden path

up to the door, where his housekeeper—and the sole co-inhabitant of his estate—had left his post.

With nothing urgent that required his attention, the gentleman granted himself a minute to check that the locks on his ground-floor windows were fastened, then he pulled on his walking boots and hurried back down the garden for what would either be his third or fourth excursion of the morning.

In a noisier estate across the water, Ophélie had barely stepped out of her bedroom when her journey to breakfast was intercepted by Adèle. That her cousin was already adorning her sun hat indicated that she and her sister were intending to spend another day on the terrace, watching the gentlemen of the village row past.

"Are you coming?" the younger twin asked, clutching Ophélie's hands. "We have so missed you this week".

Before her cousin could open her mouth, Manon waved away the maid styling her hair and groaned a response from her bedroom: "Oh leave her. She is probably going to the left wing again".

In the silence that followed, Ophélie did everything in her power to avoid eye contact with Adèle as the younger twin brushed aside her sister's remark and squeezed her cousin's hands for an answer. It was true; since being reunited with her grandfather, Ophélie had leveraged every interval between meals and activities to sit with Arnaud in his library. These visits were hardly going unnoticed by the rest of her family.

"Perhaps tomorrow", she eventually suggested, while peering over her cousin's shoulder at a familiar figure ahead.

This was not the first time Ophélie had spotted Roland at the end of the corridor when he thought nobody was looking. She would remain in little doubt as to his motive for lingering there; staring into his younger brother Henri's old bedroom, the gentleman barely noticed his niece joining him in the doorway.

Force of habit might explain why the house staff continued to keep Henri Baudin's bedroom door open to this day. Ever since Arnaud's younger son had outgrown the nursery, you see, the boy had insisted that his bedroom door was never to be closed. From childhood into adolescence, this rule had incensed Roland, who had plugged his ears with tissues on occasion to stifle the perpetual racket his brother had made in there. Glancing around Henri's room decades later, the chipped furniture and layers of ink scribbled across the wallpaper offered Roland some indication about what its source had been.

Ophélie, herself, was no less accustomed to seeing Henri's bedroom empty. In her childhood, her uncle had made a surprise appearance at Baudières every few weeks. The weather in whichever country the gentleman wished to travel to next was unfavourable, he would proceed to explain, thus Henri was simply there to tend to his father and sister at home until such time as conditions improved.

Mostly, the gentleman had remained on the right wing during his visits—playing the piano in the drawing room or reading to Gabrielle by her bedside. He had all but moved into the estate again when he had discovered that his sister was dying. The gentleman even offered to travel to Petit Pin himself to bring Roland back to see her, although like all of Henri's correspondence, this letter had gone unanswered. Finally, the morning after Gabrielle's funeral, Henri had packed his remaining bags and left the estate without a word. The gentleman had not returned to Baudières since.

"Have you heard from Henri recently, uncle?" Ophélie broke the silence in the corridor.

"What are you talking about?" Roland snapped. "I am merely reacquainting myself with the house".

With a nod, Ophélie bowed her head and continued walking, but in the heat of the moment, Roland could have sworn that he heard her whisper: 'You and I both, uncle', as she passed.

The gentleman's ears had not forsaken him on this occasion, although like most of his niece's comments, the meaning of this one would remain abstruse to him all the same. By the time he peered back over his shoulder, Ophélie had vanished from the corridor, and with a shudder, Roland, too, took his leave to return downstairs.

That night, the rowboat appeared for a fourth time during Ophélie's attempts to tire herself to sleep. Pulling her shawl tighter, she gripped the window sill once again as the silhouette glided towards Mèliez, imploring: "What is it, Étienne? What are you trying to tell me?"

In reality, her question was futile—Ophélie had known the answer ever since her return. With each repetition, her sole opportunity to act upon it moreover drew nearer.

The day before the Rinaldis' ball, Aixelles would be due to host its twenty-second annual Boat Show. According to its endorsers, this time-honoured event permitted the village's nautical aficionados to have their most handsome vessels compared by a jury. The spectators gathered on terraces with caviar and vintage champagne added a certain gravity to the competition, and everybody who was anybody would be among those crowds.

As a child, Ophélie and her grandfather had watched the show every year from his library window. 'Stick a turkey on water, and the rest of the flock is captivated', the doctor would famously snicker every time a new round of applause broke out.

Like the echo of boyish giggles that seemed to follow Ophélie around the estate, this memory was fast saturating her ears to the point that she could hear nothing else. For a further few nights, she sat by the window, transfixed on the lake. Then, as darkness fell on the eve of the Boat Show, she nodded to herself and slipped back into bed.

After awaiting those first rays of sunlight with bated breath, Ophélie greeted the morning by hurrying to the window for confirmation that the event was going ahead. To her relief, across every visible terrace were maids setting up chairs and parasols, and a fleet of glistening boats was already out on the water.

Her optimism may have been overhasty; judging by the early intensity of the sun, the pattern of hot weather had still not broken. From midday onwards, exercising any degree of physical activity would be problematic, and the journey that she intended to make had been enough to exhaust her even in the best of conditions.

Having mentioned the Boat Show at dinner the previous evening, it came as no shock to Ophélie when Manon and Adèle descended for breakfast in their finest summer dresses. Her cousins would be among the earliest spectators to take a seat on the terrace, where their mother joined them armed with her husband's binoculars.

Ophélie sat with her family momentarily at the water's edge before retreating indoors to 'escape the heat'. Promising to return to her cousins after lunch, she noted the time on the clock in the hallway and was careful to avoid her grandfather's staff as she made her way towards the back door.

Then, collecting her nerves at the bottom of the garden, Ophélie gripped her walking stick, lifted the hem of her dress, and entered the woods.

10

An Encounter in the Woods

The breeze got cooler as Ophélie meandered through the sea of ancient trees. Steadying her legs across the twisted roots and leafy carpet below, her senses gradually adjusted to that surreal silence she had grown to love as a child. With it, all the harshness of the world she was leaving behind faded into sublime tranquillity once again.

Of course, retracing that fateful route was not without its apprehensions; beyond the obvious risk of being caught, Mèliez had been closer to Ophélie's heart than anywhere. Every attempt to imagine what she might find upon her return was naturally accompanied by doubt; would its people be more impoverished than before—their livelihoods destroyed by the sanctions that Aixelles had inflicted on them for 'producing Isabelle's killer'? Would Étienne's parents still reside there, and if so, would they recognise Ophélie after all these years?

For her friend's sake, she kept her head down and battled through these fears regardless. No changes could be more alarming to confront than the enclosure-like structure Aixelles had become, surely. And then, just when she had convinced herself that she was prepared for any further surprises that time might throw her way, Ophélie approached the first historic milestone along her path and was struck motionless.

There it was—the lofty, loyal fence that guarded the Institute. Within its protection, the so-called 'closest earthly depiction of the Garden of Eden' was steeped in stillness so deathly that Ophélie could hear her pulse as she crept towards it.

Triggered by the realisation of where she was standing, an unfamiliar strain of nausea entered her stomach. Few locations in the village were featured in Ophélie's memories as often as this.

From the branches above her head, she and Étienne had spent many an afternoon watching the students of the Boarding House as they slunk in and out of the greenhouses scribbling notes in their exercise books, or the hordes of tourists pouring up and down the paths on either side, whose names and personalities the children had liked to guess.

Now, with the exception of one or two gardeners cutting at bushes, what Ophélie could see of the grounds was devoid of human movement to the point of resembling a painting. Either the students were attending a lesson indoors or they had been allowed out early to watch the Boat Show. In their absence, only a humble chorus of birdsongs and the rolling echo of the fountains cut through the eeriness as Ophélie grasped the wooden stakes and gazed inside.

Immaculately uniform, and exuding an almost military-like degree of control, the liberal conception of the flora was long gone; clearly, the capricious nature of Isabelle's murder had provoked her father to transform more than just the external visitation rights to his establishment. Even after ten years,

Charles Moreau's sorrow was palpable, both implicitly in the orderliness of his vegetation, and overtly in the hefty stone slab sticking out of the grass metres from the fence—presumably marking the spot from which his daughter had been abducted.

Of all the features vying for her attention, it was this monument that caught Ophélie's eye for a specific, albeit unusual reason. Given the angle at which she was standing, she could only speculate as to what was engraved on the front of the stone. But within her line of vision and flooding her head with questions was its second message, etched into the back and pointing towards the woods:

Forever waiting until we two meet again.

Amateurish in finish, she briefly considered whether this had been added by someone in the Moreau family as a threat to Kacper Smolak. Whatever its intention, it was the final proof necessary to complete Ophélie's analysis; if the ancestral crypt housing Isabelle's remains was her peaceful resting place, then these gardens embodied limbo, replete with the unresolved agony left behind by her death.

Thankfully, the chill running down Ophélie's spine was jolted into cessation by the rhapsodic jangle of bells signalling that the Boat Show was in commencement. Reaching her as crescendoing murmurs, the subsequent roar of the spectators served as the encouragement she needed to jump down and push on with her journey.

Twenty minutes later, the rumbles of applause from the other side of the woods began to abate, and Ophélie's ears picked up the distant reverberation of gunshots. Given Mèliez's closer proximity to the barracks of Annecy Castle, this could only mean that she was nearing the halfway point between the villages.

If tradition was to be respected, this should have been Ophélie's invitation to sit and rest her legs a little. Something in her subconscious had been screaming for her to keep moving since leaving the Institute, however, and like a stone rolling around in one's shoe, it was becoming difficult to ignore.

Until now, Ophélie had stifled this alarm by reminding herself of the remarks she and Étienne had made that if indulged with too much concentration, the captivating lull of these woods was known to play tricks on the mind. But as Aixelles fell further behind, Ophélie's voice of reason increasingly lost its gravitas, stripping her defenceless against the most daunting of female intuitions: that someone was following her.

It started as a series of rustling sounds—a branch shaking or twig snapping from a nearby thicket. Then came the more disconcerting patter of footsteps, whose weight and recurrence Ophélie struggled to attribute to an animal.

By the time she had begun her countdown of the estates left to pass before Mèliez, Ophélie had spun around on so many occasions—only to find herself staring at the trees—that she was lightheaded. Accelerating her pace, she covered the remaining distance in as fast a sprint as she could. She was moments from collapsing when she reached the gate now blocking entry to Aixelles' easternmost boundary from Mèliez.

However extraordinary it was to imagine such a construction—cutting through the trees themselves—Ophélie should have anticipated that it would never have been enough for the residents of Aixelles to cordon off the public road connecting the villages. Kacper Smolak had used these woods to gain access to Isabelle, after all.

With such an expansive area to cover, checks for structural integrity appeared to be irregular, at least. Several metres to her right, a fallen tree hitherto spliced between the gate had left a gap in the bars wide enough for Ophélie to fit through. With a wince, she squeezed herself onto the other side, then hurried towards the light.

Relieving as it was to have reentered a public domain, the cost of help should she need it would be a heavy price to pay for the physical discomfort. In the space of just over an hour, the temperature under the open glare of the sun had soared to such an intensity that Ophélie felt as though she was sucking fire into her lungs.

Weak at the knees and leaning on her cane to keep herself from falling, it took her a minute to gather her bearings. Based on the surrounding placidity—the low hum of the paper mill, the grunts of livestock flicking their heads to shoo the flies away—she could be nowhere other than the outskirts of Mèliez.

Over the horizon, the myriad of boats swanning across the water was decidedly less amusing to Ophélie from this perspective. Turning her gaze to the rows of ramshackle farmhouses drooping in the torridity to her right, she felt profoundly sorry for the people of Mèliez that their view should be sullied by daily spectacles as brazen as this. On their bank, time moved at a pace so listless that the air itself felt heavier.

All along the lakeside, inquisitive faces clocked Ophélie's arrival among them; scraggy women slinging clothes around the branches of trees to dry, men tilling fields or leading cattle to the water's edge, and the boys of conscripts lost to the war of 1871-2, gearing up to shine shoes in their fathers' place. The severity of their expressions would leave Ophélie in no doubt that something had indeed changed in Mèliez since her last visit.

As a child, the villagers had overlooked her elegant dresses and articulate speech as if these features were as undeserving of judgment as her limp. Evidently, now that Ophélie was older, her upbringing had become a choice subject to scrutiny.

Despite the recognition in some of the younger residents' stares, it was clear that this would be her only chance to trespass on their land as an adult—an impression that only reinforced the finality of the farewell Ophélie had waited so long to make. Repeating those crucial words, 'no turning back', she stuck to the shade of the trees and made her way along the main road.

The ferocity of the midday sun appeared to have driven most people indoors, at least, emptying the path that led off to Étienne's cottage of its habitual trickle of carts. Every so often a door or shutter on either side would creak open while Ophélie passed, but given both the size of the buildings and the narrow spacing between them, it was not long before the Sourdois family's sycamore tree came into sight at the end of the lane.

It was at that moment—mouth parched and sleeve damp from wiping her forehead—that Ophélie made the mistake of consoling herself that the most gruelling part of her expedition was over. Had she been a child again, she would have recalled from literature's numerous examples that the gateway to any hard-earned recompense is always foreshadowed by a final test. In this instance, the obstacle would be embodied by a middle-aged woman chopping wood in front of her house, four doors along from Étienne's cottage.

Now, you may be wondering why Ophélie's heart sank upon spotting her figure hunched over the road, but fool yourself not, Francesca Bosco was as intimidating as any ill-humoured man wielding an axe. Identifiable by an apparent inability to smile, long had a story circulated among the girls and boys of Mèliez that Mrs Bosco had scowled during a windstorm once, leaving her face permanently stuck in that position. Their parents were less kind in their verdicts, although it was quite another thing to watch them quiver behind civility in her presence.

While Mrs Bosco's surliness certainly appeared to have stood the test of time, the same could not be said about her looks. Sullen cheeks, downturned shoulders, prematurely grey hair; stress had robbed Francesca of whatever youth she had left. Its source was evident in the form of six grandchildren playing barefoot in the vegetable patch by her cottage.

The two on the cusp of adolescence Ophélie had last seen as toddlers. Their younger counterparts had no doubt joined them as the latest victims of their mother's romantic exploits—dumped on their grandmother's doorstep the minute they, too, became tiresome.

With so many mouths to feed, Mrs Bosco had made a name for herself as the only firewood seller willing to take on every village around the lake in a given working day. It was from these visits that the residents of Aixelles had come to learn about her; 'the woman so ill-bred that no level of education could make of her a respectable lady'.

By this, they were referring to the fact that Mrs Bosco frequently wore men's trousers hoisted up with a belt, swore like a sailor, and shouted at a volume capable of causing cardiac arrest in the weak-hearted, all of which led to the dubbing of her nickname 'The Banshee'. 'Let this be a warning of where lascivious conduct gets you', mothers would tut to daughters from their terraces whenever she glided by, pointing at the growing troop of children in her boat.

While Ophélie had never been privy to such slanders herself, she knew better than to stoke Mrs Bosco's temper on a day as sweltering as this. Crossing to the far side of the road, she attempted to keep her movements stealthy, although based on the ease with which 'The Banshee' detected her advancing footsteps, Ophélie might as well have been wearing clogs.

"It's ten cents for a pile of firewood", her heavy Venetian accent burst through the silence.

Ophélie stopped and shielded her face from the sun. "I suppose you do not recognise me, Mrs Bosco".

'The Banshee' winced as she raised the axe once again above her shoulders and thumped it down onto a new stump of wood. "What can I say? Everyone from your village looks and sounds the same to me. Oh don't get me wrong, I'm flattered that you addressed me by my real name. There may just be hope left in the world. If you're here for the firewood-"

"I cannot say that I am", Ophélie replied, shuffling forward. "Forgive me, I had no intention of disturbing you. I was just on my way to visit the Sourdois household".

There was an uncomfortable silence while Mrs Bosco wiped the sweat from her brow and studied her intruder. "Sourdois? Funny, I've not heard that name mentioned in a decade".

"Neither have I, as it happens", Ophélie replied, dropping her gaze. "Étienne was a very close friend of mine, though, and I am ashamed to say that I have not yet had the chance to offer his family my condolences for their loss".

"The deaf boy?" 'The Banshee' exclaimed, resting a hand on her hip. "You're a little late to see his parents. Hugo quit the mine on the day of the burial and the pair of them left Mèliez shortly after. I've not heard from them since".

These words caused a lump to form in Ophélie's throat. It was all she could do to force an answer without her voice trembling. "I see. And Étienne's grave?"

Mrs Bosco raised an eyebrow, then lifted her axe towards the road. "Over in front of his parents' old place. My little ones like to play around there when it's hot but if they get in your way just tell them to scram. I need them indoors to help with lunch soon, anyway".

Ophélie nodded and bid 'The Banshee' a terse thanks, before resuming the scorching stretch of gravel calling her onward. Sure enough, at some point during their conversation, Mrs Bosco's grandchildren had run off in search of shade and were setting up a game of marbles under the sycamore. As soon as the group saw Ophélie approaching they scattered, revealing an infant-sized gravestone whose position at the base of that tree could only make it Étienne's. No name, no epitaph; in grief, his parents had managed nothing more than a date.

Having envisaged a hundred versions of what would follow, Ophélie was sure that by the time she knelt before Étienne's grave, she would know exactly what to say to him. Her mind must have had other intentions, for every script she had committed to memory dissipated as she drew a ready breath on the grass. Never would Ophélie find herself more aphonic.

Locked in this trance—mouth shut, eyes fixed on the weathered stone staring back at her—the elapsing minutes gradually blended into oblivion. Before long, the lull of lunchtime inertia plunged the village into further desertion. And with the return of Mrs Bosco's grandchildren to the road, Ophélie's procrastination gained an audience.

Eventually, she conceded defeat and peered through the branches to gauge the hour. Presuming her aunt and cousins had not already noticed her absence, questions would be asked if she did not return soon. Facing Étienne's grave a final time, she placed her fingers on the stone, whispering: "One day I will find the words with which to close our chapter, my friend". And with this adieu, Ophélie rejoined the road, so abstracted by her thoughts that when she finally glanced aside at the building she had been lingering next to all this time, her legs buckled.

The Smolak house; 'abandoned by God first and its occupants second', the greenery at the front resembled straw now, most of the windows were broken, and with wooden bars across the door, it looked as though the cottage had been derelict for years. Apparently, no one had been tempted to call the home of Isabelle's killer their own, subsequently, and Ophélie was loath to judge people for staying away—this ruin was no longer an abode for the living.

Deprived of its primary function, there was a density emanating from the exterior, as if the secrets of the cottage's last inhabitants were expanding against the walls with intensifying force. It was these whispers that rooted Ophélie to the spot in fascination, like phantom lamentations luring her towards them from the road.

The longer she stood there, staring, the more lucid the bond became; this was a replica of the mental vault that Ophélie had created for herself years ago—the parts of her childhood she had locked away with Isabelle's murder. Confronted with its physical incarnation, the door of this vault began to loosen, and one by one, its memories escaped.

At their core was Kacper Smolak, of whom Ophélie's impressions had been bleak even before 'The Incident'. In hindsight, not one of her visits to Mèliez had gone by without factoring in the quarantine approach to village life that his reign of terror had periodically induced.

Since deals and deliveries had tended to take place at night, mornings had offered the only safe window in which it was possible to come and go without bumping into the gentleman. From midday onward, you could expect to find him lying drunk against public property, or hurling abuse at the village children. But surpassing all reasons why Ophélie had avoided 'The Polack' was the company he had kept.

Led by a man named Ivan—whose smirk alone had caused Ophélie to reach for Étienne—the gang of 'business associates' who had defiled Mèliez's streets once a week could not have better attested to Kacper's own ethos. Not even the livestock had been spared their tyranny, for local farmers lost count of the animals that went missing after the mob's visits, petrified of the consequences if they were to involve the police. Liberated from such a regime, Ophélie could only imagine how the villagers rejoiced in the wake of Kacper's execution.

As for the gentleman's wife, Mrs Smolak had seldom been allowed out of the cottage, and on the odd occasion that Ophélie had seen her staggering along Étienne's road, the woman would be sporting a fresh injury with a pretext more incredulous than the last.

In light of this combination, it should come as no surprise that all mentions of the couple had incited gratitude that these 'miscreants' chose not to procreate. Where there is drama in any community there is controversy though, and while rebuttals to such remarks were rare in Ophélie's recollection, the matter of an alleged son existing between Mr and Mrs Smolak came to mind by nature of it being the sole rumour to have made the rounds in the entire history of Mèliez.

Since the notion of befriending either individual had been repugnant, there was no proof of this, of course. For the handful of eye-witnesses who claimed to have seen an evasive child returning to their cottage from the markets once or twice, however, the conjecture was that the boy had been kept indoors most of the time—possibly for his own safety, perhaps even for theirs—before departing from the village with his mother.

These days, those who maintained the validity of this folktale made up a flimsy percentage of the ageing community. Where Ophélie's own judgment was concerned, she was inclined to believe that observers had simply perceived what their eyes had wanted them to—something she, herself, had experienced once before.

By no coincidence, her 'sighting' had taken place at the height of the story's circulation. While playing hide and seek with Étienne in his garden, she had looked up and spotted what she thought was a boy in the circular attic window of the Smolak cottage. As quickly as Ophélie's gaze had been drawn to the illusion, though, the face had vanished, leaving her with a range of explanations—the least likely of which was that the child watching her had been real.

Lost amid these flashbacks, the explosion of a woman's voice struck Ophélie like a bullet. Surveying the road ahead to locate its provenance, it occurred to her that the steady thuds of wood-chopping had ceased some time ago.

"I said, are you looking for someone?" 'The Banshee' repeated from her driveway, her eyes shifting between Ophélie and the attic window of the Smolak cottage.

Ophélie shook her head and continued walking. Based on the acerbity of the Venetian's glower, her grace period in Mèliez had run its course, and by this stage, Ophélie was reluctant to contest its terms by dawdling.

She had nearly reached the safety of the main road again when 'The Banshee' stepped forward to shout after her what Ophélie presumed was a final adieu: "I would be remiss not to tell you that making a habit of coming here is a bad idea, Miss Davenport. You know as well as I do that Aixelles is an unforgiving place".

Rarely was Ophélie caught off-guard by a comment such as this. Allowing herself an extra second to think, she turned around in the hopes that Mrs Bosco's face would provide some elucidation, only to be disappointed by its inscrutability.

"I appreciate your concern", Ophélie called back, pausing to add: "But I do not believe I am the only one to whom it is owed. Every few nights I see a rowboat that crosses from my village to yours transporting a crate. I do not suppose you know who the gentleman might be, or what his purpose is for making this journey?"

With defensive gestures, 'The Banshee' muttered something to herself, then dragged another log onto her pile. "I think it would be best that you return to your village now, Miss Davenport. I've seen no such boat".

It may have been the heat or the uneasiness of Mrs Bosco's sendoff, but when Ophélie turned back to the road, she was struck by a dizzying headache. Flustered at the notion of rejoining her family in this state, she chose to take a longer route home.

The message on the back of Isabelle's monument, the footsteps following her to Mèliez, Étienne's grave, Mrs Bosco's caution; like the snowballs she had rolled downhill to thicken as a child in winter, the momentum of these retrospections forced Ophélie to retreat into a state of quasi-consciousness to sort through them all.

As a result, the passing branches and dusty streams of sunlight soon became a monotonous blur. With no notion of how long she had been walking for—or her location respective to either village—Ophélie failed to spot the silhouette moving through the woods ahead.

By the time she had reached the clearing, it was too late to change course—her eyes shot up and were met with those of a young man staring back in equal astonishment.

Despite being impeccably dressed, his muscular frame was not what one would expect from a gentleman accustomed to sitting and dining. The sleeves of his shirt were rolled up to the elbow displaying olive skin, and his wavy hair was tousled as if he had been exercising profusely. Across his shoulder was the carcass of a boar, while a rifle hung loosely in his hand.

But of all these features, the one that struck Ophélie the most was the look on his face. Familiar, yet sublimely novel; never a more remarkable blend of emotions had she witnessed in a single expression.

When she finally tore her own gaze away and hurried home, Ophélie was unable to recall whether the encounter had lasted mere seconds or a full minute. Either way, she could hardly bring herself to look her female cousins in the eye upon rejoining them for the Boat Show's closing ceremony, or later at dinner.

To make matters worse, when Ophélie returned from taking her grandfather his nightcap, a gift in the form of a ballgown and black satin mask awaited her on the bed. As the accompanying note explained, they had been bought by Adèle earlier in the week on the apt presumption that her cousin would be too occupied to prepare a costume for herself.

Holding the mask to her chest, Ophélie sank onto the window ledge to clear her head. That night, her reflections would be preceded by the hushed words: "Oh Étienne, what have I done?"

11

The Faces Under the Masks

Unable to shake the previous day's encounter from her mind, Ophélie made herself scarce in the hours before their ferry to the ball. Mostly, this was to avoid the interminable squeals of Manon and Adèle swapping garments to try on. But in addition to these echoes—audible from every inch of Baudières in which she sought refuge from them—Ophélie's apprehension was reaching the stage whereby she could no longer control its materialisation on her face.

Having fended off questions about her aloofness all day by feigning a stomach ache, a part of her was relieved when Thomas interrupted dinner with a tantrum. It came after the news was finally broken to him that he would be spending the evening at home with Mrs Cadet. Between his screams and Camille's even louder demands for this racket to cease, Ophélie did not know which mind-numbing distraction she should be more grateful for.

Whatever mitigation she felt was fleeting nevertheless. When threats involving a belt entered the discussion, she waved Camille down and led Thomas upstairs.

Fifteen minutes later she had calmed him enough to stop his panting, and continued stroking his hair on the bed until the boy's sobs turned into yawns. No less weary from her own emotions, Ophélie seized this opportunity to change into her dress and pick up her mask in advance of their departure, then hurried to the left wing before her female cousins could seek her out again.

Unfortunately, even Dante's soothing purrs from the armchair were unable to offset the tension that she brought with her into the library. Suspecting that it was only a matter of time before her grandfather enquired as to why she looked so restless, Ophélie set about pacing the room. Then, omitting the detail that she had been on her way back from Mèliez, she relinquished the confession that someone had witnessed her wandering through the woods behind Baudières not twenty-four hours ago. By now, Ophélie had spent the best part of that interval praying the gentleman would have found himself too occupied to inform others of what he had seen.

"Highly doubtful", was Arnaud's response when she asked for his opinion on the matter, however, after which the old man cleared his throat. "Hearsay waits for no man here, Ophélie; this is the sort of place where people on their deathbed reach for a neighbour rather than a priest. Lord knows no amount of money could repair the havoc that they wreak on others. And while we are on the topic I cannot say I approve of you walking through the woods alone. Next time, I urge that you take a weapon for self-defence—a kitchen knife would do".

"A kitchen knife?" Ophélie repeated, savouring this much-needed moment of comic relief. "I half expected you to lecture me on the importance of remaining within the grounds of the estate again".

Her grandfather rolled his eyes. "Ten years on, I know better than to argue with you, young one. No, I have long learnt that if my granddaughter sets her mind to something then it is likely for a good reason, and so I concede. Now, let us find a solution to this problem of yours. There is little point in me asking, I predict, but what did the gentleman look like?"

"Well, that was the strange part", Ophélie replied, drifting towards the window. "I did not recognise him from childhood, but I suppose he was about my age; tall, athletic, with dark brown hair and the bluest eyes I have ever seen".

"How funny", Mrs Cadet muttered from the other side of the library, where she had been dusting the bookshelves in silence. "That sounds like the fellow who came to the house asking after you two summers ago".

Certain that she had misheard the housekeeper, Ophélie turned to face her. "Asking after me?"

"Quite right", Mrs Cadet called back from the top of the ladder. "Oh, about eighteen months ago. He was very polite from what I can recall. Naturally, I was reluctant to disclose your aunt and uncle's address to a stranger, so he simply thanked me for my time and left, informing me that one of the downstairs windows needed work done to it before the winter".

"And that was all he said?" Ophélie pressed.

"It was indeed", Mrs Cadet replied. "By the time the caretaker got round to the window, the woodwork had already been replaced and looked as good as new. He must have commissioned someone to fix it on our behalf. Pleasant chap, I never did catch his name".

After a minute of silence, Arnaud lit his pipe and abandoned his attempts to ascertain his granddaughter's reaction with the brusque reminder: "You do know you are under no obligation to go to this ridiculous party".

Ophélie sighed and stepped away from the window. "On the contrary, Grand-père, I fear that the only thing worse than attending would be not attending. Following yesterday's stunt, the villagers' misgivings about our family have already been confirmed, and it would hardly be fair for my aunt and cousins to bear the brunt of dishonour in my absence".

"Well in that case what does it matter, Ophélie? Believe me, I have had to endure my fair share of social engagements with these blathering trollops and booze-guzzling narcissists in the past, so I can tell you firsthand that their approval is meaningless", Arnaud beckoned her over to his bed. "Now, go to the ball and be my eyes. Keep count of the damning glares funnelled your way, give me the name of every fool who mutters censure at you as you pass, and mark my words, by tomorrow we shall be laughing about them all".

This advice might only have elicited a smirk from his granddaughter, at first, but it did allay Ophélie's nerves later when the hallway bell signalled that it was time to leave. With a deep breath, she kissed Arnaud goodnight, then hurried to the front of the house where her aunt and cousins were waiting by the water.

In Manon's own words, she had timed their journey to coincide with the most popular batch of arrivals with 'remarkable precision'. As the newcomers stepped onto the terrace and joined the crowd congregating towards a crescendo of music, Ophélie could only hope that the Rinaldis' extraordinary abundance of decorations would draw attention away from her family.

Miraculously, this did seem to be the case at first; whether it was the staggered rows of multicoloured lanterns or the ribbons draped across the trees, something garish loomed at every angle. The exterior would pale in comparison with what was in store beyond the footmen at the door, though.

While packing the entire festival-filled city of Venice into one estate might sound like an overambitious goal for any host, Mr and Mrs Rinaldi had clearly pledged to execute this plan or die trying. From the fifty-piece orchestra lining the back wall to the scattered cast of street performers, never had a greater throng of shapes or colours been assembled in a ballroom.

With matching feathered headdresses half a metre high, the Rinaldis themselves had more than embraced the carnival spirit. Judging by the manner in which they were scanning the crowd, the couple moreover appeared to have been on the lookout for their 'guests of honour' for some time now. As soon as they spotted Ophélie, her aunt, and her cousins hovering by the door, they made a beeline for the ladies to ensure that they would be the first to say hello, before launching them on a guided tour of the ballroom to greet the other attendees.

This would be one in a series of acts that left Ophélie dubious as to whether yesterday's mishap was public knowledge. As the first hour drew to its close, pleasantries were exchanged and small talk was conducted without any cause to suspect that perceptions of her family had been sullied since the villagers' welcome visits. On the contrary, not insobriety nor ballroom etiquette could account for the apparent thawing of their demeanours.

And with this observation, Ophélie relaxed further behind

her costume. Since her incapacity to join the quadrille spared her from dancing, she poured her eyes over the sea of figures surrounding her instead. If only Étienne could be here to witness them too, she sighed, for never had she encountered a more willing sample of humans displaying their inner beasts.

Visions obscuring alongside inhibitions, night's seductive invitation for the mischievous to come out and play settled like a narcotic fog. Each round of champagne flutes stripped the Rinaldis' guests of another layer of defence, until everywhere Ophélie turned, she felt as though she were looking at birds in a menagerie.

Scattered around the ballroom were the flashy macaws like Jacques Saunier, squawking to be heard above everyone else. Then there were the unblinking owls such as Adèle and Marguerite Veaux, ever-questioning what the louder ones might be thinking about them. The lazier storks like Eduard de Corbiac, on the other hand, were content to smile and nod, as if their presence alone was sufficient contribution to a conversation.

No less prominent were the seagulls such as Camille, who slunk off early on to inspect the Rinaldis' estate for comparison with Baudières, or Solène Ozaman, who lent back during every conversation to pick up delicious morsels of gossip from behind her. Julien Girard and Nicolas Belmont from the Institute all but played dead to elude passers-by, whereas the Boarding House students who approached Ophélie and her cousins to dance reminded her of peacocks.

Yet, as quickly as the villagers had grown plumage came the detail that rendered them unmistakably human again; the bitter cry beneath every roar of laughter, longing to be acknowledged, and in turn, liberated.

In one look shared between the wrong dancers, Ophélie saw the forbidden pinings of desire; into every ear that names were whispered, her gaze was drawn not to the sinful subject of their exchanges, but to the faces of the whistle-blowers. Only more jarring was her observation that a certain individual did not appear to be present among them.

Despite the stiffness in Ophélie's neck, every glance over her shoulder to catch sight of the gentleman from the woods had been fruitless so far. Towards midnight, she grew tired of waiting for a chance encounter. Using the next break in the orchestra to split from her cousins, Ophélie secured her mask, then went about circulating the room.

Face after face, group after group; irritation began to set in towards the end of Ophélie's third round, and with it, the inevitable haze of doubt. Could the gentleman have been a mere figment of her imagination? Or had he come and gone, perchance, without making his presence known? In reality, all speculation led to the same conclusion regardless: that Ophélie might never receive an explanation for why this stranger had kept her secret.

An hour later, she found herself fatigued in the corner of the ballroom, staring at the row of gold-framed paintings protruding from the wall. Awash in a sea of Neoclassicism, the biblical scenes and sashaying maidens before her were almost enough to drown out Ophélie's surroundings. Regrettably, there could be no hiding places in an environment such as this, though; a minute later, a wobbly pair of hands grasped her waist from behind.

"You are something of a celebrity tonight, Miss Davenport!" Mrs Rinaldi's voice slurred between hiccups. "Even Mr Romain Lavarre has been requesting to speak with you, which is most extraordinary given that we seldom have the pleasure of his presence at social events like these. He surprised us all with his arrival just now".

"Did he indeed?" Ophélie replied, while searching for something to mop up the champagne soaking into her dress from her host's glass. "I am not familiar with the gentleman".

With a deafening squeal, the host nearly knocked Ophéle to the floor once again as she spun around, demanding: "Giulio! Where did Mr Lavarre scamper off to? Find the chap and bring him to us at once!"

By the time the sensation had returned to Ophélie's ears, Mrs Rinaldi had leant in so closely that Ophélie could feel herself becoming inebriated from the sour fumes in her breath. The host continued in as low a pitch as she could manage: "Between the two of us, you would do well to keep in Romain's favour, my girl. Rumour has it his ancestry dates back to Russian Tsars themselves. Very good blood there. Many a young lady has tried for his affection, but his work and travel schedule are a most discouraging hurdle in the love department. Of course, you will find out all about that once I introduce the two of you. Someone fetch me that husband of mine!"

For better or worse, her cries were interrupted by an unfamiliar voice that appeared from behind Ophélie at that moment. "There is no need for that, Mrs Rinaldi. As it happens, Miss Davenport and I have already met".

Having instantly summoned to mind an image of who this gentleman might be, it came as no shock to Ophélie when she turned around and lowered her mask, only to look up at the hunter from the woods. With a polished costume and his hair swept neatly back, he blended seamlessly into the crowd. There was something in his expression that suggested otherwise, though.

Sensing that an interjection from Mrs Rinaldi was imminent, Romain handed Ophélie the napkin he had brought over for her dress and added: "Allow me to elaborate. We came across one another yesterday in the village centre, but Miss Davenport left in such a hurry, we were not able to be properly introduced".

"Heavens, well I shall leave the two of you to become better acquainted then", Mrs Rinaldi giggled, before tearing off towards her husband with the painfully loud refrain: "I hear wedding bells, Giulio!"

On the bright side, the mutual humiliation of this exit awarded Ophélie an extra minute to think while she dabbed herself down. Based on Romain's silence, the gentleman was waiting for her to make the first move. In the aftermath of Mrs Rinaldi's comment, all of Ophélie's pre-devised strategies for how to tackle this situation nevertheless fell apart.

Setting the napkin aside, she eventually opted for directness and began: "Mr Lavarre, I would like to thank you for keeping my whereabouts yesterday private. I would hate for people to jump to the wrong conclusions".

To her surprise, a look of confusion entered Romain's face as he responded: "Miss Davenport, you may rest assured that I have no interest in spreading your affairs around the eyes and ears of ballrooms. I only wished to apologise for startling you. You looked somewhat out of sorts when our paths crossed. I certainly hope my presence did not aggravate this".

"Oh no, not at all", Ophélie muttered, "I was simply not aware that anyone hunted in that part of the forest".

A smile was not the reaction she had expected from this

comment, let alone one whose warmth carried an air of curiosity about it. Romain took a sip of his champagne. "Hunting? Is that what you think I was doing?"

"Well, you do not strike me as someone who counts taxidermy among his hobbies", Ophélie raised an eyebrow.

"I am certainly glad to hear it", Romain responded. "The truth is somewhat less amusing, though. I am afraid the boar in question was dying long before my involvement—victim to an old snare that someone had left in the woods. Both of its back legs were gone when I came across it during a morning walk, so I returned to put it out of its misery with a bullet to the head yesterday. I can assure you that it was a quicker and more dignified death than dehydration.

"As for the rest, when you saw me I was in the process of taking the animal to an associate of mine in Mèliez. What with the drought we have had across the region this summer, I am sure you can understand that I thought the carcass would serve better use keeping children from hunger than rotting in the woods. And now that you have my explanation, might I ask what you were doing so far from the village yourself?"

Ophélie paused. "I was on my way home from saying goodbye to an old friend".

"I see. Well, I shall press you no more on the topic", Romain reassured her. Tilting his head towards the wall, he continued: "I noticed you were taking in the Rinaldis' art collection before I walked over".

"Yes", Ophélie shrugged, "it is impossible not to marvel at the precision in each painting. My grandfather would certainly approve—he is a great believer that art should be as accurate a depiction of reality as possible".

"But you find fault with his theory", Romain suggested.

Ophélie smiled, then turned back to study the gentleman's face once again. Having sought an appropriate occasion to bring up Mrs Cadet's earlier comment, she proceeded to enquire: "I must ask, Mr Lavarre, have we met somewhere in the past? Our housekeeper is under the impression that you came to my grandfather's estate some time ago".

Just as Romain went to speak, something in the middle of the ballroom caught his attention and the gentleman shook his head. "No, Miss Davenport. I can confirm that before tonight, you and I had never met one another".

Then, without explanation, Romain handed his champagne flute to a passing waiter, adding: "Please forgive me, I have a pressing matter at home that I must attend to. It was truly a pleasure to have met you".

And with a bow, the gentleman turned and made for the exit, providing Adèle with the window of opportunity she had been waiting for to reappear at her cousin's side, poised to interrogate her about him.

It was for this very reason that Romain resisted the urge to look back over his shoulder until he was past the Rinaldis' entrance hall and out the front door. By this point, Ophélie had been reabsorbed into the crowd, and her impression of their interaction—still visible on her face—would remain just out of sight. The frustration of not knowing what she might be thinking was a necessary sacrifice, though it made Romain's journey home all the more solitary.

Aided by the breeze and the silvery light of the moon, he released this tension with each turn of the ores. Unlike the guests who would soon be staggering onto the Rinaldis' terrace and passing out in boats on their way home, Romain's night was far from over. If the plethora of eyes watching his discussion with Ophélie had served a positive purpose, it was convincing the gentleman not to delay the journey he had intended to make at dawn.

Upon entering his estate, Romain went straight to his drinks cabinet to pour himself a glass of wine, then pulled out his suitcase. From the pile of letters on the desk, his destination called to him: Lise Duclos, that evasive ex-employee of the Institute, whose location he had gone to the lengths of hiring an investigator to track down.

The gentleman was not thrilled at the prospect of another potentially unsuccessful trip across the country. Several attempts to locate Isabelle Moreau's nurse over the past eighteen months had led to a string of dead ends in his search. That afternoon, however, Romain had received a new lead indicating that Miss Duclos was lying low in a tavern in Rennes. Being the only name and city left on his list to check, this might be Romain's last chance to find her.

Coordinates in hand, the gentleman made his way down to the road where his carriage was waiting for him. Though mild in temperature, there was a faint undercurrent of change in the wind that had not been present the previous week. If Romain's intuition was right, the lake and mountains would not look the same upon his return.

As the gentleman set off—accompanied only by the echo of hooves—he watched the village fade into darkness from the carriage window with replenished strength. The hardest phase of battle lay ahead, but for the remainder of the journey, Romain lifted his head to the sky and allowed himself to hope again.

12

Voices

There were few complaints about the weather turning sour in the days that followed the Rinaldis' ball. In part, this was because the heatwave of recent months had driven people to embrace the prospect of autumn with greater gusto than ever, but predominantly, it was due to the groggy aftereffect of the night's escapades.

For the younger generation of villagers, the queasiness was nothing that two hours' sleep and a spot of hearty food would not solve. While their elders darted from the sunlight like cockroaches, the Boarding House students could barely wait until breakfast the following morning to commence their assessment of the event.

Of the three newcomers to their pool of analysis, the students were divided in their preferences. For those drawn in by Manon's neckline, the elder twin was quickly rising to the ranks of a coquettish goddess. Not only had her ballgown been tighter-fitted than her sister and cousin's, but she had exuded such an air of vanity in their eyes that the meeker-inclined among the gentlemen were reluctant to contribute an opinion right away.

Until that morning, countless debates had culminated in the agreement that Eloïse Monnoyeur was Aixelles' greatest beauty—that is, before her figure was 'tarnished' by pregnancy. Now, a revolutionary dialectic was emerging among one faction of the Boarding House that Manon's fuller lips might afford her an edge in this contest. More compelling, Victor Chappaz pointed out, was Miss Baudin's comparatively wanton nature, from which comment Corentin de Lastelle proposed a wager based on who could bed her before the first snowfall.

On the opposing camp, the other half of the students turned their noses up at what they considered to be mere mistress material. Manon Baudin undeniably embodied the barefaced lustfulness of woman, but there was something altogether more seductive to them—more deliciously tempting, about Ophélie Davenport.

They had, of course, been briefed about 'the doctor's granddaughter' long in advance, which only fuelled their fascination at how 'unscathed' she had turned out. A second Gabrielle Davenport would certainly have shaken up the village atmosphere after such a tedious summer, but it was clear from the pleasure that the students took from their interactions with Ophélie that this would not be the case. That she required a cane and looked upon each of her listeners with extraordinary attention only sealed her image as the angelic antithesis of her cousin.

And then there was the younger Baudin twin, whose name only surfaced into the discussion via a remark that a 'mousy girl' had spent the night latched to Ophélie like a limpet, rendering all private exchanges with Miss Davenport arduous.

Mercifully for Adèle, the jeer led to an instant rebuke of the bigger stumbling block they had encountered in this respect.

Indeed, it was inconvenient enough for the bachelors of Aixelles that Romain Lavarre had 'swanned into the village' two years prior to become the unattainable object of desire for its female population, but verging on an affront that he had made a surprise entrance at the Rinaldis' ball. More alarming yet was the observation that for the first time, the gentleman appeared to be displaying an interest in one of their young ladies. If those inclined did not act soon, it was advised, Miss Davenport might be lost to his enigmatic allure.

Towards the end of breakfast, their mutterings were picked up by one of the professors and with a bemused roll of his eyes, passed along his table at the back of the hall. Having fantasised about shedding their robes and crawling back into bed from the moment they had sat down, the teachers welcomed this excuse to swap onerous attempts at scholarly discourse for a respite of mindless jabber. And so the boys' comments were relayed from ear to ear until they reached a certain individual at the far end of the bench.

Elbows resting on the table, chin poised atop his hands, he had been leaning towards the gentleman opposite him in growing captivation over the course of the meal. At this point, he could not be sure how long they had been talking for, or what turns their conversation had most recently taken. He did, however, know that he had spent the last four minutes imagining what would happen if he were to pick up the silver goblet by his elbow and smash it over the man's head until his skull cracked open like an egg.

As soon as the subject of Ophélie Davenport tore through the blanket of background noise, his body stiffened. Shifting his hands into his lap, he adjusted his position subtly enough to hear what was being said about her by the gentlemen to his right.

For this individual, such tattle—like most human behaviour—was merely the guidon of the unremarkable. And yet, the articulation of Ophélie's name in correlation with Romain's caused his jaw to lock.

At the next appropriate opening, the gentleman bid his colleagues a pleasant morning, then stood up to exit the hall. With a greeting to each of the house staff he passed along the corridor, he proceeded to take the western stairwell to the top floor, tapping the space between each baluster with his index finger to check that the end count was still the same.

Finally in the safety of his favourite room, the gentleman removed his notebook from its drawer and slunk into his chair by the front-facing window.

Little mid-morning activity to follow; other than the Rinaldis' maids bundling the decorations from their ball into carriages to dispose of them, both the road around the village and the lake itself appeared to be empty. At 10:15, Marie-Charlotte Saunier would no doubt make her way into town for another 'private session' with her choirmaster—as she did twice a week—and Albert Godefroy's housekeeper should be returning home from fetching his daily tobacco any minute now.

Happy that there was nothing more to report here, the gentleman gravitated over to the window on the opposing side of the room and he took a seat, ready to check in on the gardens. Before he had reached for his binoculars, though, the subject of his earlier eavesdropping reentered his head and he hurled the notebook against the glass, pulling at his hair with both hands until two sizable clumps floated to the ground.

Eventually, he regulated his breathing and riveted his gaze on the largest members of his taxidermy collection across the far wall. From the buzzards in-flight on one end to the perching condors at the other, he took in each expression with a series of reluctant nods. Then, turning back to the window, the gentleman placed both hands atop the ledge.

It was a decade since he had allowed himself to evoke the memory that had instigated everything—fourteen years prior in that very spot. Back then, his observatory had still served as a classroom, and it was midway through a lesson when the outline of a girl limping through the woods behind the gardens had caught his attention from the window. Having disappeared into his subconscious, the gentleman was unable to remember what had happened next in the physical world, but he did recall a prickly heat that rose from his toes to his forehead.

Jolting away from the window ledge, the gentleman spared himself the torment of reliving the weeks that had followed this sighting by bending down to retrieve his notebook from the floorboards.

Where the scope and regularity of its content was concerned, he had come a long way since that first sleepless entry. It was impossible to imagine that what had begun as mere observations were now the opening chapter of a diary so intricate that it had spilled across thirteen subsequent note-books. Even more unthinkable was the fact that the diary's denouement—the page to which the gentleman returned and re-read each evening—was at last in sight.

And yet, he began to consider, might it have to end differently?

When the burning exposure of his eyeballs caused tears to erupt, 'The Watcher' forced himself to blink. With deepening breaths, he eventually lowered himself back into the chair as if his body were weightless. Then, he lifted his pen to the notebook, and from this fluid movement emerged the words:

Ortus, my friend, I have finally seen the light.

II

Autumn

13

From the Ashes

25 September 1879, Mèliez.

As a woman whose visitors largely took the form of children goading each other to approach her porch, it had come as a surprise to Francesca Bosco when there was a knock on her door one morning in the autumn of 1879.

'The Banshee' had no idea of whom to expect when she unhooked the latch in her nightie, but it was certainly not a tall, well-dressed gentleman claiming to derive from Mèliez. Now in possession of a fortune 'too considerable for one person', he pledged to provide the villagers with a constant supply of food and money thereafter, in exchange for anonymity.

At first, Mrs Bosco thought her guest was quite mad. The gentleman spoke with such earnestness, though, his face eliciting a semblance of familiarity. Then, like a shock to the system, 'The Banshee' stepped back in the doorway as if she were gazing upon a ghost.

For lack of words, she beckoned him inside, but the gentleman declined, insisting that he could not stay long. This visit, he explained, was one of two he intended to make in Mèliez that morning. With a bow of his head, he left Mrs Bosco with the promise of returning at nightfall with his first delivery, then continued along the road to complete the journey he had begun eight years ago.

Wandering through his childhood cottage again, he might have thought that no time had lapsed at all. His parents had come to France with one suitcase, and they had long sold most of its contents. Now, save the crucifix above the fireplace and the dog-eared copy of *Pan Tadeusz* hidden behind the coat stand, there was little evidence of who had lived here—their private habits, aspirations, or legacies. Probably, this was for the best, their son remarked to himself—posterity would not have looked on the pair kindly.

Indeed, every inch of that cottage evoked a memory the gentleman had willed himself to forget the day he walked out; the sofa on which he had once been beaten so hard that he lost consciousness, the stove that his mother had twice set fire to, and the habitual snort of his father wiping the vodka from his chin, then slamming the front door behind him.

"There's no such thing as justice in this lifetime, boy", he had grunted to his son the very last time they saw each other. "I sacrificed everything I had for the greater good, and in return, I was given a grey lump from the waste pile as a child".

His metaphor was inspired by a pottery maker whose workshop was located in the village marketplace. Forever smiling at the crowd, the old man would sit and turn the wheel, moulding the clay into a pot that perfectly resembled the one before. Inevitably, there were one or two pots in every batch that did not turn out like the others, and the boy's likeness to these unpliable masses was perhaps the only subject upon which he and his father had ever agreed.

When he reached the staircase, the gentleman's eyes narrowed and he turned back to re-scan the living room. The evidence was undeniable; someone else had been there since his departure. This was not the work of mischievous youths, mind you, but a person who had scoured the place then gone to great lengths to return the interior to its previous state. The position of each piece of furniture—embedded in his mind with photographic accuracy—was ever-so-slightly askew, from the angle of the table legs to the corners of the rug.

Presuming that whoever it was had been searching for valuables to pilfer, the gentleman shook his head in pity, then ventured upstairs to collect the keepsakes he had come for.

The first—an item he had carved from the back of a chair—he found beneath his bed in the attic where he had left it. His intruder had drawn the line at rifling through the affairs of a penniless child, at least, he reassured himself. Upon crossing to the circular window where he had spent most of his infancy, however, the gentleman recanted this assumption.

Staring into the wooden chest beneath the sill, he could think of no justification for why its contents would have captured the interest of a robber. Then again, he was no stranger to having these private possessions stolen; on his ninth birthday, he had learnt that his mother was regularly taking them to sell at the market on her husband's orders. Oddly, only one object appeared to be missing from the collection, this time.

Between this observation and his noticing of the smeared, bloody imprint of a fist on the wall, the gentleman's desire to linger there swiftly waned. The individual who had broken in must have been desperate for money, he told himself. But conducting a final check on the other rooms, he was perplexed to find his mother's jewellery untouched in its drawer, as well as what remained of their family heirlooms.

When his housekeeper opened the door to welcome him home an hour later, her smile instantly faded. To her accompanying question as to whether something was wrong, the gentleman relieved his arms of the chest he had carried back.

Staring down at the broken lock on the lid, once again, he proceeded to respond: "I rather fear so".

14

The Cabin in the Woods

Hidden half a mile behind Aixelles, there lay a derelict log cabin that Ophélie and Étienne stumbled across once while exploring the woods. It was not clear who had built the cabin there, or why, for this lonely refuge had long been relinquished to the wilderness.

With vines creeping in through its windows, nature seemed to have accepted this gift with open arms, reaching out to reclaim what was once hers. On one of the ceiling joists, a family of finches had made their nest, and the cylindrical rays of sunlight pouring through the roof lit up a carpet of moss coating the floorboards.

For Ophélie and Étienne, the cabin's functions were limitless; it could be a pirate ship, a castle in the clouds, or a lost underwater kingdom. Occasionally, Ophélie would bring props from her grandfather's estate to aid with their games, and across the walls, the children hung drawings of each new universe that they conceived. For a little over a year, this den remained theirs alone—until the day an external pair of eyes claimed it.

After hearing the plod of footsteps approaching, the children had ducked beneath the window to hide. The minutes that they lay there waiting for the figure to depart had felt like hours to Ophélie, but she would never cease to wonder whom she might have seen on the other side of the wood if she had just lifted her head.

Retribution came the following week when they returned to discover that their illustrations had been removed from the cabin walls. The children could only presume that its previous owner had decided to take it back after finding them there, and not wishing to trespass any longer, they were forced to move on to other exploits.

Outside of her memories, Ophélie never imagined that she would have a chance to see the cabin again. Had her morning not begun with another of Manon's jeremiads about her shortage of suitable dinner party attire, she might not have seized the opportunity to evade her family's bickering and disappear through the garden.

After ten years, she half expected to find the cabin transformed—a fully functioning woodshed or a cosy winter retreat. To Ophélie's surprise, the framework was barely visible through the mesh of greenery camouflaging its exterior. Moreover, the person who had been responsible for taking down the children's pictures must have foregone their venture of restoring the cabin to its original function, for it looked more squalid than ever.

Cautious not to disturb the surrounding peace, she slid the door open and crept into the jungle-like interior as if entering a stranger's home in their absence. Even in the dimness, Ophélie was struck by the reminders of a hundred youthful adventures, alongside that dank, earthy aroma clogging the air with ever-fiercer pungence. Walking its floorboards alone for the first time, the silence was disquieting, broken only by a creaky piece of timber dangling off the roof and the occasional flutter of birds taking flight through the holes in the ceiling.

As a child, it had slipped Ophélie's attention that there may be a reason why she had felt comfortable playing in an environment that, upon reassessment, would unnerve most adults; this cabin was about the same size as the bungalow in which she had lived with her parents in Orléans, before being brought to Baudières.

Even now, Ophélie could remember the smell of the soup simmering atop the stove, and the patter of rain like miniature hooves on the roof on the last evening the three of them were together. Frederick would be rejoining his garrison at dawn, and through his attentiveness to his wife and daughter, seemed to foresee that he would not be returning from this trip. Time and again, he asked Gabrielle to sing to them while she braided Ophélie's hair by the fireplace, but it was her parents' unspoken exchanges in these moments that had most stuck with her.

When they received news of Frederick's death a week later—the result of a blunder during a training exercise—Gabrielle had dropped to her knees and with an ear-splitting wail, offered her soul in place of her husband's. Looking back on this image as she neared the age her mother had been at the time, Ophélie often wondered whether such depth of companionship can only be shared with one person throughout our lifetime. For her own sake, she could only hope that this was not the case.

When she approached the far wall, Ophélie stopped and stared ahead in confusion. It may have been her first visit to the cabin in a decade, but judging by the items across the floorboards, someone else had been there since her departure—possibly a vagabond travelling through the mountains and seeking shelter from the elements.

In the corner, a moth-eaten blanket lay strewn in a heap collecting leaves and spider webs. Next to it; pieces of old newspaper with the faint traces of human excrement, a weathered pile of books, decaying chicken bones, and one or two wisps of long, golden hair stuck to a heavily stained pillow.

In an odd way, it was reassuring to Ophélie that somebody other than herself or Étienne had found comfort in their little hideout. Then, as she glanced aside to inspect whatever else this drifter had left behind, something more unusual caught her eye.

Peeking through the floorboards to her right was a colourful, handwoven bracelet that had been pulled loose at the clasp. Being the last item Ophélie had expected to find there, she bent down and ran her fingers across the braided straw, striving to recall where she had seen similar such jewellery before.

Unable to locate this memory, she lifted herself back up and tucked the bracelet into her coat pocket to examine later. Something about the presence of a woman's trinket in a place as secluded as this suddenly made Ophélie uneasy, and in any case, her family would be wondering where she was by now.

With a final pause to reposition her shawl, she went to turn back, but the walls were rattled by the reverberation of footsteps charging towards her. Before Ophélie could open her mouth to scream, she was tackled to the floor by Thomas, who proceeded to roar with laughter and throw his arms around her.

"You scared me half to death!" Ophélie cried. "What are you doing here, Thomas?"

"I was bored so I followed you, just far enough away that you wouldn't see me", he grinned, jumping to his feet. "What is this place? Does it belong to Grand-père, too?"

"No, it does not belong to anyone", Ophélie snapped, hauling him back, "and you should not have followed me".

Despite the manner of his arrival, she could not deny her relief that of all the Baudins, Thomas had been the one to discover her there. If nothing else, the boy was unlikely to divulge Ophélie's whereabouts to the others. The last time he had left the estate without his mother's permission, Camille had sent him to his bedroom for several hours, then instructed Roland to march upstairs and beat him. A second transgression would inevitably warrant worse.

After a minute of trying to calm her cousin's excitement, Ophélie lowered herself to his eye level, whispering: "Thomas, you have to leave right away. Your mother will be furious if she finds out that you were alone in the woods. Promise me you will never run off from home like that again—regardless of where I am".

Her cousin folded his arms and rocked back and forth on his heels. "Fine, but only if you come with me. Adèle is asking where you are. She says you have been invited to the theatre tonight by the Ozanams. It's not fair, Ophélie, Maman never lets me come with you to these things. I will have to spend another evening with no one but mean old Mrs Cadet, who cannot stand to be in the same room as me. She hates me, I know it".

"You are being silly. There is a reason Mrs Cadet is distant with children, and it has nothing to do with hatred", Ophélie's voice trailed off into a sigh.

According to her tally, this would mark the eleventh consecutive day that their family had been summoned to a decadent breakfast, afternoon excursion, dinner party, or all three. Between both cousins' predicaments, she would have given anything to trade with Thomas.

"Come, breakfast will be served soon. This outing will just have to remain our secret", she eventually forced herself to say, before taking her cousin's hand and leading him back through the woods.

15

Captivity

Summer's transition into autumn began early across the Alps that year. By mid-September, the nights were drawing in and the air turning crisper, as if carrying with it the news that winter was on its way. From terraces, chairs and parasols were brought indoors, while the aroma of bonfires began to replace the scent of freshly-cut grass.

And, as tradition dictated, with the start of a new month came the Baudins' first experience of the Residents' Council. At the end of the session, the family was formally welcomed to Aixelles via a toast by Eduard de Corbiac.

"Ghastly. Just ghastly", was Manon's response upon relaxing the smile from her face and embarking on the boat back to Baudières. "Did you see how he followed me around? I would sooner regard a dog a paramour".

Only then did Ophélie grasp that her cousin was not referring to the two-hour meeting to which they had just been subjected, but Alessio Lettiere, a Sardinian lawyer who had been enthusiastic in his pursuit of Manon since the Rinaldis' ball.

Of all the suitors to court the elder twin in recent weeks, Mr Lettiere was, in fact, the only one to whom Ophélie wished any success. In terms of his credentials, the lawyer may have inherited 'the worst physical features of both parents'—a running slight coined by Manon—but his humour was infectious, and his affection appeared sincere.

Mockery of the gentleman continued well into the journey home regardless, until somewhere between Eduard de Corbiac's marina and their own, Camille thought that she saw Marguerite Veaux peering into their boat.

"Enough, Manon!" she hissed, kicking her daughter's leg to silence her. "Unsightly or not, Mr Lettiere is a respected man in Aixelles. What will I say to the others tomorrow if they catch wind of your gibes?"

By 'the others', Camille meant her Book Club, of course, to which she had signed up after learning that catering was provided in each session. Outside its members, little was known about what was discussed during these private exchanges. Being an avid reader, Ophélie had been invited to attend one herself the previous week, whereupon the ladies spent more time picking apart the rumours that Albert Godefroy's youngest daughter might be pregnant out of wedlock than they did review Madame Bovary. Needless to say, Ophélie declined their next meeting, and her grandfather nearly passed out from laughing at her account later that day.

By the time they reached Baudières, Manon's complaints had shifted to the bruise forming on her shin. Between that and the plummeting temperature, the prospect of a quiet evening in Arnaud's library had never been more appealing to Ophélie.

No sooner had she stood up to mount the pier, however,

than Adèle ceased staring at the boats behind her and pulled her cousin aside to whisper the soul-shattering words: "Do you think Mr Perez will be at the Sauniers' tonight?"

Suddenly, a reminder of their dinner plans was the least of Ophélie's worries.

The gentleman to whom the younger twin had alluded was Pierre-Alexandre Perez, the godson and protégé of Charles Moreau. At thirty-one, Mr Perez had completed his education at the Institute ten years prior before joining its teaching staff. With his fellow scholars stationed around the globe, Ophélie could only imagine that the botanist had chosen to remain by his godfather's side as a result of 'The Incident', but this was a subject she sought to avoid by all measures.

Where certain residents of the Institute were concerned, her discretion was justified; having found herself alone with Nicolas Belmont at one point during the Rinaldis' ball, Ophélie had walked away with a sour taste in her mouth after the professor replied to one of her comments with the warning that: 'God is always watching us, in judgment of our sins'.

As for the Moreau family itself, neither Charles nor his godson appeared to hold anything against her—alas, quite the contrary. Ophélie had not been ignorant to being at the centre of Mr Perez's eyeline throughout the entirety of the ball, or any of the subsequent events they had both attended.

When Adèle repeated her question in the hallway minutes later, Ophélie calmly expressed her inability to speak on behalf of the gentleman's schedule, then picked her coat back off the stand and prepared for a walk into the village. Even the gates around the road would prove a welcome distraction from Mr Perez's name.

Entering the main square—a street that once buzzed with

tourists from the bakery to the florist—the view was somewhat less solacing. At its heart, the tattered, lemon awning of
the Bon Acceuil hotel waved at her in the breeze. The lights
from its interior had long been extinguished. Built in 1866 to
coincide with the arrival of Annecy's train station, the inn had
enjoyed five years of business until it was taken down at the
residents' request—the next precaution to follow their ban on
public boats to their banks in the autumn of 1871, Ophélie
supposed.

Then, passing her grandfather's old tailor shop, she stopped
and looked up at what had, to her surprise, been converted
into a library. Rumour would tell that Mr Aninat, its previous
owner, was unable to afford the rent after losing the services
of Kacper Smolak, who had imported his fabrics cheaply from
a source in Eastern Europe.

With the exception of the Book Club ladies who occasionally
pottered in to pick up whichever novel had the least number
of pages, it looked as though the library was hardly ever used,
yet there it stood, promising passers-by shelter from the wind.
Intrigued to find out more, Ophélie unbuttoned her coat and
stepped inside.

Her entry was heralded by the tinkle of a bell, and the sight
of a rotund man popping his head up from the back of the
room.

"Please come in", Mr Bernard chirped, "we have quite the
collection here!"

Ophélie smiled at the gentleman and removed her shawl.
She did not have the heart to inform him that her grandfather's
library might be five times the size of this one. Its musty
aroma was a universal language to her, though, and on closer
inspection, there may be more to this little repository than

first met the eye.

Midway down the second aisle, Ophélie's gaze began to dart from shelf to shelf with increasing speed. How extraordinary, she told herself, that every one of her favourite childhood books should be there—arranged with a randomness that would have sent Arnaud into a cold sweat, but that Ophélie found oddly endearing. From the Greek myths she would read to Étienne to the works of François Rabelais that she could practically recite, the pages of worlds in which she had loved absorbing herself flooded her memories as she ran her fingers along their spines.

Lethargic, too, in the undulations of heat spewing from the fireplace, Ophélie had almost forgotten where she was when Mr Bernard's voice broke the silence.

"Let me know if you are looking for something", the librarian called out, lifting a box of new arrivals onto the desk. "We only have fiction here, mind you. Mr Lavarre was very specific about that".

As soon as Ophélie heard his name, she emerged from the aisle. "Mr Lavarre owns this library?"

"He does indeed, though it is not common knowledge", Mr Bernard replied. "He purchased it about a year ago and is quite diligent with its upkeep. Sometimes, I catch him down here consuming book after book in the middle of the night. I am quite sure I have never known anybody to get through literature so quickly".

Ophélie glanced away to gather her thoughts. Ever since their meeting at the ball, she had searched for Romain without success at every social engagement. "I have not seen Mr Lavarre in the village for some time now".

"You are quite right, Miss. I believe he is travelling at

present", Mr Bernard answered, "then again, he never does talk much about his private life. All I know is that until his return, I am to leave bread out for the birds and start sorting through this new shipment of books from England. Not that I understand a word of it myself".

"England?" Ophélie enquired, approaching the desk. "I should very much like to go there one day. My father was half English, but he died long before I had the chance to explore that part of my heritage".

"In that case, I suggest you begin with this", Mr Bernard exclaimed, pulling a tattered book off the shelf behind him. "*Wuthering Heights*, by Emily Brontë. It is Mr Lavarre's favourite. He takes it home every few weeks".

"I am much obliged to you, sir", Ophélie responded, before accepting the item and making her way back to Baudières.

With Manon and Adèle already preparing for the evening's festivities, Ophélie went straight to her grandfather's library and spent the remainder of the afternoon reading her new book while Arnaud napped. An hour later, she allowed herself a break to stroke Dante's chin, while mulling something over intently in her head.

Ophélie's ruminations would continue throughout dinner, all the way back to her bedroom window on their return. And there, alone at the sill, she finally drifted off to sleep, looking for the rowboat that never appeared.

16

The Hunt

It would be another week before Ophélie saw Romain again, at Eduard de Corbiac's hunting party. This annual ceremony required an early start as multitudes of boats made their way over to the gentleman's estate, where a team of Savoie's most expert trackers and dog handlers was waiting to guide them into the wilderness.

After a buffet-style breakfast, the group was led out into the grounds, composed of the dozen or so families who had not been deterred by the rain clouds sweeping down the mountains. Romain's unexpected entrance was met with a wave of delight as he passed through the crowd, explaining that he had been unwell of late.

With dark circles under his eyes and an air of agitation about him, it certainly looked as though their latecomer had not slept in days, yet this 'brooding regard'—as Manon put it—seemed to suit Romain in some strange way. When he approached the Baudins, Ophélie's gaze met with his momentarily in concern, but before she could ask after his health, the whistle was blown and battle positions were demanded by the party's guide.

Tradition dictated that the women and children march ten metres behind the men at all times, an arrangement that suited Ophélie inasmuch as it meant remaining at a safe distance from Mr Perez's 'surreptitious' attempts to woo her. On the last three occasions that she had come face-to-face with the gentleman, Ophélie had all but hidden behind furniture to avoid him. Their game of cat-and-mouse could not continue indefinitely, but as far as Ophélie was concerned, each evasion might grant her a few more days of Adèle's ignorance.

With another blow of the whistle, the hunt was called to a start.

Given its geographical limitations, a private hunting ground was a feature that few households in the area could boast. Eduard de Corbiac had his ancestors to thank for his. Some decades earlier, an onset of gout had rendered his great-grandfather unable to travel long distances. With no intention of abstaining from his favourite pastime, he had cleared much of the forest behind the estate to accommodate man-made lakes and a pavilion for storing his firearms. Having passed away before the project was completed, his heirs had considered it their familial duty to make regular use of this creation in his stead.

After a scorching summer, the fields were an unhealthy amber colour, and only the sound of the hounds barking provided solace from the stillness as the first flock of birds took to the sky. The ensuing explosion of bullets was met by a round of cheers from the spectators.

Based on the hunters' level of accuracy, some of the birds might stand a chance, at least, Ophélie consoled herself while the guns were reloaded; Jacques Saunier had let his fringe grow a little too long, for example, obstructing his vision to the point of having to use his wife's hairpins to tie it back. Giulio Rinaldi's incessant pauses to compare shooting techniques indicated that the gentleman was something of a novice. And then there was Charles Moreau, whose recent onset of arthritis caused his shaky arms to miss every shot.

Despite his apparent affliction of a respiratory problem, the professor was in admirable form notwithstanding—particularly compared to his contemporaries. Locked in a lunge by his side was Nicolas Belmont, whom you might be forgiven for mistaking for an owl by effect of the skin under his eyes seemingly drooping off his face.

According to the women of the village, Mr Belmont had been quite handsome in his day. The professor was even engaged, once, though the wedding had never come to fruition. Now, decades of reading in candlelight had left him with him a downturned mouth on which frivolity was as unfamiliar as the embellishment of youth.

As the morning progressed, so, too, did Ophélie's perception that someone was watching her again. Locating the likely cause ahead, she shuddered. Mr Perez seemed to have grown in confidence since their last meeting, and was edging nearer to begin a conversation. Having lost the sensation in her arm following Adèle's excited tugs, it was all Ophélie could do to will that the storm would unleash itself.

When Mr Moreau's pillbox and flask were flung from his pocket in the recoil of his next shot, her hopes were dashed.

"As you can see, my godfather is rather inept at this. He is of the sort who is made for academia, not for sport", Mr Perez laughed, striding alongside Ophélie and her cousins while the group moved on. "If time allows, I should be glad to show you ladies how to shoot today. There is really nothing so liberating".

Without another word, Mr Perez waved the women back and cocked his gun up at the broken formation of geese following one another into a shower of pellets. Ophélie's reaction would not go unnoticed by Romain, who glanced over his shoulder at her from the other side of the field, before firing twice, slightly off-target.

After an hour of shooting, the air became humid and fat raindrops began to fall. Led by Mr de Corbiac, the party retreated towards the house, where alternative entertainment would be provided for them indoors.

Of all the group, Thomas was the most disappointed by this turn of events. The hunt was the first outing that Mrs Baudin had allowed him to attend since their arrival, and he had been on his best behaviour all morning. Mr Moreau agreed to lend him his gun to play with on the journey back, at least, and those minutes while Thomas waved the weapon around seemed to compensate for weeks of boredom. And yet they would be short-lived.

Just as the party reached the de Corbiacs' pavilion to pack up their belongings, the air was pierced by the reverberation of a final shot. From the side of the crowd, Romain proceeded to lurch forward, clutching the top of his arm. Within seconds, the collar of his shirt and half of his right sleeve had turned a deep crimson colour.

Thomas froze to the spot while Eduard de Corbiac rushed over to snatch the gun out of his hands. As the gentleman expected, there had been one cartridge accidentally left in the chamber.

With the group encircling Romain in greater numbers, Ophélie pushed her way to the front to inspect the damage.

Miraculously, one of the pellets had just grazed his shoulder, splitting open half an inch of skin on either side. Immediate action was needed to stitch it back up, but compared to the injuries that had been dragged from the barracks through the threshold of Baudières when Ophélie was a child, Romain's would be simple to treat.

On one occasion, she had opened the door to a soldier whose foot was cut so badly that she could see a silvery bone beneath the gash. Having noted the concern on his granddaughter's face, Arnaud had insisted that she stay in the front room to watch him work on it, after which Ophélie had professed: "You never told me you were an artist, Grand-père".

Given the storm gurgling above them, she knew it would be impossible for a doctor to reach the de Corbiacs' estate from Annecy before the lake became too choppy.

A first flash of lightning exacerbated the villagers' whimpering, and Ophélie stepped forward with a proposition: "I can do it. I will sew it up".

As the stunned crowd looked on, she turned to their host, urging: "Mr de Corbiac, the weather is about to break. Send everyone home and have a medical kit brought to the pavilion at once. I will take it from there".

The gentleman nodded and did as he was instructed, while two guests helped Romain into the pavilion.

With the initial shock over, Ophélie was relieved when the door was finally shut behind them. Heating the needle with a match, she turned away, allowing Romain to remove his shirt and take a preparatory swig of alcohol.

Only then, as she peered over at the scars on his lower back, did Ophélie realise she was nervous—succeeding this, that she might never be further from knowing who Romain was. By the look on his face, the gentleman's wound had caused him no more pain than a scratch, and now that they were alone, he seemed to relax for the first time all morning.

"Mr Lavarre", Ophélie began, "I cannot express how sorry I am. I should have watched Thomas more closely".

"Please, Miss Davenport, your cousin did me a great favour", Romain muttered. "Another minute of listening to Albert Godefroy's advocacy of our 'riveting success in the Africa campaign' or Renald Ozanam's passion for fourteenth-century Italian fencing techniques, and I would have pointed the shotgun towards me myself".

"I will reserve my sympathies until you have partaken in a session with Aixelles' Book Club", Ophélie answered.

Romain gave a deflated laugh, then shook his head. "You must be wondering at my reserve today".

"Actually, I find it oddly refreshing", Ophélie replied, dabbing away a layer of blood. "Although I would be lying if I said I had been convinced that your aloofness is the result of a mere cold. Is something else the matter?"

"The easiest way for me to answer that is to tell you that I am having trouble sleeping at present", Romain explained as the needle entered his shoulder. For a moment he winced, but at the touch of Ophélie's fingers on his skin, he turned calm again. "It is a strain of insomnia that I am regrettably unable to foresee, much less control. I had not initially planned to join today's excursion, but I have been keen to ask how you are enjoying Aixelles since our last encounter. I believe you are not as taken by the village as your aunt and cousins".

Ophélie smiled. "Was that an observation, or a question?"

"Both, I suppose", Romain responded. "Posing the right queries is the best way to understand one's listener, is it not?

I once met a man who claimed that you can know everything you need to about a person via just three questions".

"An interesting philosophy. I am tempted to suggest that four is the ideal number though", Ophélie answered, preparing the next stitch. "Let us find out. Where does your family come from?"

"Kraków, originally. In their youth, my parents were driven out to France after the Uprising. They changed regions many times before settling in Savoie, and by then, the man my father had been pre-exile was long gone. When I was born, my mother spoke to me in Polish, for example, but he refused to hear or read it. All questions regarding his 'previous life' were forbidden", Romain replied. "After his death, I moved to the city to try my lot in business and found that I excelled at it. There was something here I had left behind that I needed to return for, though".

Ophélie nodded. "And what is it that you do in the village? Given your nonattendance at so many dinners and parties, I find it difficult to believe you could be so enamoured by the place yourself".

"No indeed, you might say I reside in Aixelles out of necessity, not inclination. Exceptions exist, of course, but broadly speaking, it is the avarice attached to power that disagrees with me, here", Romain responded, shifting in his seat. "As for my latest absence, I returned just yesterday from a trip to Rennes, where I was obliged to spend a number of weeks on business. I hope your final question will satisfy you, Miss Davenport".

Ophélie paused. "What caused these scars on your back?"

There was a prolonged silence while Romain moved his gaze to the window. "When I was nine, I decided to leap from the tallest branch of the tree in my parents' garden. I cannot recall hitting the ground, but when I came to, my back was numb from landing on a pile of stones. It took me several weeks to walk properly again, in fact.

"By jumping, I hoped that I would open my eyes to find myself somewhere far away—in another body altogether, with no reminiscence of who I had been before. To my surprise, the longer I lay there, the more I realised something—that the view of the sunlight through the branches was more beautiful than the one from the treetop. I have carried that epiphany with me ever since".

At the end of Romain's explanation, Ophélie's hand dropped, and it took her a moment to conjure a response. "It would appear I was right; had I one question left to ask whether the change in temperament you are disguising as an illness was the same ordeal you were jumping from, my analysis might be complete".

The gentleman smiled and lowered his head. "You have a rare gift, Miss Davenport. Most people see of their surroundings only a fragment".

Ophélie waited until the final stitch was in place before offering her response: "Well, perhaps therein lies the 'avarice' you spoke of".

Whatever Romain had intended to reply when he turned back to face her, his words were interrupted by the sound of voices approaching the pavilion. The gentleman slipped his shirt back on and pushed himself upright just in time for the door to swing open, revealing Mr and Mrs de Corbiac accompanied by a troop of maids holding umbrellas. Their terror was quelled when they saw their patient's shoulder bandaged, but this would not delay them from whisking their guests around to the front of their estate, where two carriages had been ordered to take them home.

By now, Thomas had been banished to his bedroom for the afternoon while his mother devised an appropriate penalty for his recklessness. Flouting Camille's order that he was not to be given dinner, Ophélie put together a plate of food for him and took it upstairs in the expectation that the boy would be desperate for company. This time, Thomas requested to be left alone.

As soon as his cousin departed, he turned onto his side and ran his finger along the wall, tracing a message of contempt to Mr Moreau for handing him that shotgun.

Not far from the boy's bedroom, words in an equally personal language were in the process of being composed. Rounding off his evening report, 'The Watcher' reached inside his desk drawer until his fingers met with the item he sought. For over a minute he stared at the trinket in his hands, then delicately slid it into an envelope.

17

Liberation

Around three o'clock that morning, Ophélie was drifting off to sleep when she was woken by the sight of Mrs Cadet standing over her bed in her nightie. In a frantic whisper, the housekeeper implored her to come to the library at once because her grandfather was in some sort of crisis and was asking for her.

With the weather turning bleak, Arnaud's coughing fits were becoming more violent. There were times when he thought he would never breathe again, clutching at the sheets and retching until his lungs felt as though they might implode. Then, he would lie back in the darkness—mind utterly blank—and extend his arm towards Dante. The sensation of the feline's fur beneath his fingers was usually comforting enough for the old man to close his eyes and fall back asleep. But on nights like these when his dreams were plagued by otherworldly visions, Arnaud required the company of his granddaughter.

There was a chill in the air when Ophélie entered the library. It was made eerier by the sound of the rain pounding on the windows, and the intermittent flashes of lightning illuminating the bazaar-like objects scattered around the room. Turning to her grandfather, she asked Mrs Cadet to prepare the fire, then pulled a chair over to his bed.

Hand still resting on Dante's head, Arnaud waited until Ophélie was sitting beside him before beginning: "Do you know, I once believed the age-old lie that dog is man's best friend. Nonsense invented for the needy. As pack animals, it is in their nature to follow and obey without question, just as a child idolises its parents. A cat's spirit, in contrast, is as free as the wind. When they enter a human's life, they look into our souls as our equals and they see everything—our flaws, our mistakes, and our weaknesses. And what is more, they choose to remain by our side in spite of them. There is no stronger bond between man and beast than that".

Ophélie smiled and pulled Arnaud's blanket up to his chin. She was no stranger to these endearing monologues by now, and liked to think of them as her grandfather's way of ridding his conscience of clutter in the lead-up to death.

"Is your defence of Dante's honour what has been preventing you from sleeping tonight, Grand-père?" Ophélie asked.

"Well, it is cruel that most of us spend our youth absorbing information but achieve elucidation solely when it is too late to apply any of this insight—almost as cruel as the state of childhood to which one reverts at about the same age. The last time I felt this useless I was a dribbling, mewling infant", Arnaud took a sip of water. "No, no, to tell you the truth, my being awake is because I dreamt of your mother, for the first time in longer than I can recall. It put me out of sorts. I had forgotten the extent to which her presence could be foreboding".

Ophélie nodded. "Yes, she often spoke of humanity being

doomed".

"Doomed indeed", Arnaud responded, staring at the flames crackling in the fireplace. "Throughout my life, I have seen victims of misfortune so arbitrary that their nature would frighten the devil himself. Consider four brothers and three sisters ravaged by scarlet fever, in the blink of an eye. An uncovered sneeze between siblings—that is all it took to wipe out an entire generation of Baudins with the inexplicable exception of myself.

"But the most harrowing example came five years after your departure when I travelled to Chamonix—the only time I left the estate in your absence. I was reluctant to make the journey, but a dying ex-colleague had requested to see me, and I felt that I had committed enough wrongdoings by then to incur endless penance if I were to refuse.

"When I reached Saint-Laurent en route, the road was blocked and the entire village was on the hunt for a missing girl. She was sixteen—the daughter of a local dairy farmer. I will forever be marked by her family's wretchedness as I watched them from the carriage window, and all I could think was this: what if the girl had been you?

"Now, there are perhaps two or three moments in a person's life when even the most sceptical of believers realise they are being called upon by a higher power to act. I joined the search party without a second thought, and on the eighth day of trudging high and low through freezing mud, I found the girl's body floating in a reservoir. Would you care to guess what happened? She had broken her leg, fallen into the water, and drowned—the result of a mere slip or lapse of concentration. Easily done, yet so avoidable. I fear your mother was right; our lives are as tenuous as leaves falling to the ground in the wind".

Another flash enveloped the library as Arnaud reached for his pipe, and in its aftermath, those ensuing seconds felt eternal to Ophélie. Unsure of what to respond, she looked towards the window, waiting for the grumble of thunder in the hopes that it would inspire a way to lead their conversation to cheerier territory. Upon its arrival, her thoughts were drawn to something else, though—a memory of the time she and Étienne had been caught outdoors amidst similarly turbulent weather, and forced to use their cabin for refuge.

Minutes into the storm, Étienne had decided to alleviate the tension by telling Ophélie a 'silly story'. It started with Jean Sourdois, the eldest son of a blacksmith in the south. Having fallen into hard times, his father had signed him up for a stint at Entrevernes—just across from Mèliez—in response to an advertisement that they needed youths for a particularly narrow section of the mines. When the boy's shoulders were deemed too broad for the job, however, his brother Hugo had been sent to work in his place. It was there, weeks later, that the youngest Sourdois son had met his future wife after witnessing a woman drop her baguette in a puddle in the marketplace.

"To think I would never have been born if my mother was not so clumsy", Étienne had concluded, to which Ophélie added: "Or if your grandfather had missed that poster for the mines, and your father's frame not been so slim". In the end, the children extended these scenarios all the way back to Étienne's oldest known ancestors, until before they realised it, the storm had cleared and it was safe for them to leave the cabin.

Turning to face her grandfather again, Ophélie went to

speak, but the dejection in his eyes caused her words to dissolve.

Eventually, she dropped her shoulders and began: "Grand-père, you mourn for a gift whose very value lies in its fleetingness—and one you were extraordinarily lucky to have been given in the first place. Of the infinite humans who might have existed in your stead had the odds been tilted in their favour, *you* were the single grain of salt plucked from the ocean. No, the unborn are the only ones deserving of pity".

Lips parting, Arnaud proceeded to stare at her in silence, before replying: "I have never been sure of whether to envy or feel sorry for you, Ophélie. Either way, my life might have been different with your counsel sooner".

"And yet we would never have known each other had that been the case", Ophélie answered, prodding the embers in the fireplace. "Would you like me to read you a passage to help you sleep, Grand-père?"

"You and I both know that the time for stories has long gone, Ophélie", he muttered, sinking into his pillow. "It will not do. If I am to hold out until spring, what I require is a project to work on. Otherwise, I shall be left to fester in my thoughts like the philosophers of old. I am adding a new clause to our arrangement; for goodness sake find me a final task—something meaningful. My sanity—or whatever is left of it—depends on it".

His granddaughter smiled. "I have let you down once, young one—nothing in the world could persuade me to do so again".

The doctor sighed, and with his breathing steadier now, he appeared to be ready to close his eyes again. Ophélie waited until he had fallen sound asleep, then snuffed out the fire and tiptoed back to her bedroom. This time, she lifted herself onto the window sill and pulled the shutters open to meet the storm head-on.

Whirling with enough force to knock her off the ledge, the gale clawed at her hair and the rain lashed against her skin. But tilting her face towards the blackened sky, Ophélie had never felt so alive. Her mother had done this whenever the weather was fierce and shouted words into the wind, maintaining that this was the only time that one could speak with those who had passed into the next life and know they were listening.

Grabbing hold of the sides of the window for balance, Ophélie uttered something inaudible against the backdrop of thunder, then stepped down from the ledge and closed the shutters, comforted that her message had been heard.

Weariness would not enter here for the rest of the night; retrieving her old diary from beneath the bed, she sat and poured through every adventure she had shared with Étienne as if she were experiencing it anew. By the time she had finished, only the remarkable scope of everything they had seen and done together imbued her memory.

On the other side of Aixelles, Romain had never been further from sleep, either. Unable to carry out the nightly search he had been conducting since his trip to Rennes, he embraced the storm as a source of creativity by sitting under the shelter of his terrace with his axel.

Eyes fixed on Baudières in the distance, he ignored the bandages wrapped around his shoulder and pushed through the discomfort, moving his paintbrush across the canvas in harmony with the lightning. As its frequency increased, Romain, too, began to feel the life force coursing through his veins. Then, with a last surge of energy, he found himself emerging from the darkness.

18

The Calm Before the Storm

In the week that followed the hunting party, Aixelles became invisible beneath a curtain of rain. Enslaved to their homes, the Rinaldis huddled by the fireplace, complaining that the weather was denying Cornelius his daily walks. Eduard de Corbiac's pipe was refilled more times than he had needed it in months, and Jacques and Marie-Charlotte Saunier's son even took to injuring himself on purpose, just to end their squabbling.

In the Baudin household, 'family time' meant Camille convening a council of war in the drawing room.

"My behaviour at the hunting party was anything *but* inappropriate", Manon snapped in response to that morning's subject matter. Shifting her position on the sofa, she proceeded to elbow her cousin for reinforcement of this defence.

Her appeal was in vain; for the best part of an hour, Ophélie's attention had revolved around the contorted body of a mayfly on the window sill. It must have flown in the previous day and not been able to find its way out, she thought, pitying the insect for having spent the remainder of its life thrashing against a glass barrier. She could not help but wonder how humans would act if, like mayflies, they had only twenty-four hours to live.

After ordering the maid to fetch another pot of tea, Camille marched back to the sofa. "You and that hussy Solène Ozanam spent the day cosying up to those Boarding House students like women of the night and had many of the mothers making comments. There is a fine line between flirtation and indecency, and it takes a more subtle approach than yours. How much can you expect them to earn from learning *botany*, in any case?"

Manon scoffed. "I will have you know that each one of those gentlemen is worth a fortune in inheritance; Victor Chappaz's father owns half of France's silk industry, Corentin de Lastelle boasts more land than the residents of Aixelles combined, and not that I care for the man in the slightest, but from succeeding Charles Moreau as head of the Institute alone, Pierre-Alexandre Perez will receive everything from his godfather".

This remark triggered something in Ophélie's memory, and she turned to Manon in confusion. "How can that be so? Does Mr Moreau not have an elder daughter to whom some proportion of his assets is owed?"

"Mr Perez did mention her once", Adèle interjected. "Troubled girl; she received a marriage proposal from a highly adequate suitor—for which she should have been appreciative because from what I have heard, Florence was no oil painting—but she turned it down, claiming that she wished to study botany at the Institute. Naturally, her father could not allow it, so she left the village years ago and has not spoken to her family since".

Incensed that her sermon was being hijacked, Camille seized this occasion to recover her position as orator. "Quiet! You will control yourself in public from now on, Manon—everything you do is a reflection of me".

"Oh", Manon cried, "and I suppose it is acceptable for Adèle to trail at Mr Perez's heels like a dog, and for Ophélie to dally in pavilions with Mr Lavarre, but when I split my time between Victor Chappaz and Corentin de Lastelle in a harmless endeavour to gauge which of the two I wish to consider for marriage, I am accused of prostitution!"

Thankfully, a knock on the front door broke up the commotion. Moments later, Mrs Cadet stepped in carrying an envelope and a parcel that had just been dropped off from the Institute. The former was addressed to the family, containing an invitation to their Botany Display that December. The latter was a personal item sent by Mr Perez. It was not the first gift of its kind that Baudières had received—Manon's jewellery box alone had doubled in size recently. This one, however, had Ophélie's name written on the front.

Anticipating what would happen if either of her cousins were to see it, she grabbed the parcel and stood up to leave, but it was snatched out of her hand by Manon before Ophélie could reach for her walking stick. Sniggering to herself, the elder twin hastened to the opposite side of the room and tore it open to reveal an enormous box of Swiss chocolates. Within the lid was a note from Mr Perez requesting the pleasure of sitting next to Ophélie at Émile Veaux's upcoming poker tournament, to afford them 'more intimate conditions for a tête-à-tête'.

Adèle's eyes widened just in time for her sister to begin delivering jokes about 'Ophélie's new beau'. With a howl, she proceeded to storm up to her bedroom, stopping at the top of the staircase to assert that she never wished to see or speak to her family again. Ophélie's own departure to the right wing would immediately follow, if only to prevent herself from retaliating with a remark to Manon that she might later regret.

Curled up in the corridor, she sat begging Adèle to let her in for so long that her muscles became dormant. It was no use. Morning faded to noon, until finally, Ophélie retreated to her room and flopped onto the bed.

Unfortunately, she was no stranger to seeing Adèle in this state. The last such occasion had involved their neighbour Thibault in Petit Pin, when the twins were fifteen. Despite her cousin's warnings, Adèle had made herself available to perform his chores night and day, adamant that this would win his affection. In her diary, she had signed off entries with his surname, and Ophélie even caught her draping a white shawl over her head in front of her mirror, once. In the end, it had taken the shock of walking in on Manon and Thibault kissing in his family's barn for Adèle to comprehend where his preferences lay. As for Mr Perez, Ophélie was unlikely to be so easily forgiven.

Longing to block out Adèle's sobs on the other side of the wall, her cousin sandwiched her head between two pillows and squeezed her eyes shut. When that failed as a barrier, she sat up and peered around the room in search of a distraction. It was only then that Ophélie thought to open her bedside drawer for the first time since her return. In doing so, her gaze fell on something that she could scarcely believe she had forgotten.

There, hiding in the darkness, were the wooden figurines

Étienne had carved for her when they were children. Or, at least, she always presumed he had been their creator, no matter how fervently he denied it. The first—based on a character in *Gargantua and Pantagruel,* which she had been reading to him at the time—Ophélie had found waiting for her beneath the sycamore tree one afternoon, with no note or explanation. Each week thereafter she had discovered another, then another, until her collection of characters was complete but one.

Reunited with these souvenirs of her friend, Ophélie upheld her latest promise to reminisce on their time together with a smile, then returned the figurines to the drawer and stretched out on her back. Within minutes, her mind started to gravitate, as minds do, to the topic preoccupying her subconscious.

It embarrassed Ophélie to admit that she had never given much thought to what had become of Mr Moreau's elder daughter. From what she could remember, Florence had excelled tremendously in science, harnessing an appreciation of the natural world that was rare in one so young. When she was not landing in scuffles with boys, Florence would be studying the weeds growing in the schoolyard, or tending to the plants in the classrooms. She had seldom spoken about her little sister, but then again, nor had anyone else. In all Ophélie's time passing behind the Institute, she might have doubted Isabelle's existence, in fact, had the girl not been rushed to see her grandfather in the summer of 1871.

Ophélie had watched from behind the bannister as Isabelle's nurse carried her into the front room. Whatever had caused the girl to thrash, scream, and clutch her shin like that, the puddles of blood on the parquet had led Ophélie to suspect that it was serious. So, too, did the brace on Isabelle's leg when she eventually re-emerged into the hallway, and the look on Arnaud's face once she and her nurse had left. The doctor had cancelled all other appointments and locked himself in the front room for the rest of the day.

After a while, the sound of Thomas' voice barking Ophélie's name from the corridor brought her out of her thoughts and back to the monotone stretch of ceiling above her. Evidently, the boy had cut his hand while fashioning a device to pick the lock on Adèle's bedroom door—at Manon's request—and he now required Ophélie's aid to stop the bleeding.

With calming breaths, his cousin counted to ten, then stood up to leave.

19

The Autumn Festival

When Manon awoke the next morning, a recollection of her quips about Mr Perez triggered a niggling feeling of guilt that lasted the five minutes it took her to comb her hair. She flirted with the idea of going to Adèle's room to apologise, but cast it aside in the knowledge that as always, her words would not have been taken to heart.

As the elder twin opened her curtains to a newly azure sky, her thoughts whirred to Émile Veaux's poker tournament the following week, and she could hardly resist breaking into a dance. She envisioned the looks she would attract, the compliments she would receive, and the jealousy of the other young ladies opposite her. Then, taking a seat at her dressing table, Manon swept her fringe back and pressed her face to the mirror.

Her hopes were futile, for it was still there—the reminder that when she smiled baring her teeth, her left eye appeared marginally smaller than the right. In public, it was a defect she had learnt to correct by raising the corner of her mouth. This would not stop her from questioning whether others had noticed it during a momentary lapse of focus.

Even so, Manon reassured herself, the left side of her face was more than attractive enough to compensate for its right counterpart. And with a sigh, she began planning her outfit for that evening's function.

Despite the fact that the residents of Aixelles would sooner hang themselves than set foot near farmlands, they upheld the tradition of Alpine transhumance each year. The 'retour des alpages' (return from the Alpine pastures) was an event that celebrated the cattle and sheep being herded back down the valley before winter, upon which a grand festival was organised throughout Annecy. From craft demonstrations to a parade of livestock through the city centre, there could be no greater way to commemorate the rebirth of the harvest than this.

The festival had always been Ophélie's favourite day of the year as a child. With the sky turning dark and all manner of stalls lining the waterfront, it was a rare occasion when traders, farmers, and artisans from outside the village could come together—not to mention the sole annual tradition she shared with Arnaud that involved them leaving Baudières. Pumpkins, berries, and seasonal produce of every colour were laid out like a feast for the senses, and the sharp autumn air would be filled with the ethereal melodies of folk bands.

Adèle took the carriage into Annecy in advance of her family. By the time they caught up with her by the entrance to the Old Town, she had already vanished into the crowd. Having been forced to assist Manon in her fastidious hunt for necklaces over the past hour, Ophélie, herself, was moments from staging a getaway.

Aside from the tedium of watching her cousin hold various

pendants to her nape, her interest in this field was so limited as to make her opinion void. The sole piece of jewellery Ophélie had ever owned—or wished to—was an old silver locket with her initials on it.

The item had been given to Ophélie by her mother at birth, and as a child, she had refused to remove it even to bathe. Upon realising that the locket had fallen off somewhere in the woods one spring, Ophélie had searched for it behind Baudières for almost a year, before finally accepting that her mother's gift was lost.

When the cousins approached the next row of merchants, Ophélie waited for Manon to begin haggling over a brooch, then continued towards the Italian gentleman selling cannolis at the end of the road. This would complete the list of items her grandfather had requested that she bring home from the festival. Before she had neared the stand, however, Ophélie came to a halt.

To her left, an array of straw trinkets drew her attention, as did the poster hanging above them—'Saint-Laurent', the village from Arnaud's story on the first night of the storm.

Inching closer, Ophélie patted her coat pocket. In the flurry of recent weeks, she had forgotten all about the bracelet from the cabin. Not only did it bear a striking resemblance to the ones on the table, but moreover, Ophélie realised precisely where she had seen it before: in that same spot, on the wrist of a golden-haired girl whose family would come to the festival to sell products from their farm.

Aside from them having been the same age, more than one passer-by had commented on the girl's similarity of appearance to Ophélie's. It was the girl's affection for her brother that stood out most in Ophélie's memory, though. She had enjoyed watching them behind the stand in the minute or so that it took Arnaud to purchase Beaufort from their father.

Frustrated not to have made this connection sooner, Ophélie felt a lump form in her throat. In her confusion she was not alone, and after several seconds, she peered up at the young man observing her from behind the table.

"Do we know each other, Miss?" he enquired, sweeping his hair off his face in the unconscious manner of a tic.

This movement alone was enough to confirm that Ophélie was standing before the farm girl's brother once again. Ten years later, his expression was so changed that in her state of shock, she had to collect her thoughts before answering: "We have never been introduced, but I came to your stand each year when I was younger".

The gentleman nodded. "Matthieu Lacroix, pleased to meet you. Are you looking for something?"

"Not exactly", Ophélie murmured, casting her eyes back over the table. "Forgive me, but I seem to recall that your primary merchandise was butter and cheese in the past".

"You're not mistaken, but we no longer trade that stuff at this festival. After my sister Madeleine's death, our village made it a tradition to honour her memory by weaving straw necklaces and bracelets to sell here instead. She loved making jewellery of this kind", Matthieu's voice trailed off into a whisper.

In the seconds that followed this remark, the blood drained from Ophélie's face. As if anticipating his next response, she swallowed, before uttering: "I am extremely sorry for your loss. May I ask when your sister passed away?"

"Five years ago, almost to this day. She fell into a reservoir further up the mountain and drowned", Matthieu answered, dropping his gaze. "Anyway, did you want to buy something,

Miss?"

With an uneasy nod, Ophélie pointed to the first bracelet she saw and handed him the coins. No sooner had he fastened it around her wrist, though, than Manon detected a change in the music and raced up to grab her arm from behind. Ignoring Ophélie's protests, she proceeded to drag her cousin towards the city centre, squawking that the parade was about to commence and that she wished to have a front-row view.

At the footbridge, Manon let go of her hand and allowed Ophélie to catch her breath by the railing. Her choice of places to stop was unfortunate; directly across the water, the Palais de l'Isle—that triangular fortress isolated between two canals on the Thio River—had historically been Ophélie's least favourite sight. Even after its function as a prison had ended, she could sense the horrors of all it had witnessed via a paralysing heaviness in the air, from the two hundred inmates incarcerated there during the Revolution to the last band of prisoners to call it home in 1863.

Upon spotting Nicolas Belmont skulking across the bridge ahead, a chill of another kind ran down Ophélie's neck. Suspecting that Pierre-Alexandre Perez, too, might be nearby, she parted from her cousin and meandered back through the crowd until she was alone by the lakeside. There, perched on a bench, she looked to the stars oscillating on their obsidian stage for clarity, but even they could not distract her from Madeleine Lacroix's name.

Now that most of the festival stands were being packed away, she pulled the straw bracelet out of her pocket to study it properly. Could it be possible that Madeleine had come to the cabin at some point before her death, she asked herself? If so, why had she left behind the one object Ophélie had never seen her without? And what series of events had transpired for her to have ended up floating face-down in a reservoir?

With such little to go on, Ophélie's questions rapidly led to a dead end. Twenty minutes later, she abandoned her speculation and glanced aside, spotting a familiar silhouette hovering by the water's edge. The woman's face was barely visible beneath the hood of her jacket, but between her muttered profanities and the five children wedged into the boat that she was trying to untangle from some netting, Ophélie was in no doubt as to who she was.

By now, Mrs Bosco's fingers were numb from dipping in and out of the water. In her concentration, she nearly tumbled off the side of the boat when she heard Ophélie's voice offering to help her.

"God almighty, Miss Davenport!" 'The Banshee' cried, "it's not the done thing to sneak up on people like that".

"Forgive me", Ophélie responded, "I saw you from the footpath and I thought you might need assistance".

"Well, it's not such a bad thing that we bumped into each other. I have something for you", Mrs Bosco reached into the lining of her coat to retrieve a small parcel. "I hope you know I am not accustomed to making deliveries as a favour. Mr Lavarre asked me to bring this to you once the storm was over".

"Mr Lavarre?" Ophélie repeated, striving to comprehend the improbability of these two individuals being associated.

Mrs Bosco reached back to throw a blanket over her grandchildren. "Don't look so surprised. The gentleman might be modest, but I can more than attest to his generosity. In fact, from what you interrogated me about back in Mèliez, you have witnessed it yourself without even knowing it. Three nights a week he makes that journey in a rowboat—to bring us money and food we'd be hard pushed to live without. And all while the rest of Aixelles sleeps soundly in their satin sheets. But enough now, I have said too much".

Without another word, Mrs Bosco picked up the ores, leaving Ophélie to call after her: "Wait! Is there a reason Mr Lavarre could not give me this himself, Mrs Bosco? Is he still unwell?"

"Unwell? No, not at all", 'The Banshee shouted back. "His boat was destroyed in the storm so he is hard at work fixing it. Besides, he's even less fond of participating in events with the people of Aixelles than I am. Honestly, you'd have thought the Revolution never happened in their eyes".

Ophélie nodded, then held out her basket. "Will you please take this home with you, Mrs Bosco?"

After an uncomfortable pause, 'The Banshee' rowed back and extended a hand to retrieve Ophélie's peace offering. From the way she inspected the cheeses and pâtés inside, her grandchildren might have thought these items were poisoned. In silence, they proceeded to watch as Ophélie's silhouette disappeared back along the road towards her family's carriage.

In view of her latest episode involving a parcel, she waited until she had returned to her bedroom before opening Romain's gift, to reveal a book—*Jane Eyre*, by Charlotte Brontë. Inside its cover, a note was inscribed:

Dear Miss Davenport,

A happy and, I might add, tragically underworked associate of mine by the name of Guillaume Bernard informs me that you recently became one of the first customers of our little library. For this, I must offer you my sincerest gratitude. I can only hope that

'*Wuthering Heights*' has lived up to your literary expectations.

Between the works of the Brontë sisters, I find myself torn in my partiality. I enclose this book to you in the hopes that you might assist me with coming to a decision on the matter.

I look forward to hearing your thoughts next Thursday during Émile Veaux's poker tournament, at which I would wager money on your table finding you a fierce opponent.

Romain Lavarre.

When she reached the end of his message, Ophélie set the book down and moved to the window ledge. Staring out at those first layers of snow coating the mountain peaks, the hint of a smile entered her face.

20

Poison

"Ophélie! Wake up", Thomas' voice nearly perforated her eardrum in the darkness. His cries were followed by the icy grip of his hands tugging her arm beneath the blanket, and the explanation: "The ghost is back!"

With a groan, Ophélie sat upright and lit the lamp on her bedside table with even greater speed than she had the previous week. "We have spoken about this many times, Thomas. Grand-père is not dead".

"But I saw him in the garden from my window", her cousin insisted. "Come with me and look for yourself!"

"What we think we are seeing at this hour is often false", Ophélie repeated, folding back the blanket for him. "You may stay here now if you are frightened, but we need to conquer this fear of yours".

Gaze flitting between her face and the door, Thomas eventually crawled onto the bed. He would return there at the same hour for five consecutive nights. By the time Émile Veaux's poker tournament came around, it felt like a blessing in disguise to Ophélie, if only because the event promised a brief respite from her new sleeping arrangement.

The Veaux family were the sort of people whom you might expect to see on the cover of a chocolate box. As guests flooded their drawing room, Mrs Veaux signalled for the orchestra to commence, and her children adjusted their posture on the sofa, dressed as if they were ready for the Paris Opera. A self-proclaimed 'Renaissance Man', Émile himself was the next to enter, ushering each group over to their table as indicated in his seating plan.

For most of the villagers, their host was best characterised by his diatribes against 'the barbarous Boche'—whom he had still not forgiven for the purloining of his ancestral Alsace-Lorraine—and his unparalleled poker skills. Ophélie herself had known the gentleman solely in an intimate context involving her grandfather's solicitor. And based on the speed of his grimace when he saw her arriving, Émile's memory in this respect was just as sharp.

In his reaction he was not alone; before Ophélie had even crossed the threshold, she noticed that Marguerite Veaux—sixteen years her husband's junior—was unable to refrain from staring at her. This expression was replicated by all three of her sons. From the edge of the sofa, the children's eyes pursued their guest as she passed them to inspect the mammoth painting above the fireplace—the latest family portrait from Christmas day.

"Maman said not to speak to you", Philippe, the youngest Veaux boy, proceeded to whisper when she turned to ask after them. "She said your mother was not right in the head".

Out of his parents' earshot, Ophélie bent down to his level and smiled. "And what is your opinion, sir?"

Between his brothers' elbows nudging him to keep quiet on

both sides, it took the boy several seconds to decide. "Well, you don't look dangerous to me. You can't even walk properly. I feel sad for you".

"There is no reason to feel sad", Ophélie reassured him. "You see, I count my riches in the number of places to which my mind has travelled, for unlike my feet, it knows no boundaries".

The grin that entered Philipe's face coincided with his father's announcement that the first round of poker was about to start, at which point Ophélie bid the children goodnight and joined her fellow guests at their table.

Émile's seating plan would do her no favours; while both Baudin twins glowered at their cousin from their places either side of Alessio Lettiere, opposite, Ophélie found herself coupled with Victor Chappaz and Corentin de Lastelle to her left, and none other than Pierre-Alexandre Perez to her right.

However intolerable a composition, she was largely able to distract herself with the empty chair staring at her from across the room. As one round of poker rolled into the next, Ophélie's eyes became increasingly drawn to Romain's name tag on the table in front of it. When an interval was called at midnight for the men to smoke cigars, she slunk to the bathroom for a moment of privacy to ponder the gentleman's whereabouts.

Between Ophélie's departure and her return, a dozen more carafes of wine had been doled out. Her own name tag had also found its way onto the floor, by virtue of Manon having claimed her seat in her cousin's absence.

Left with only Manon's previous place by Adèle, Ophélie hurried to the back door and stepped outside. The breeze met her with the wrong sting of bracing, but each step through the garden would be a welcome one.

A minute into her walk, the hum of laughter from the house dulled to silence, and Ophélie glanced to her right at the fence she had been following along the path. With a set of greenhouses visible above the top, this must be the midway section between the Veaux family's land and that of the Institute, she supposed.

Squinting ahead, Ophélie peered down at what looked like footsteps in the dirt leading away from the path. They ended at a gap beneath the wooden panels, on the other side of which the sounds of an animal chomping were audible. Wary that a boar might have forced its way in from the woods, Ophélie held her breath and crept through the fence.

Emerging into the gardens of the Institute, she could not contain her amusement when her face was met with the moist snout of the Rinaldis' terrier. Evidently, he had evaded his master's clutches earlier in search of something to satiate his appetite. Patting Cornelius' head, Ophélie sat with him for a minute while he sniffed at the ground and licked his lips, until the dog's ears picked up a noise and he scampered back through the fence.

In his departure, Ophélie stood up to gather her bearings again. Before her, she could just make out the rows of plants drooping from their pots in the nearest greenhouse—presumably the specimen that Mr Moreau had imported in his earlier career. With many of the pots empty and a nauseating odour seeping out from under the glass, his staff members were clearly not doing as good a job at looking after them these days.

As it happened, Ophélie knew this part of the gardens well. Metres to her left was the fence separating the far corner from the woods, and as children, she and Étienne were forever finding objects forgotten by tourists on the other side. Receipts, lipstick, and the odd bonnet had been their most common treasures to come across, but among Ophélie's more unique discoveries was a biscuit tin she had picked up once from a pile of leaves.

No sweet treats had greeted her inside, but rather, scraps of paper on which words had been scribbled in another language beneath the same, strange symbol. The tin must have fallen from a foreign tourist's bag long ago, Ophélie had presumed, slipping it into her satchel to examine later. Unfortunately, her return to Baudières that afternoon was intercepted by Arnaud, having recently been informed by a neighbour of how his granddaughter spent her free time. The confiscated tin had sat in a cabinet in his study ever since.

From the section of woods nearest her, a sudden rustle of footsteps sent a shockwave down Ophélie's spine. Hastening back to the fence, she caught her foot on something and fell to the ground. The impact was made all the more unpleasant by the sensation of wet earth soaking into her dress, but before Ophélie had managed to rise beyond her knees, a beam of light approached from nowhere, and she was pulled to her feet.

When the gentleman lowered his lantern, she found herself staring once again into the eyes of Romain Lavarre. Ordinarily, Ophélie might have been relieved to see him, but something in his discomposure put her further on edge.

"Mr Lavarre, what are you doing here?" she asked once she had caught her breath.

"Forgive me, I was walking in the woods and I saw your fall", Romain replied, handing Ophélie her cane. His expression hardened when she winced to retrieve it, and the gentleman took her arm. "You are hurt".

"No, I am alright, I simply scraped my elbow on something", Ophélie responded. "In any case, it cannot be worse than the wound with which Thomas left you".

"Thanks to you my shoulder has made almost a full recovery, Miss Davenport", Romain insisted, holding out his lantern to inspect the ground below. On the patch of grass next to the greenhouse was a tree root jutting out of the earth. It was covered in the speckles of a jet-black liquid that appeared too dark to be blood.

With a final shake of her dress to remove the soil, Ophélie bent down to examine her attacker. It was the flower lying next to it that caught her attention, though. The deflated shells of its berries were still visible on the tree root from where she had fallen on top of it, and its juices were now percolating Ophélie's sleeve at the elbow.

"In all my years, I have never seen a flower like that", she remarked, running her fingers along its bell-shaped petals.

"With any luck, it only grazed the skin", Romain answered. Eyes unmoving from the fence, he proceeded to wrap his coat around Ophélie's shoulders to shield her from the wind, and his voice turned grave. "Miss Davenport, I must leave. Your absence will already have attracted questions and we cannot be seen together".

"You are beginning to frighten me, Mr Lavarre", Ophélie replied. "Why did you not attend the poker tournament? And what were you really doing out here? Please, if there is something troubling you, I may be able to help."

Romain's response was cut short by the sound of someone gasping, as Pierre-Alexandre Perez's flushed grimace poked through the fence behind them.

"Miss Davenport! Mr Lavarre! Is that you?" he cried.

As an excruciating silence elapsed, Ophélie felt her legs weakening. Devoid of an explanation for the gentleman, she brought her hand to her forehead, but the echo of a scream startled her to the point of having to clutch her cane.

Before she and Romain had shared a glance of confusion, the outburst was proceeded by a cacophony of wails, whose provenance Ophélie instantly recognised as her aunt.

While Mr Perez sprinted towards the commotion, Romain offered Ophélie his arm and helped her back through the garden. By the time the pair had caught up with Mr Perez at the entrance to Émile Veaux's drawing room, a crowd had gathered around one of the tables. At its centre, Manon was writhing and sputtering on the floor.

"What happened?" Ophélie demanded Solène Ozaman between Manon's groans.

Solène shook her head. "I cannot say! She collapsed and started clawing at herself like an animal".

Ophélie dropped to her knees to check her cousin's windpipe. No sooner had she joined her aunt on the parquet, though, than Romain appeared at her side, scooping Manon into his arms. With the help of their host clearing the crowd, he rushed her out of the house and towards the water, then handed her to the Baudins' ferryman.

"I have seen this before", Romain explained to Ophélie. "Your cousin needs urgent aid to bring down the swelling in her throat. She will be delirious for a number of hours, and will likely be confused when she wakes up. Take her home and put her to bed—if necessary, tie her arms down and keep her restrained until assistance arrives. I shall travel to Annecy and bring a doctor to your grandfather's estate right away".

Befuddled spectators were now assembling across the terrace, but on Ophélie's orders, her aunt and cousin leapt into the boat next to Manon. While the ferryman fumbled for the ores, Romain bent down to help push them away from the marina.

"Miss Davenport", he whispered, "I will call on you at Baudières just after dawn".

Then, upon Manon's next whimper, the gentleman lent in to utter the promise that Ophélie would cling to as their boat drifted into the darkness: "Please trust me—I will not let any harm come to you or your family".

21

Notes in the Darkness

Upon returning to his observatory, 'The Watcher' lent back against the door and massaged his temples with his forefingers. Not since his aunt had he known a woman capable of caterwauling at the same pitch as Camille Baudin, although the former had probably displayed greater gumption in the face of panic, he decided.

It had been during a family holiday in the south one summer, when the gentleman and his cousin, Théodore, were both six. From the front of the boat, their parents had been so enraptured with the view of the coast that nobody had noticed Théodore leaning over the side, or the delicate splash when he slipped into the water.

Instinctively, 'The Watcher' had bent down to grab his cousin's sleeve, but the look in Théodore's eyes as he was gradually sucked beneath the surface became so gripping to behold that it rendered him immobile. By the time he had called for an adult, the boy's floundering limbs were still, and no amount of resuscitation could breathe life into the stony pallor on his face. While Théodore's mother and father bawled, his cousin had slunk away to find someone to whom he might entrust this experience, which he did, in the form of a seagull perched on the mast.

Once the ringing in his ears had ebbed, the gentleman sat down to fasten his boots for another trip through the woods. After the evening's hysteria, the tension in his chest should have loosened upon the mere notion of making the journey; the path to Baudières was one that he could walk in his sleep, after all, and no aspect of his daily routine did the gentleman look forward to more. As he tightened his second lace, though, he felt his airways constrict and was forced to grip the desk for equilibrium. It would seem that even after fourteen years, he struggled to shake loose the memory that would claw its way back to him every so often pre-departure.

The incident had transpired shortly after his first sighting of Ophélie, whereupon the gentleman had emerged from the trees amid a storm, only to be met by Gabrielle Davenport standing in her father's garden metres ahead. With a skeletal body protruding from a smock—soaked to the point of being transparent—she was the most peculiar being he had ever seen. Revelling in each clash of thunder overhead, she swayed in the wind like the trees anchored to the soil, stepping barefoot through the flowerbeds and howling at the sky.

Frozen to the spot, 'The Watcher' had anticipated the screams that would surely follow the moment this spectre noticed him gaping at her in the darkness. Instead, Gabrielle's face had become as pale as a ghost and her eyes jutted from their sockets. Without uttering a word, she had waited for the next flash of lightning to strike, then lifted a bony arm towards him as if condemning his soul to Hell. The image had caused the gentleman to hurtle home with such speed that he almost slipped and dropped his lantern multiple times in the mud.

Back on the top floor of the Institute, he had drained a glass of cognac to calm himself down, before wrapping his head around the question of what to do next.

The woman is clearly demented, he had written as a preamble. Even if she were to inform the police of what she had witnessed, her story would more than likely be treated as fictitious. Then again, what if she were believed and the security around Baudières tightened as a result?

The instant this hypothesis had so much as emerged as a thought, the gentleman's mind had temporarily blacked out. When his consciousness returned, he had found himself blinking down at a new entry in his notebook, whose concluding line read:

There can be no risks—no interference. She must be removed.

Once the final lace on his boots was secured, 'The Watcher' kept his breathing sufficiently steady to check his pocket watch. Eighteen to twenty minutes from now, Professor Boissonnet would be leaving his bedroom to use the first-floor lavatory, and he would be free to descend the stairs without being bothered by fellow staff. In the meantime, the moment had come to transcribe the evening's events while they were fresh in his memory.

Succeeding this, the gentleman went to stand up. Lifting his lantern off the desk, he tarried only to add two final words in the form of a hieroglyph:

Adèle Baudin.

22

The Figure Beneath the Window

The following hours would constitute one of the longest nights of Ophélie's life. At two o'clock the doctor arrived, determining that Manon had reacted unfavourably to a canapé she had eaten during the poker tournament. He concluded his visit by giving her a powerful dose of medicine and instructed the Baudins to keep her temperature stable until morning.

Breath by breath, Manon's panting gradually softened. After sending her aunt and cousins to their rooms, Ophélie wrote a note for her grandfather informing him that she would be unable to come to his library for breakfast, then pulled up an armchair beside Manon's bed. Every so often she would wipe her cousin's forehead with a damp towel, using the thuds of the clock on the wall to gauge the intervals between her fits.

Both Manon and Adèle had been susceptible to allergies as children, but never to this extent. Only once had Ophélie witnessed such erratic behaviour in another person, in fact—along the corridor in her mother's old bedroom.

Three weeks before her grandfather had pronounced Gabrielle Davenport dead, Ophélie had suspected that her mother's health was taking a downward turn. It had started with the sight of two maids restraining Gabrielle on the bed, whereupon Ophélie had noticed scratches all over her mother's arms. Arnaud had ordered that Gabrielle's bedroom be locked from the outside after that incident, but even the heavy oak door could not muffle the sounds that Gabrielle had produced in those final days. Neither her groans nor her wheezing would ever depart Ophélie's memory, and to hear the same distress from Manon's lips was enough to rattle her to the core.

Ophélie's nerves were thus wearing thin by the time Thomas ran into Manon's bedroom claiming that their grandfather's ghost had returned to the garden. Before the boy had finished his sentence, Ophélie began escorting him back down the corridor to put an end to this once and for all.

When she reached the boy's window which overlooked the rear of the estate, however, the words she was preparing to speak fell from her mouth into the void before her. Ophélie's muscles stiffened as a double-take confirmed what she was seeing; standing between the trees at the back of the garden was the figure of a large, hooded man.

Visible only via the flickers of the lantern dragging at his side, he lifted his head to the window and remained perfectly still. Then, he turned and retreated into the woods with such placidity that Ophélie felt as if time were decelerating.

Despite her pulse stifling her hearing, she eventually pushed herself away from the window and tucked Thomas back into bed. Based on the boy's expression, her insistence that he had simply woken from a nightmare and imagined the intruder was as unconvincing to its recipient as it was to its fabricator. Ophélie maintained it regardless.

Returning to Manon's side, she attempted to regain her composure. In her state of bleary-eyed exhaustion, had she simply been hallucinating, Ophélie questioned? If not, who was the man Thomas had been seeing in the garden all this time, and what could he be doing there?

Like the pebbles she had skimmed across the lake with Étienne as a child, the impact of the disturbance would grow before it subsided. Upon every subsequent creak of the floorboards in Manon's bedroom, a new doubt would unfurl in Ophélie's mind, until finally, the sheepish slivers of sunlight under the curtains alerted her to the imminent passage of daybreak.

With morning came a muffled knock on the front door. True to his word, it was Romain whom Ophélie found standing in the hallway when she descended the stairs. In stern silence, she proceeded to lead the gentleman into the front room where she knew that their conversation would go unheard by her grandfather's staff.

The icy draught of the ground floor was unrelenting as the pair stood opposite one another, subdued by the mutual understanding that what was about to be said would likely change everything between them.

"Miss Davenport", Romain began, "I hardly know where to start. How is your cousin?"

"I believe she is recovering. Her fever is going down and she is no longer struggling to take in air. I cannot thank you enough for bringing the doctor so quickly, Mr Lavarre", Ophélie responded, her voice still shaky.

Romain nodded and turned to glance away. "Forgive me, I have spent many nights pondering how best to proceed. I am sure you are aware by now that Aixelles is far from the fairytale village it is portrayed to be in the tea salons and smoking parlours of high society. Every community, however fanciful, has its flaws, but I have come to regard the utopian vision here as being based on a complex mosaic of secrets—secrets that remain safe so long as we are all distracted long enough not to notice them. You must think me quite absurd".

"Actually, I discarded all notions of absurdity last night", Ophélie cut in, "but to which secret are you referring?"

"One so distasteful that after hearing it, I fear you may regret asking me that", Romain answered. "You must be wondering how it is that I was familiar with your cousin's condition. I only had to look at her to determine that something was slipped into her drink—a muscle relaxant or drug which, in big enough doses, can cause phantasms, madness, and in the worst-case scenario, death. I know this because I, myself, have suffered the effects of the toxin before, no doubt administered by the same individual who sought to harm your cousin".

Ophélie gripped the window sill and squeezed her eyes shut. "No, it cannot be true. Who on Earth would poison her?"

"If I knew that I can assure you the reprobate would already be behind bars. His motive in targeting your family, I am profoundly sorry to say, is to intimidate me. Ever since your return to Aixelles I have done everything in my power not to involve you in this, Miss Davenport, but I believe that you may now be in the same danger as I", Romain removed a silver necklace from his pocket. "Yesterday I found this in a parcel on my doorstep, one week after my boat was destroyed by a blunt instrument. Given the initials, the item is yours, if I am not mistaken, and I would be remiss not to interpret this 'gift'—alongside last night's demonstration—as a warning for your safety".

Ophélie felt her stomach turn as she reached for the locket from her mother that she had lost as a child. In vain, she scoured her mind for an explanation as to how it could have ended up in an envelope at Romain's door, before admitting: "I find myself at a loss for words, Mr Lavarre. Setting aside the implausibility of someone having had this in their possession, what desire could anybody have to menace you like that? Have you contacted the police?"

"The police would be useless at this stage, Miss Davenport; we are dealing with the most powerful and manipulative individual I have ever come across", Romain replied. "What he wants, I can only presume, is for me to end my two-year investigation into the framed murder of Isabelle Moreau, through which a man was wrongly executed for her death while her killer—my oppressor—remains at large in the same establishment that she called home".

As soon as she heard Isabelle's name, Ophélie was forced to take a seat on the sofa. Eyes locked in a vacant stare, it was another minute before she could bring herself to utter: "How is that possible?"

"There is much I have to tell you and very little time", Romain answered, perching down next to her. "I can only imagine how you must feel at present, Miss Davenport, but please know that I meant what I said yesterday evening about not allowing any harm to come to you or your family".

Mrs Cadet's abrupt entry into the front room propelled Ophélie to her feet. According to the housekeeper's breathless cries, Manon had just woken up, and the doctor would soon be coming back to check on her.

"I shall be there right away", Ophélie promised, to ensure Mrs Cadet's departure. She waited until the door was closed again before whispering to Romain: "Mr Lavarre, I must go to my cousin. Will you wait here an instant?"

"I am afraid I have risked your safety by coming to Baudières as it is", Romain replied. "My every movement will be scrutinised over the coming days, so I must leave before anybody sees me here".

"And when will you return?" Ophélie asked. "I have so many questions I can scarcely think straight".

"Next Tuesday marks the tenth anniversary of Isabelle Moreau's death. I am on good authority that the villagers will be spending the weekend laying their wreaths and tributes by the lakeside in preparation, including your own family. It should provide a diversion for us to continue this discussion unseen", Romain spoke. "If you are willing to meet me at sundown in the village library on Saturday, I give you my word that I will explain everything".

"Yes, of course", Ophélie whispered, just as Mrs Cadet's furrowed brows reappeared in the doorway.

Nodding to the housekeeper, Ophélie picked up her cane and led their guest back to the entrance. And with a final bow of his head, Romain slipped through the door, plunging the hallway into a deafening stillness.

In the wake of his departure, Ophélie slowly moved her hands to her mouth. Another few seconds might have helped the throbbing sensation in her head to subside. Instead, the clatter of a maid dropping a tray on the stairwell prompted her to fasten the locket in her palm around her neck, then join Mrs Cadet upstairs.

23

Revelations

Three days into Manon's recovery, the Book Club met in Camille's absence to exchange what was known about the situation thus far. Confusion would best characterise the consensus, with memories skewed and questions left unanswered—namely how Romain Lavarre had swept into Émile Veaux's drawing room to 'save the day'.

Some maintained that he had been there with them all along. Others surmised that the gentleman must have received an affront early in the game, hence spending the remainder of the evening cooling off in the garden.

Then there was the suggestion that Camille might be intending to pursue legal action against Mr Veaux, followed by the rumour that 'the jealous, plain twin' had somehow been responsible for Manon's fit. 'And no doubt the confirmation that his daughter's condition was not fatal provided sufficient reassurance for Roland's backside to return to its indentation in his office chair', was added while the second round of tea was served.

The ensuing chuckles gave way to a comment regarding

how spiteful the Baudins' housekeeper must feel in having to 'mollycoddle' Manon at present—Mrs Cadet being famously impotent herself—and the ladies concluded with the agreement that it would be best to pay the family a visit in the coming days, to offer their well wishes.

Within Baudières, conversation was reduced to a minimum that week. While Adèle took it upon herself to man the entrance, Ophélie refused to vacate her seat by Manon's bedside, so much so that Mrs Cadet began to worry about the number of hours she was spending there, ruminating in silence.

The housekeeper's efforts were nevertheless in vain; each morning the doctor would stop by to affirm that the elder twin's health was improving—his words wrought with the same aplomb with which Ophélie had heard Arnaud diagnose his own patients—yet when she looked upon her cousin's ashen face, she saw only the product of duplicity.

Nightfall could afford little respite, either; twilight brought with it the risk that whoever tried to poison Manon would return to the garden, or worse, attempt to enter the estate.

Soon, the passage of time began to lapse, and in her lassitude from patrolling every ground-floor window from dusk to dawn, it took Ophélie longer than it should have to notice two new developments unfolding around her. The first was the graze on her elbow that stung when her sleeve brushed the skin; the second was the sound of Adèle's laughter as she recited the afternoon she had spent at the Institute to her mother within earshot of Manon's bedroom.

Evidently, amid the recent flurry of visitors, Pierre-Alexandre Perez had stopped by with an offer for Ophélie and Adèle to attend lunch, on the grounds that 'a dose of good food overlooking the gardens' would raise the ladies' morale. From the finery of Mr Moreau's chinaware to how attentive Mr Perez had been, Adèle's encyclopedic accounts of this experience—the invitation for which had never reached her cousin—would continue throughout the week.

For this reason, as much as her own restlessness, Ophélie could barely contain her relief when Saturday evening came around. No sooner had her aunt and cousins left for the lakeside than she donned her coat and hurried to the back door.

Creeping around the house, she strayed from her path only to take in the view from the terrace—a trickle of lanterns congregating around the spot where in a matter of days, Isabelle's remembrance ceremony would be held. From here, each step forward signified a journey from which there was no turning back. In acceptance of this fact, Ophélie pulled the hood of her coat over her head and continued along the road, her breath billowing out like smoke in the darkness.

Under the oil lamps, the trees lining the streets were skeleton-like without their auburn jackets, and the jingle of the library bell echoed across the square as piercingly as a scream.

Stepping inside where Romain had been expecting her behind the desk, the gentleman was quick to lock the door and draw the curtains behind them, then gestured Ophélie towards the table he had set up for their meeting. Days prior, both parties might have expected a wave of apprehension as they took a seat opposite each other. Now, after more sleepless nights than either cared to count, there was a mutual readiness in their faces to put solicitude to rest.

"I gather Mr Bernard has been kind enough to take himself

elsewhere", Ophélie observed.

Romain poured her a glass of water. "Believe it or not, we receive even fewer guests here when the sun goes down, so I do not flatter myself that our literary services will be missed tonight. Had I been a true businessman, I might have opted for a more lucrative trade in my retirement—selling Persian carpets, or crockery from the Americas, perhaps".

Ophélie smiled and took a sip from her glass. "Why did you buy this place, Mr Lavarre?"

"Because I wanted somewhere to escape to", Romain replied. "When the world feels remote, I come here to be surrounded by the writers who have turned its obscurities into art. Their company is something of a solace".

"I understand", Ophélie answered. "I once had a friend who provided that level of comfort, but he is no longer with us".

"This person was taken from you?" Romain asked.

Ophélie went to respond, then brought her hands together atop the table. "Mr Lavarre, I have little doubt that since your arrival, you will have heard a plethora of theories about my family's involvement in 'The Incident'".

Romain shook his head. "Everything I could wish to know about the matter I have waited to hear from you".

"Allow me to clarify what happened then", Ophélie began. "The night of the murder, I was in Mèliez visiting Étienne—my aforementioned friend—in what would be his final moments. He was beside me when I discovered Isabelle's body, and had my grandfather not pulled me away, I might have been spared from witnessing Étienne receive a fatal blow to the head minutes later. Until today, I had never spoken his name to another soul, and I am sure that whatever you have to share with me will be of similar gravity for you. So, here we are;

now that I have entrusted you with my secret, I commit to hearing yours with the same compassion".

In apparent cooperation, Romain glanced down, then unfolded a newspaper extract he had been hiding in his shirt pocket. "What do you make of this, Miss Davenport?"

"It is a copy of Kacper Smolak's ransom note to Isabelle's parents, if I am not mistaken", Ophélie answered.

"You are quite right. It comprises the contents of the envelope discovered in his coat shortly after he was arrested—credible enough, yet it was not written by Kacper Smolak", Romain lowered his voice. "I am under no illusion that you have not spent this week deliberating how an outsider such as myself could have been implicated in this affair. I am afraid the question was never how I came to be associated with Isabelle Moreau, but rather, my relationship with her alleged killer. Kacper Smolak was my father".

In stunned silence, Ophélie sank into her chair and inch by inch, re-examined the gentleman's face as if the missing piece to this puzzle was finally exposing itself. The revelation that she was staring into the eyes of Kacper's son should have felt impossible, but somehow, she could only reprimand herself for not having suspected this link all along.

After a minute, Ophélie shook her head in disbelief. "Mr Lavarre, I spent a great deal of my childhood in Mèliez—how is it that nobody knew anything about you beyond rumours?"

"To put it lightly, my father saw my temperament as an unholy mark", Romain replied. "During his darkest hours, he spoke of God punishing him by virtue of me. As such, I saw very little of the outside world until my mother ran away and I left the village myself".

Detecting the subtext of Ophélie's stare, Romain wasted

no time in adding: "Before your opinion of me is clouded by consolation, Miss Davenport, please know that I have never sought pity for myself, nor would I wish it now. Any commiseration I feel regarding my childhood is directed at my father, in fact, if only for my admission that when the verdict about Isabelle was given, I did not think to question it".

Ophélie nodded. "How did you discover that he was innocent?"

"Thanks to this", Romain responded, placing a blue journal on the table. "It is no secret that Kacper Smolak was a man of very little means. When I returned to Mèliez two years ago to find his cottage ransacked, I was at a loss to comprehend what asset he had owned that would be worth stealing. After a lengthy check of the chest in which I kept my old sketches and paintings, the only item that was missing was a self-portrait I had made as a boy. That was when I knew there was more to this break-in than a simple attempt to loot. Then it dawned on me—the notebook in which my father noted his clients' orders.

"Recreational drugs, money laundering, illegally-sourced artefacts, erotic homosexual artwork; within these pages are sufficient scandals to expose many a prominent family to defamation should they see the light of day, hence why my father had taken to hiding the notebook at home for safekeeping during deals and deliveries.

"At the end of that week, I went back to the cottage to check the fireplace, where I had once seen my father stash a bag of coins. As suspected, the notebook was there, but as I picked it up, I was alerted to the presence of a man staring at me through the window. Despite my haste in following him outside, his departure was too quick; I arrived at the opening of the woods seconds too late to catch whoever had been watching me. After a decade, I could only fathom that there was something in the notebook still capable of causing him irreparable damage, though, thus I set about studying each order for clues as to his identity.

"To my confusion, the sole cause for alarm was this", Romain flicked to the end of the notebook. "22 October 1871; 'The Incident'. Having expected to find a blank page here, I was perplexed to discover that a delivery had indeed been requested of my father. The item in question? An envelope—instructed to be brought to a specific location behind the Institute where one shipment of a bag of seeds had previously been transported. If this is not unusual enough, I invite you to examine the text here and in his ransom note, and tell me if you notice the difference that served to be my second indication that something was amiss".

Ophélie lent over the table and cast her gaze across Kacper's pages confirming the completion of several deliveries, which he had done by scribbling the word 'payed' under every concluded transaction. Then, she glanced back at the copy of the letter that had sentenced the gentleman to death in three lines:

I have taken Isabelle over the mountains where nobody will ever find her. Your daughter is safe and will stay that way until I am paid the sum of 20,000 francs, which must be delivered in one week to an address that will be sent to you imminently. Alerting the police or failure to execute this request will result in Isabelle's death.

"The spelling of 'paid'", Ophélie remarked, lifting her head. "But surely he could have checked this against other books or solicited another opinion, it being such an important letter?"

Romain raised an eyebrow. "I once overheard my father having his pronunciation of 'bouteille' corrected by a passer-by in the street. He pulled a knife to the man's throat. No, Kacper Smolak would have slit his own wrists before requesting assistance with the French language. And then there is clue number three, Miss Davenport: an issue of timing.

"According to documentation that I subsequently reviewed, the evening of Isabelle's murder transpired as follows: between 17:10 and 17:17, her nurse launched a search party in the Institute and its grounds after discovering that the girl was missing, then left to fetch Isabelle's parents. At 17:28 she arrived at the Sauniers' estate and a village-wide campaign was called. At 18:14, the police came to Mèliez where Isabelle's body had been found some twenty minutes earlier. Only at 18:18 did my father re-emerge from the woods.

"On numerous occasions, I have traced the path to the coordinates at which Kacper was instructed to carry the letter. At my fastest running pace, it takes me a minimum of fifteen minutes to sprint from the gardens of the Institute back to Mèliez, yet based on the accepted timeline, my father—far from having been in his physical prime—had managed to kill Isabelle, carry her to his village, dump the body, and flee in just over half an hour".

Ophélie rubbed the sides of her head. "But your father was covered in scratches when he was arrested".

"Yes", Romain answered, "not dissimilar to the ones on your arms from the night of the poker tournament".

Ophélie paused. "Are you saying that Isabelle, too, was poisoned?"

"What better way to stage an abduction than by directing your frenzied victim into the path of her 'assailant'?" Romain replied. "Based on my own reaction to the toxin—which was slipped into a bottle of milk I bought at the market—I believe the child was drugged and driven from the gardens into the woods by some method, at which point dehydration would have led her to seek the nearest water source. A fatal seizure likely struck as she reached the banks of Mèliez, where her death could be mistaken for drowning. As for the real cause, I have approached countless apothecaries, but none have been able to identify the substance".

"And what do you know about the person responsible for creating or procuring it?" Ophélie pressed.

"With what words can I describe a man more similar to a shadow?" Romain lent back in his chair. "His failed assassination attempt was only the beginning. From the moment I retrieved my father's notebook, I perceived indications that my estate was under surveillance; on multiple nights my housekeeper reported to have seen a man looking in through the ground-floor windows, and soon, objects on my terrace started to shift in position to give the impression that they were being tampered with. Had I not been swift to put security measures in place, I might not be alive today".

"You are no longer the only one he is watching", Ophélie muttered, dropping her gaze. "I so wanted to believe that none of this could be true, Mr Lavarre, but on the night that Manon was poisoned, I saw someone at the back of our garden—a figure, cloaked in darkness, staring up at the house with no concern for being acknowledged. On the contrary, he appeared to *desire* it. What do you know about this man?"

Romain clenched his fists. "Well, at first, I was foolish enough to believe that I was looking into the open-and-shut case of a child's murder, but I have learnt to doubt that theory".

From one end of the table to the other, Romain proceeded to place rows of paper. Each page contained nothing but a symbol that had been drawn with extraordinary accuracy: an equilateral triangle with an eye at its centre.

"From his perseverance in leaving me these illustrations, I am persuaded to believe that this person's agenda is unfinished", Romain explained.

The gentleman could not decipher Ophélie's reaction as she took in the symbols, but there was an apparent flicker of familiarity behind her stare.

After a long pause, she shifted forward to ask: "During our last encounter, Mr Lavarre, you told me that the culprit resided in the Institute, did you not?"

"I did. Acquiring that fact required patience, since asking Charles Moreau for information would have raised suspicions, added to which most of the residents who might have known Isabelle had left long ago", Romain replied. "The year that I moved to Aixelles, I attended her remembrance ceremony. It was there that I heard the name Lise Duclos—Isabelle's nurse from 1863 until 1871. Instantly, I knew that she would be the key to this enigma".

"Your string of 'business trips' across France", Ophélie answered, "they were to locate her, were they not?"

Romain nodded, then relit the candle fulgurating in the draught beside him. "Miss Duclos disappeared overnight after Isabelle's murder. She proceeded to go into hiding—a telling sign, in itself, that she possessed information she should not have. I found her during my most recent journey to Rennes, and in exchange for my promise of her protection, the nurse shed a harrowing light on the connection between my stalker and the Institute.

"In the six months leading to Isabelle's murder, bizarre phenomena began to occur around her. Miss Duclos would notice the silhouette of a man in the girl's bedroom at night, for example, followed by a tapping noise that went away when she came close to the door. The child also became aggressive in the presence of men. But most jarring of all, the nurse told me, was her increasing sense that her every movement was under scrutiny.

"To one of the maids, Miss Duclos eventually voiced her concerns, after witnessing someone leave Isabelle's bedroom at dusk, then slink upstairs to one of the abandoned class-rooms on the top floor. What happened next sealed her suspicions; the ensuing week, the maid to whom Miss Duclos had confided this account went missing, and the staff were informed that she had left without notice to start a job elsewhere.

"Naturally, Miss Duclos feared for her life at this stage. During a moment of bravery, she crept up to the top-floor classroom and searched every drawer until she came across a notebook. 'Like something from an ancient manuscript' is how she described its form—the language unintelligible, but with evidence of fresh ink smudges suggesting that it was being regularly updated. Knowing that she would only have one chance to share its contents with the world, Miss Duclos copied the last few entries onto scraps of paper she had on her person.

"For weeks she held onto them, wondering how best to get this evidence—whatever it meant—outside the Institute. Finally, she stuffed the pieces of paper into a tin and threw it over the back fence, hoping that it would reach and make sense to someone. Then came Isabelle's murder; the point at

171

which Miss Duclos realised that her own days were numbered. As soon as the trial was over, she fled the village and changed her name. I am afraid, Miss Davenport, that whoever killed Isabelle was preparing to do so long before her death".

The trigger of a memory caused Ophélie to nod and glance away. "Have you narrowed down a list of suspects?"

"I cannot be certain, but of the existing residents who were both at the Institute on the evening of Isabelle's murder and whose status allows them to come and go as they please—including to Émile Veaux's poker tournament—there are only two credible candidates", Romain stated. "The first is Nicolas Belmont, the Institute's senior plant pathologist. The second is Pierre-Alexandre Perez, Charles Moreau's godson".

Ophélie's gaze moved slowly back to Romain. "And other than locating the tin containing Miss Duclos' copies—which I presume was what you were doing in the woods the night of the poker tournament—what is your plan for how we are to proceed?"

"Miss Davenport", Romain hesitated, "the last thing I could wish to do is to put you in any further jeopardy. That said, I have come to understand that you are not the sort of person to eschew a situation for fear of its difficulty, and that it would be futile for me to offer you the opportunity to walk away from all of this now".

"No indeed", Ophélie confirmed, "and what is more, I believe I may possess something of great importance to the case".

An hour later, she returned to Baudières and made straight for Arnaud's study.

Lightly snoring while his candle dribbled wax onto the desk, Mr Girard was lying face down in a stack of papers when Ophélie entered the room. Tiptoeing around him, she brought the candle over to her grandfather's filing cabinet and slid the bottom drawer open.

Sure enough, the dusty cotton of her old satchel awaited her inside, carrying, to her relief, the outline of the biscuit tin in its pouch. Hoisting herself back on her feet, Ophélie lifted the bag and hurried up to her bedroom.

24

Remembrance

On the day of Isabelle's remembrance ceremony, the sky was an opaque, sunless whitewash. It seemed as though the clouds, too, were gathering to pay their respects. Across the mountains, the birds keeping snug in their nests ceased to sing, and a first flurry of snow descended on Aixelles—the wonderfully soft kind that makes a crunching sound beneath the feet.

Thomas was the first Baudin to don his boots and sully the pristine trail from the front door to the water's edge. The boy's enthusiasm for the weather might not have been mirrored by his sisters, but after a week of bed rest, Manon was rearing to be seen out again—albeit for an event of a morbid kind. With Adèle apparently occupied with a caller, the elder twin spent most of breakfast sifting through her wardrobe for a suitable black dress to wear at the ceremony.

Having woken up before her family, Ophélie embraced winter's arrival in the same manner that she had as a child: by walking through the garden to witness nature's transformation.

From the animals commencing hibernation to the flowers closing their buds, it had always struck her as extraordinary that these preservative reflexes were so innate to flora and fauna. This—compared to the humans grumbling about the cold or wrapping themselves in woollen cladding—had fuelled many discussions with Arnaud about mankind's spiralling disconnection from nature.

That morning, Ophélie had to shield her face from the brightness when she stepped through the back door. For the third night in a row, she had sat by her window until the early hours striving to make sense of the copies Lise Duclos had transcribed from the notebook.

Sadly, as far as progress was concerned, the most that Ophélie could claim from these efforts was that the language had been written in a complex code. Her grandfather's aptitude for cryptology could prove indispensable to deciphering it, but at this stage, so little was known about the notebook's author that Ophélie did not wish to risk involving Arnaud.

Her caution was validated when she followed Dante's paw prints to the end of the garden.

There, in the same place where she had seen the figure, lay three thorny stems—plucked of their petals and arranged atop the snow in the form of an arrowhead pointing to the woods. Surrounding them was the outline of boots that looked to have been made only hours before, accompanied by two rose petals on the ground ten and fifteen feet through the trees ahead.

Scooping up a shovel from the flowerbeds, Ophélie accepted their invitation.

This time, the acoustics in the woods were alarmingly vacant. Each rose petal in the chain jarred a reminder that her screams were less and less likely to be heard, yet for reasons she could not explain, Ophélie sensed that an attack was not the objective of this game. Then, after twenty minutes of ducking beneath dripping branches, she realised where she was being taken.

The final rose petal stopped a metre in front of Ophélie and Étienne's cabin. Propped slightly ajar, the door groaned to and fro in the breeze. But more disconcerting a sight were the thick black panels covering the sides of the cabin from the roof to the ground.

Ophélie's hand coiled tighter around the shovel as she pushed the door open and stepped inside, whereupon she was greeted by what could only be described as a work of art.

Scattered across the floor lay the blood-red petals of hundreds of roses. Above them, lining every wall, ledge, and corner were drooling candles of every size. The items that had been there during Ophélie's last visit had all been removed, and in the centre of the cabin, a new one was being showcased atop a stool: an identical straw bracelet from Saint-Laurent.

Fighting the urge to run, Ophélie's eyes shifted to the back wall as if knowing what to look for in advance: a gigantic mural of an eye within a perfectly geometric triangle. Beneath it, a message had been drawn in slick black letters, fresh enough that the paint was still runny:

Every bird loves to hear himself sing...

With the next fluctuation of the wind, Ophélie dropped the shovel and doubled back through the woods.

Over the ensuing hours, multiple staff members would spot her breathlessly dragging logs onto a pile from the kitchen window. Of what they were witnessing, nobody could be sure, but when Ophélie finally threw a match onto the heap and backed away from the flames, it sounded as though she might be shouting something into the trees themselves.

At five o'clock, the bells of Saint-Maurice clanged back and forth to signal the commencement of Isabelle's remembrance ceremony. In single file, the shivering residents of Aixelles made their way down to the stage that had been erected by the lakeside, where a string quartet would inaugurate proceedings with a macabre rendition of 'Ave Maria'.

Four rows to the Baudins' left, Romain strived to avoid being seen glancing in Ophélie's direction throughout Charles Moreau's opening speech. The gentleman could only speculate as to what she was pondering. Based on the intensity with which her glare was darting between Pierre-Alexandre Perez and Nicholas Belmont in their pride of place behind the professor, he nevertheless feared that something grave had occurred since their last discussion.

Under her breath, Ophélie appeared to be repeating the same four words as she took in their expressions: 'Why Isabelle and Madeleine?' Both victims were female, yes, but they had been five years, several miles, and an entire social class apart. Beyond the fact that their bodies had been found in water, she could see no logical connection between the pair. Then, as Ophélie scanned the stage for answers, something drew her attention.

Battling to be seen above the bouquets was a large, framed painting of Isabelle sitting on a stool. Despite the artist's beautification efforts, the child's glaring discomfort in the image suggested that this was one of only a few portraits created of Isabelle. Based on her age and the gardens in the backdrop being in bloom, Ophélie dated the painting to the spring before Isabelle was murdered. And from this realisation, a certain detail stood out—the girl's legs, dangling in a pair of brown boots on either side of the stool. No brace or indication of an injury to her shin; either the artist had glossed over this feature, or the portrait had been commissioned before Isabelle was taken to Arnaud's practice.

Whatever the case, Ophélie's eyes did not move from the image for the remainder of the service.

The snow started to fall while the last candles were placed on the lake. One by one, the thickening flakes snuffed out these lights until the glassy surface was black again. Despite petitions for the municipality to do something about the disruption of local transport and communication routes, it would not be long before households were forced into isolation.

When the carriage returned to Baudières, Ophélie made straight for the left wing. Her grandfather was being served dinner as she entered the library, but despite Mrs Cadet's repeated offer to make up a plate for Ophélie, the notion of food left her queasy.

Having failed to elicit more than a monosyllabic response from his granddaughter thirty minutes later, Arnaud waited until the housekeeper had departed with his tray, then demanded: "Well, what is it then—this terrible dilemma you are perpending?"

With hesitant movements, Ophélie turned to face him. "Grand-père, I need you to tell me what happened the day Isabelle Moreau came to Baudières. She had injured her shin, had she not?"

"Is this because of her service, or is there something else behind your query?" Arnaud probed, lighting his pipe.

"Please", Ophélie insisted, "if you have as much faith in me as you claim to then I beseech you to ask no questions until I have heard your full account".

Her grandfather rolled his eyes. "Yes, as you may recall, she was brought to me with lesions across her right leg".

"And what did you make of her?" Ophélie enquired.

"Physically tenuous", Arnaud responded, "and unstable in her disposition. I will never forget her outburst of violence towards me that seemed to have been caused by the sound of my pen tapping against the desk. Having clawed my arms, she tried to run for the door, grunting and hissing like an imp. I had little time to examine her after that, but I would infer that this was due to a sensory processing disorder of some sort".

Ophélie nodded and stood up to pace the room. "What was the cause of her injury?"

"If I remember correctly, she had trapped her leg in a snare that was left in the woods. Extremely clumsy on the part of the hunter to place it so close to the Institute. I did suggest to her nurse that the authorities be made aware of this issue to prevent future such accidents, but she simply nodded and lifted Isabelle away the instant I had applied the brace", Arnaud answered. "Am I now entitled to hear the motive behind this inquisition?"

"I give you my word that I will explain everything shortly", Ophélie replied, "but first, the farm girl you told me about from Saint-Laurent—Madeleine. Am I right in saying that she, too, had sustained a wound to her right leg before she drowned? If so, do you believe there is any chance this injury could have been inflicted on her deliberately?"

Arnaud tutted. "Her leg was broken, yes. Since her cause of death was drowning, I concluded that she had given her shin a nasty bash while tumbling into the reservoir, thereby rendering herself incapable of clambering back out. At the time I had no reason to suspect otherwise, and it would be inappropriate for me to do so in retrospect. I must say I am becoming unnerved by these queries, Ophélie—I do not believe I ever told you the farm girl's name".

Ophélie crossed the room and reached into her pocket to hand him the copies from the notebook. "This shall be my final question. Does this language mean something to you? Have you seen anything like it before?"

"I would say decisively not", Arnaud responded, pouring over the text. "The dots at the start of every line are likely dice cypher—numbers or dates, perhaps. As for the rest, it could be a shifted alphabet code, hence why the characters resemble gibberish in their current order. Then there are these rather curious bird hieroglyphs dispersed throughout. There must be seven or eight in total, although the difference between each bird is subtle. This one here, for example, looks to be of significance judging by the fact that it is repeated. The use of the symbol above the text is also interesting.

"According to Christian iconography, this is known as the 'Eye of Providence'—the all-seeing eye of God. You will find it replicated across political imagery throughout history, including our very own Declaration of the Rights of Man and the Citizen, but I doubt there is any connection to such doctrine here. What is going on, Ophélie? I have answered your questions and waited long enough. I must know the meaning of all this".

After a long pause, Ophélie sank into the armchair by Arnaud's bed. "Weeks ago you asked me for a project to work on, Grand-père—something to give you a reason to continue fighting. I think it is safe to say I have found one".

III

Winter

25

Into the Belly of the Beast

'A man claiming to have mastered a skill is unqualified to do so until he has demonstrated his proficiency in even the most unfavourable of conditions'.

These were the words with which Charles Moreau began each lecture on the first day of term, from the stern eagle lectern that loomed over the Great Hall of the Institute. A challenge to his pupils would famously follow, to ratify their status as France's brightest future minds in their field.

That year's Botany Display—an annual contest whereby the students were allocated an individual section of the gardens to create a sumptuous exhibit—was thus announced to take place in December. The frosty climate would need to be surmounted should the competitors wish for their works to shine when they were unveiled to the public.

As the gap before the event in her calendar shortened, Ophélie awoke to find her cheek pressed against the uneven wood of her grandfather's desk. Inches from her nose, the odour of Arnaud's morning brew caused her stomach to grumble, and his pen hovered above Lise Duclos' copies as if the old man were fishing with it.

Disregarding his pleas for her to continue sleeping, Ophélie straightened her neck and forced herself upright to continue their decryption. Staring down at the progress they had made so far, her shoulders slumped once again.

Since joining the investigation, Arnaud's input had led to the comprehension of a handful of dates and times. No matter how many letters he substituted in the body of the text, however, there seemed to be no pattern in the repetition of vowels or popular consonants that could make the words discernible. If unravelling the motives of Isabelle and Madeleine's killer did indeed hinge on cracking this code, then Ophélie could only hope she would have more luck hunting for clues as to his murder weapon during her imminent trip to the Institute.

An eventual onset of giddiness drove her to the dining room, where the empty seat at the table opposite did little to restore her humour. By now, Ophélie needed not enquire as to Adèle's whereabouts; after three outings and more dinners with Pierre-Alexandre Perez than her cousin cared to count that week, the younger twin had no doubt been escorted away by the gentleman for another 'pre-lunch stroll' around the lake.

Sure enough, when the front door opened an hour later, a rosy-faced Adèle entered with an envelope bearing the Institute's seal.

Having demanded that it be handed to her at once, its contents were first examined by Manon, then relayed to the rest of her family via the repeated vaunts: "Oh how delectably bitter Solène Ozanam will be! Mr Moreau has granted us the honour of selecting the winning student at the Botany Display".

The clock ground to a halt for Ophélie while her cousins danced around the table. Initially, she thought it possible that the Baudins might have the professor's old friendship with her grandfather to thank for this offer. But as Adèle stopped to adjust the new bracelet on her wrist, Ophélie's suspicions veered elsewhere. Clenching her jaw, she abandoned the piece of fruit she had been pushing around her plate, then hurried back to the library.

No closer to deciphering the copies on the morning of the Botany Display, Ophélie ventured onto the terrace early to prepare herself for their journey.

Cleared of all boats, the lake was like an exquisite wasteland. Its surface resembled a colossal mirror reflection of the sky, broken only by the sporadic addition of ice skaters from neighbouring villages. All across the horizon, rooftops disappeared beneath thick dollops of snow, and there was a peacefulness emanating from the mountains that was both consoling and unsettling to Ophélie.

Despite her reassurances to Romain the last time they had met, the notion of infiltrating the Institute caused her hands to grip the railing tighter. More perturbing, however, was the knowledge that this would be her sole opportunity to do so.

"Let me find *something*", she whispered as the sun's tip poked through the clouds.

The family set off in the carriage after lunch to join the thirty or so champagne-clad guests in the hallway of the Institute. Their arrival was met with a demand for the invitees to write in the guestbook being passed from household to household, and a series of murmurs as their peers took note of which families had been asked to the occasion.

The Ozanamas, the Sauniers, the de Corbiacs; all the

usual socialites were there, yet Ophélie was surprised to hear that Mr and Mrs Rinaldi—Aixelles' most decorated party-goers—would not be attending. If Marcelle Arminjon's accompanying explanation was to be believed, their dog Cornelius had eaten something to make his stomach swell on the night of the poker tournament. The couple had not been seen outside their estate since.

In recalling her last sighting of the terrier, Ophélie gravitated from the group's sighs of sympathy towards the French windows backing onto the gardens.

Until that moment, it had slipped her attention that someone with access to pesticides and chemicals might have cultivated a toxin unknown to those outside the world of botany. Or perhaps the answer was more obvious than that, Ophélie proceeded to consider; rolling up the sleeve of her dress, she stared down at the rash still covering her elbow.

Could it be possible that the bag of seeds referenced early in Kacper Smolak's notebook was that of a plant the individual had sought to keep off the Institute's records, she wondered? The same strange flower that she—and as it appeared, the Rinaldis' terrier—had encountered by the greenhouse on the night of the poker tournament.

Resolved to test this theory, Ophélie pulled her sleeve back down and returned to her family.

At two o'clock, the group was let out into the grounds. While Manon waited with growing impatience for volunteers to take her arm, Ophélie followed Mr Perez down the steps towards Adèle and requested to join their tour.

There was no denying it; the gardens were more magnificent on this side of the fence than Ophélie and Étienne had envisaged. Trails merged into endless white corridors, and the stone features of the statues guarding them would never be more striking beneath that delicate outline of snow. Mr Moreau's challenge to his students had moreover worked delightfully; not a shrivelled petal or barren stem lay in sight. On the contrary, despite a blustery wind shaking their beds, the carefully-chosen primroses, pansies, and camellias vying for the swoons of passers-by were all the more endearing in their resilience.

But amid that impossibly verdant scenery, nothing appeared more in its element than their guide. Free from the crippling reticence with which he approached most conversations, Mr Perez would bestow upon his listeners a stream of pedagogical narration so smooth that each word might have been scripted. Evidently, it was easier for the gentleman to delve into matters of science than it was to discuss his weekend plans.

From the back of the group, Ophélie shadowed Mr Perez to the midway point of the eastern path, where—just as she had hoped—the gentleman changed course and led them through the orchards. Seizing her opportunity to shirk the crowd, Ophélie fumbled around with her walking stick until the other guests had moved on, then turned her attention back to the empty trail.

Perhaps it was merely the change in perspective, but she had never much noticed the lone pine tree looming ahead until that moment. Granted, its height rendered the pointy branches at the top visible from almost every corner of the gardens. Only when passing directly beneath the tree could Ophélie appreciate its strangeness, though.

Unlike the surrounding stumps that had succumbed to the groundskeepers' axe over the years, this pine had clearly been left there by design. Nothing in its otherwise ordinary appearance hinted at an explanation, yet from that proximity, Ophélie felt a shiver of familiarity as she poured her eyes over the rigid twists of its limbs—a sense that if she could ask the tree what it had witnessed over the years, the answers would contain equal measures of warmth and darkness. This might be the pine that Isabelle had climbed before her leg injury, for example, or one whose shade Charles Moreau's grandparents had picnicked beneath at the peak of their love.

A red crossbill returning to its nest cut Ophélie's contemplation short, sending a shudder down the lower branches that made her jump. Whatever the nature of the Moreau family's affinity with the pine tree, she was suddenly loath to be spotted standing next to it. Stepping away from the trunk, she continued to the far end of the path.

The moment the gardens' iconic glass structures came into sight, Ophélie's movements ground to a halt once again. Not only was the greenhouse nearest Émile Veaux's estate locked, but the same black material that had been used to cover the cabin was draped over the walls, apparently due to it undergoing fumigation.

This defence tactic may have foiled Ophélie's plan to obtain a sample of the plant, but she would never be more convinced of her theory regarding its utility. As long as she could produce an accurate description of the species from memory, she and Romain might be a step closer to identifying their killer. In the meantime, only thirty minutes remained before the Baudins would be expected to choose a victor. With her family still dispersed around the grounds, Ophélie doubled back to the Institute.

Peering up at the chandelier suspended a floor's height above her head, the hallway seemed to have expanded since she last stood there. Rooted to the centre of its vacuity, the decor alone was enough to raise the hairs on Ophlie's neck, from the row of gnarled, stuffed birds lining the mantelpiece, to the towering faces watching her from weathered portraits. So intense was the silence, in fact, that she felt as though the sound of a pin dropping might attract a hundred vigilant stares from Charles Moreau's ancestors.

After a minute of warming herself by the fireplace, Ophélie's ears were alerted to the undulation of chanting from one of the reading rooms to her left. From what she could discern, its provenance was Nicolas Belmont, who appeared to be seeking refuge from his guests through meditation. Moving discreetly past the professor's eye-line, Ophélie cast her gaze ahead to the stairwell leading to the top floor. As she inched forward to mount it, though, something along the corridor wall commanded her attention instead.

For whatever reason, the painting—a young portrait of the Moreau sisters sitting on the terrace—practically screamed for Ophélie to approach it. Transfixed by their expressions, she tiptoed closer until she was standing directly beneath the canvas, at which point a door swung open behind her and two maids scurried out carrying bundles of sheets.

No sooner had their faces met than the first let out a loud gasp, hurtling down the corridor.

"Forgive her, she meant you no offence", the other maid quickly whispered, "it is just...you look so similar to Isabelle. It was quite a shock to see you standing there like that. My apologies, Miss, I should be upstairs with the others, but Mr Moreau did insist that I tend to the ground floor this afternoon. I shall leave you be".

"I should not have trespassed. Please, do not go on my account", Ophélie implored her, gesturing towards the painting. "You knew the Moreau girls well, then?"

"Isabelle, no, but I was her sister's nurse from birth. She was like a daughter to me", the maid murmured. "Their mother had that painting commissioned just before we lost her to a chest infection. It took several attempts for the artist to complete it—only one that exists of the two girls together".

Ophélie nodded. "I attended school with Florence. Although we were a number of years apart, I regret not having taken the time to know her better".

At this, the maid's chin started to quiver. "That is most comforting to hear, Miss. Florence had very few friends, you will no doubt recall. Most children amused themselves by making jokes at her expense. Broke my heart, it did. I always said that girl was born in the wrong place at the wrong time".

"It must have been difficult for you when she left Aixelles", Ophélie replied, raising a hand to add: "Rest assured, I have no intention of asking you to discuss the Moreau family's private affairs. I whould, however, very much like to visit Florence one day. Do you know where I might find her?"

The maid took a step back as if searching Ophélie's face for confirmation that she could be trusted. Then, with a careful glance over her shoulder, she disappeared around the corner, returning a minute later holding a letter.

"This was sent to me in confidence in the months following Florence's departure", the maid whispered. "If she is still at this address then it is your best chance of locating her. I need not tell you that should Mr Moreau discover that I had shown this to you, or that I knew where his daughter had run away to all those years ago-"

Ophélie took the maid's hand. "I promise that your secret

will remain safe. Thank you".

The maid bowed her head, then turned away to resume her cleaning. That would be the first and last day she ever saw Ophélie Davenport—or, for that matter, that she would read Florence's letter in the peaceful moments before slumber. By the following morning, the staff would receive an announcement that after decades of faithful service, the maid had decided to move back to her hometown to live out her final years with her own family.

We will never know what words she had attempted to utter when her eyes had opened to 'The Watcher' perched at the end of her bed that night—eyes glinting in the darkness as the poison started to take effect. In her fleeting prelude to death, it would nevertheless be comforting to imagine that she had thought only of Florence.

26

Florence Moreau

Manon and Adèle's birthday fell on the second week of December. Habitually, it culminated in Camille purchasing one box of chocolate éclairs for the family to share for pudding. This was 'more than their mother received as a child', lay the excuse for her so-called stinginess. In reality, Mrs Baudin had drawn the line at presents after the girls turned six, whereupon she had handed them two china dolls that she snapped up from a travelling toymaker for next to nothing.

Having played together all afternoon, Manon had waited until Roland and Camille were out of the nursery before smashing her doll's face with a rock. When the family later gathered for dinner, she proceeded to inform her parents that this vicious act had been Adèle's doing, and the younger twin was ordered to give her own doll to Manon.

The sisters' twenty-second birthday would look somewhat different; Mr and Mrs Ozanam were marking the occasion by asking a handful of friends to Florence for the weekend, where a famous fencing bout was due to take place.

Never had there been a more opportune trip from which

Ophélie could exempt herself on the grounds of mobility. As for her own intended excursion, the address on Florence Moreau's letter had been from a dairy farm on the other side of the Alps—half a day's ride in moderate snow conditions.

Once her aunt and cousins had departed on the Friday morning, Ophélie waited for Roland to settle at his desk, then she hurried out of the estate to meet Romain.

The road to Florence's village was hazardous. Beneath them, the wheels of the carriage screeched at every bend as they ascended the path over the mountains. Yet despite the dangers raging from the other side of the window, Ophélie felt more at peace sinking into the upholstery opposite Romain than she had in a long time.

Every so often, the gentleman's gaze would catch her attention during pauses in their discourse, and she would remark to herself that winter suited him, somehow—the crystal-blue of his eyes emphasised by its glacial hues. More surprising, perhaps, was her accompanying realisation of how much she had been looking forward to their journey.

By the time they emerged onto the other side of Savoie, only a few hours of sunlight remained, and the wind had picked up enough speed to threaten the prospect of a safe return to Aixelles. As she stepped down from the carriage in front of the farm—boots sinking into the snow—Ophélie lifted her head and said a prayer that their efforts had not been in vain and that they would find Florence Moreau on the other side of that door.

After several knocks, someone stomped towards the entrance. It appeared their risk had paid off when the owner's face came into sight; hair cropped short, stockier than the average woman, and with a flicker of recognition in her eyes, as if trying to locate Ophélie in her memory. By her side, a red-haired boy followed her to the door, bearing such a resemblance to Étienne that Ophélie lost her train of thought as she took him in.

"Can I help you?" Florence enquired.

"Miss Moreau, my name is Ophélie Davenport and this is Mr Romain Lavarre", Ophélie answered. "You and I went to school together in Aixelles, although it was so long ago I imagine you will have forgotten me entirely".

Florence lent against the doorway. "Sure, I remember you—the doctor's granddaughter. People called your mother the 'Mad Lady'".

"Yes", Ophélie responded, "I believe they did".

"Don't be offended", Florence replied, pulling off her gloves. "They said worse about me".

Their host stood aside and beckoned Romain and Ophélie into the house, while Matteo, as she introduced the red-haired boy, led their horses to the stables.

The interior of Florence's farm was basic to say the least. Chance had brought her there after she ran away from the Institute aged seventeen, hitching a ride with a travelling theatre group. They got as far as La Féclaz before Florence had decided to go her separate way in search of work, whereupon she had stumbled across the farm.

Its owner was an elderly Italian widow whose family had raised livestock for generations. Having lost her daughter to illness, she lived there with only her grandson, Matteo, whom she had long feared would find himself without a carer once she passed away. As a result, she had offered Florence a job instantly, departing from this world months later comforted that her grandson had all the family he would ever require.

"So, what brings you to my neck of the woods? I presume you have a reason for venturing this far in the thick of winter. Which is it, though—madness or bravery?" Florence asked, clunking two mugs onto the kitchen table.

"Desperation", Ophélie admitted, warming her hands around the tea. With a nervous glance towards the window, she continued: "Miss Moreau, please allow me to be candid; we came here to ask for your help in identifying a plant which I believe possesses certain properties that are highly poisonous to humans".

This seemed to be the last excuse that Florence had expected to hear. Arms folded, she looked her guests up and down in bewilderment. The silence that followed was so arresting, in fact, that Ophélie could hear the cows shuffling around the barn outside.

Romain removed the sketch he had made of the flower from his coat, then placed it on the table to prove that their request was legitimate.

"Good God", their host chortled, "did you really come all this way just to ask me that?"

"Miss Moreau, we would not be here wasting your time if it were not important", Romain insisted. "Miss Davenport's cousin fell extremely ill recently, and we have reason to suspect that this plant was responsible. If Miss Davenport is not mistaken, you are something of an authority in this area. Do you recognise it?"

As she narrowed her eyes at Ophélie, it was not clear whether Florence was touched or startled by this question, at first. The former sentiment appeared to prevail, for she eventually took another look at Romain's sketch.

"How much do you know about the Romans?" Florence

asked, resting her arms on the table. "You will be familiar with the names Claudius and Augustus, I presume, among the most famous Roman Emperors. Few are aware that in both cases their deaths are rumoured to have been ordered by their respective wives. Even fewer people know what poison was allegedly used—that of an untraceable plant known as *Atropa belladonna*.

"As you have illustrated here, it resembles an ordinary flower and grows across hedgerows in many parts, but its berries and roots can be deadly. If your cousin ingested this and survived, then she either consumed an insufficient amount to cause serious damage or she was unimaginably lucky. What were her symptoms?"

"She had trouble breathing, initially, then dehydration, confusion, and aggression set in", Ophélie replied.

Florence nodded. "Well, that sounds consistent with the effects of *Atropa belladonna*. It can cause powerful hallucinations in its victims, so much so that ancient armies purportedly used it to lull their enemies into a mindless trance before battle. In any case, I would strongly recommend that you discourage your cousin from eating unknown fruits and berries she comes across in future, Miss Davenport, however tempting they look".

While their host stood up to fetch more wood for the fire, Romain gave a nod to confirm Ophélie's suspicion about the contents of the greenhouse. His action did not go unseen, and when Florence resumed her place at the table, there was an air of curiosity in her voice.

"Not that Matteo and I don't appreciate the company", she began, "but you are aware that there are books in which you might have found this information closer to home?"

"I have no doubt, Miss Moreau, but as you have insinuated, there is another, more significant reason for our visit today", Ophélie paused. "You and I did not know each other well, but Isabelle's murder touched everyone in the village. I could never forgive myself for not expressing my condolences to you in person".

"Condolences?" Their host tilted her chair back. "Don't take this the wrong way, Miss Davenport, but you might have spared yourself the trip. I barely knew my sister—none of us did. 'A hummingbird inflicted with a broken wing', my family used to call her. If we were in the wild she would have been rejected at birth, but then again, compassion is the one thing that separates us from the animals. At what cost, though? What life could she have had? Make no mistake, I will forever condemn what happened to Isabelle, but in some strange way, I cannot deny my relief that she is at peace. It would have been kinder than watching her struggle as an adult".

"Do you believe this is the view of the rest of your family, also?" Romain asked.

Florence shrugged. "Isabelle's passing hit my father the hardest. I am not convinced he ever loved my mother. Like so many, marriage seemed nothing more than a rite of passage to him—a convention that afforded certain advantages. I don't even recall him having cried when my mother died. But my God did he mourn Isabelle's loss. The Institute turned into a mausoleum—everyone keeping their heads down, not daring to utter my sister's name. It was one of the reasons I left in the end. Well, that, and the dreadful ultimatum I was given by my father to accept his godson's marriage proposal or consider myself homeless".

"Mr Perez asked you to marry him?" Ophélie exclaimed.

197

"That he did", Florence muttered. "I am not sure why he bothered in hindsight. It was no great secret that the only calling I ever wanted to pursue was to become a botanist. Alas, my father insisted that it was not an appropriate path for a lady of our class, and I suppose Mr Perez was impressionable enough to misapprehend that with sufficient persistence I would submit. As you can see, I chose otherwise, and have not looked back since".

As Florence said this, the clatter of a branch falling outside caused Ophélie to jump, affording her a few additional seconds to formulate a follow-up question. When she turned back around, however, Matteo was sitting in Florence's lap blowing bubbles in her tea.

Suddenly, any inclinations to continue her inquiry melted into the beauty of that moment. Instead, Ophélie took a mental image of the pair interacting, then went to stand up. There would be ample opportunity to discuss Florence's revelation with Romain later, but time was rapidly running out to begin their journey back.

"Miss Moreau, I cannot thank you enough for your hospitality, but we must be on our way", Ophélie spoke.

Her words were greeted with dubiety by Florence, who proceeded to open the kitchen window, letting half a foot of fresh snow tumble onto the floor. Before anybody could react, the room was filled with a sharp polar blast, beneath which Florence's hearth battled to remain lit. All across the meadows outside, the fences were no longer visible, and the snow was showering down in such quantities that it made patterns in the wind.

"I'm afraid there's little chance of that, Miss Davenport", Florence answered, using all her force to slam the window shut again. "We are in the middle of a blizzard. You and Mr Lavarre will have to stay the night".

27

The Blizzard

At eight o'clock that evening, Arnaud awoke in a state of panic. Fumbling for his glass of water, he called Mrs Cadet into his library and pushed himself upright on the mattress. While it was uncommon for the doctor to contemplate the significance of nightmares, this was the third time in four months that Arnaud had dreamt of his daughter.

It was always the same scenario; he would find himself standing opposite Gabrielle in a vast, burning garden. At first, she would do nothing but stand and stare into his eyes. Then, as if fixating on something behind him, she would slowly lift her arm and point.

Like clockwork, Arnaud's thoughts were drawn to Ophélie each time he emerged from this dream, and the doctor would have to spend the ensuing minutes reassuring himself that his granddaughter was not in grave danger as he had feared.

When Mrs Cadet informed him that Ophélie had not returned home, Arnaud's back stiffened and he cast his eyes to the window. Despite his nerves, something in the way the snow was falling led him to believe that wherever she was, his granddaughter was safe and thinking of him at that moment. With no choice but to trust this instinct, the old man eventually dabbed his forehead and picked up the copies from the notebook again.

On the other side of Baudières, Roland ate dinner alone at his desk. The gentleman's eyes had not moved from the windowpane rattling beside him since he had sat down.

The last time he had been snowed into the estate like that was many decades ago when he and Henri were young. In reliving the memory, Roland was reminded of his little brother's excited comment that they might never be able to leave Baudières again, to which he had rolled his eyes. How things had been different then, he thought.

The following summer, Henri had come to his brother on the terrace to announce: "I am going to move far away from this place one day—move far away and never return. I shall start my own piano show, and invite the kings and queens of the world to hear me play. Papa will be sorry when I'm a rich and famous musician".

"Why do you care what he thinks?" Roland had muttered while turning another page in his book. "One day, you won't remember this village, this house, or the people in it".

"You will always remember me though, won't you?" was Henri's wide-eyed response, "and Gabrielle?"

As Roland poured himself another goblet of wine to keep warm, it occurred to him that he had never answered his brother's question that day. Still, the patch of missing paint on the helmet of one of his figurines demanded his more immediate focus. Heaving himself back into the armchair, the gentleman set about rectifying this oversight.

In a tavern several miles away, meanwhile, Henri Baudin

201

slammed an empty pitcher onto the table, then ordered another round from the barmaid who had been smiling at him since his arrival. With bedraggled curls stuck to her forehead, she was older and larger than the women who typically attracted Henri's attention. Then again, now that the gentleman's hairline was receding and his belly expanding, the gentleman would relish in whatever coquetry was aimed at him.

His hands, at least, appeared to be immune to aging, Henri often told himself. It was remarkable how many women—including the barmaid—seemed to fixate on the strength and steadiness of his fingers. Showcasing this asset to the best of his ability, he proceeded to reach into the breast of his coat where he had taken to storing Mr Girard's letter.

Between the sodden lining of his pocket and the growing puddle of beer beneath his elbows, the ink on the paper was so smudged as to be unreadable now. Four measly lines to notify him that his father was dying, Henri cursed under his breath; clearly, Mr Girard's dubiety that the letter would reach him had justified his composition of a message no doubt half the length of the one Roland had received.

How many copies had the solicitor bothered to dispatch, he further wondered? There were dozens of addresses from which Henri had sent correspondence over the years. Had the younger son not returned to his favourite inn in Rouen weeks ago, he might never have seen Mr Girard's warning and known to hitchhike his way to Aixelles before it was too late.

Having decided against announcing his arrival at Baudières, a part of Henri was looking forward to taking his father by surprise. Extending a sticky hand to his tankard, he even chuckled to himself at the notion. Then, he adjusted the gold signet ring on his baby finger—the emblem of the Baudin family that he had found beneath Roland's bed as a child—and the gentleman re-read Mr Girard's letter, just in case he had missed something during his last lecture.

Across the mountains in La Féclaz, Ophélie and Romain waited out the blizzard by helping Matteo prepare dinner, while Florence set up a bed for Ophélie in her spare room and fetched a pile of blankets to line the barn floor for Romain. There was something wonderfully simple to Ophélie about eating a bowl of stew at the kitchen table; no embroidered napkins, no maids hovering by the walls with silver trays. Of the new life Florence had made for herself she became more enamoured as the evening drew on.

After dinner, the four of them moved to the living room and spent the next few hours exchanging stories around the fire. Towards midnight, Florence took a reluctant Matteo off to bed, leaving Ophélie and Romain to admire the snow-enveloped scenery from the window. Neither of the pair noticed their host's smirk as she shut the door behind them, and probably, this was for the best given its insinuation.

Florence Moreau did not consider herself to be a romantic by anyone's definition, but it had been impossible for her to overlook the smiles of affection shared between her guests throughout the evening. If she had been the nosy kind, she might have satiated her curiosity by enquiring as to their situation. Instead, Florence sensed that the kindest thing she could do would be to give them the space to work that out for themselves.

By now, a veil of white powder shimmered like satin atop the mountains, and the wind had slowed to a gentle breeze, carrying with it dust-like particles of snow. Eyes unmoving from the view, it took Ophélie several seconds to notice that Romain was glancing at her every so often in a manner she had seen only once before.

"Do you know", she whispered, "if my grandfather were standing in your place, he would accuse me of being distant and demand to know where I had disappeared to".

"Sometimes, silence speaks louder than words", Romain responded. "That said, it can also prove grossly provocative to the wrong recipient. As a boy, my father once found me curled up in the corner of my bedroom rocking back and forth. He removed my mattress for a week when I was unable to provide an explanation".

Ophélie dropped her gaze. "I must say, I cannot fathom how you survived it all".

"Well, my father's heavy hand was easy to endure. Those periods of emptiness, however... They are comparable to a loss of vision—the world around me withering away, along with any notion of my place within it. At a young age, I was simply lucky enough to find something to hold on to in the darkness", the gentleman replied.

Ophélie nodded and fell silent. With circumstances as uncertain as they were, she knew that she and Romain might never have another moment together like this.

Suddenly, of all the topics preoccupying her, there was only one that she wished to address: "It is strange, even though we are still in the thick of it, it has just occurred to me that there is an end to all of this—our investigation. What do you plan to do when it is over?"

Romain rested his back against the window. "I have given much thought to that question these past months. Some time ago I wrote to an association that organises humanitarian missions to areas in conflict. It can be dangerous work, which is why they are always in need of new volunteers to distribute food and medical aid, but I can think of few causes more worthy to dedicate whatever is left of my time".

Ophélie parted from the window, attempting to conceal the bittersweet quake in her voice when she answered: "Were other people to adopt your philosophy, the world would certainly be a more gracious place".

"My philosophy? Miss Davenport, I can assure you that any magnanimity you identify in my actions, however flattering, is miscredited", Romain insisted. "This decision was wholly inspired by you, as it happens".

After a long pause, Ophélie searched for the words with which to respond. "You hold me in such high regard, Mr Lavarre, yet I am not ignorant of what you are doing for the people of Mèliez. Even before we became so well acquainted, your kindness towards me surpassed anything I could have expected from a stranger".

"Maybe so, Miss Davenport", Romain turned to face her, "but we have never been strangers, you and I".

As he watched the corners of her mouth break into a smile, the gentleman fought the urge to add to his response the confession that would have rendered it complete, then returned to his place in front of the fire.

His assiduous maintenance of the cinders was interrupted moments later when Ophélie joined him in the next seat, with a question she had long yearned to pose: "Mr Lavarre, that day in Eduard de Corbiac's pavilion, you said you had returned to the village because you had left something behind, yet you only found out that your father was innocent upon your arrival. What did you come back for then, if not to clear his name?"

"I fear that is a story for another time and place, Miss Davenport", Romain suggested. "I promise to tell it to you one day, though".

With that, the gentleman bid Ophélie goodnight and waited for her to leave, before slipping out of the farmhouse to his own bed. The chill in the barn was unpitying, and Florence's blankets offered minimal relief from the rickety floorboards or the sprigs of hay sticking into his back. Romain cared not at all, though. For the entire night he stared up at the stars through a small hole in the ceiling, until before he knew it, the sky was turning an airy shade of pink, and Ophélie appeared at the door to help him lead the horses out to the carriage.

The road to Aixelles was difficult to navigate in yesterday's snowfall, but they made it back to the village just as Roland was tucking into his lunch. On the presumption that his niece had already eaten, the gentleman was enjoying his filet steak far too much to notice the door opening as Ophélie crept in and hurried upstairs to change. It was fortunate that she arrived when she did nevertheless, for there appeared to have been a last-minute alteration to her cousins' weekend itinerary that resulted in the party returning home a day early.

Presuming that a crisis had arisen when she heard her aunt's voice shrieking demands from the ground floor, Ophélie rushed into the corridor and, to her confusion, was met with the sound of cheering. When Manon's expressionless face floated past her on the stairs, she should have anticipated what was to come.

Clinking champagne glasses in the front room were her aunt and uncle, Adèle and Pierre-Alexandre Perez, and Charles Moreau. The group called Ophélie over as soon as she entered the doorway, whereupon her cousin stretched out her hand.

If the emerald ring on Adèle's finger was not alarming enough, Ophélie had to steady herself as the younger twin proceeded to utter the words: "Mr Perez and I are engaged".

28

An Unexpected Visitor

On the morning of Christmas Eve, Manon found herself alone in the sitting room, sewing a holly leaf onto a cushion. The trill coos of a pigeon had driven the elder twin out of bed an hour earlier, but not before she had hurled her perfume bottle against the window to scare it away. Between the oily mess it had made on her carpet and the drone of her parents arguing about Adèle's wedding finances, Manon had not dared return upstairs since.

Eyes bearing into the tangled nest of threads, the elder twin nearly punctured her hand with the needle when the knocker on the front door boomed across the hallway. Setting aside the cushion, she rose from the sofa.

Probably, this was another well-wisher stopping by for Adèle, Manon warned herself as she edged towards the window to check. How her future brother-in-law could have had the gall to announce their engagement before the entire Residents' Council that month was quite beyond her. If she had to endure one more evening affirming her delight at Adèle's situation to a room of crooning faces, Manon felt as though she might explode.

On the other hand, could this be a male caller, the elder twin queried? The notion quickened her movements, at first, then brought them to a standstill while she took in her warped reflection in the windowpane.

Having been rendered mute by Corentin de Lastelle's invitation to 'slip upstairs' at a recent dinner party, Manon had waited for the gentleman to speak to her again with growing impatience. Corentin had simply caught her off guard, she insisted to herself upon each occasion that she replayed his question in her mind. And yet, only more startling than the entry of his hand sliding up her dress beneath the table had been her subsequent discovery that Mr de Lastelle had requested to sit next to Solène Ozaman at Adèle's wedding.

Of the remaining names on her list, there was always Victor Chappaz as an alternative companion, she reassured herself. Given the manner in which he had been leering Christiane Alarie of late, it nevertheless seemed likely that the gentleman would ask her soon.

Unable to discern the identity of their visitor from behind the curtain, Manon concealed her nightie under a blanket, then tiptoed to the hallway. She arrived just as Alessio Lettiere was stepping through the threshold.

To the inquisitive maid who had opened the door, the gentleman's reason for calling would remain a mystery; no sooner had he lifted his head to speak than the elder twin ran to the bathroom, clutching her stomach.

At that same moment above her, a fresher-faced Baudin was bounding along the corridor with equal speed. Today, Adèle's preliminary rehearsal for the role of Mrs Perez entailed helping her fiancé to select Christmas decorations for his cottage.

The bride-to-be hummed to herself all the way downstairs imagining the ensemble of colours she had planned, then abruptly turned her head to coincide with her cousin drifting past the hallway.

This was, at least, an improvement on the tone of their last interaction. Instigated by Ophélie's appeal for her cousin to reconsider rushing into marriage, the argument had incited accusations of envy, before resulting in the proclamation that nothing could change Adèle's mind on the subject. Between the various dress-fittings and food tastings the younger twin had since been called to attend, the pair had scarcely spoken a word to one another. As far as Adèle was concerned, there was no reason to begin doing so again until after the wedding.

Ordinarily, Christmas dinner in the Baudin household was characterised by three distinct sounds: Roland's lips smacking together as he slurped down mountains of oysters, Manon gracing her relatives with variations of her New Year's resolutions, and Ophélie quietly instructing Thomas to stop rocking his chair back and forth, lest Camille evict him from the dining room. None of these traditions would feature in this year's celebration.

Trickles of conversation were exchanged between Adèle and her mother on the topic of flower arrangements, but otherwise, only the intermittent screeches of cutlery scraping against plates cut through the sullenness of six individuals wishing they were anywhere else. If you had removed the rather sad-looking tree strung up in the corner, in fact, a by-stander would have struggled to believe they were observing a Christmas festivity at all.

In many ways, the tension in the air offered a perfect prelude for the surprise that came midway through the meal, when the cheese course was interrupted by an almighty ruckus from the hallway. Before Roland had registered the noise, Camille stormed out of the dining room to demand the source of the commotion. Her mouth dropped open at the sight of her brother-in-law bending down to lift the statue he had just knocked over.

"Well I'll be damned", Henri grinned. "How long has it been, Camille—twenty-five years since your wedding day?"

"What in God's name are you doing here?" Mrs Baudin cried as her husband appeared at her side.

"I might well ask the same to you", Henri hiccuped. With lumbering movements, he tossed his jacket over the coat stand. "Mr Girard informed me that father's not well. Now that I see how comfortably you two have settled into the estate, the mind starts coming up with its own conclusions".

There was an uncomfortable pause while Roland stuttered his words out. "It is Christmas Eve, Henri, and this is not the time or the place for such quarrels. I think it would be better if we moved to my office-"

"'My office'", Henri repeated, "you've not wasted any time. I'm almost impressed by your canniness, Roland! Where was this Machiavellian streak when we were boys, eh?"

"Have some decorum", Roland pleaded, ushering him over to the right wing.

Henri went to laugh, but his smirk faded the moment he spotted Ophélie standing in the doorway.

Clearing his throat, he eventually slapped his palm across Roland's back, crowing: "Fret not, brother. I did not come here to argue over the division of doilies and chinaware. Mine is a nomadic life—you and your lady can keep this dustheap and everything in it for all I care. Now, I am longing to hear what I've missed since our last get-together".

The gentlemen set off down the corridor just as Thomas appeared by Ophélie's side to ask: "Who is that?"

"Your uncle", his cousin whispered, peering over to gauge the extent of her aunt's indignation.

"That can't be Papa's brother", Thomas giggled, "he looks like a homeless man".

"Yes, he does", Ophélie sighed, before leading her cousin back into the dining room.

An hour later, their meal concluded with Henri joining the family at the table. He had barely finished pudding before requesting that his belongings be brought to one of the spare rooms on the right wing.

"Damn the abolishment of primogeniture", Mrs Baudin hissed at her husband when they crept into bed that night. "The minute your father is in the ground, your parasite-of-a-brother will be out of this house quicker than he can lift his flask—whatever it takes".

Little did Camille know that as she said this, the person on whom her warning hinged was jolting upright and reaching for his candle, in a manner suggesting that his own departure from Baudières might not be imminent.

The doctor was no stranger to the physical perception of a breakthrough. At the height of his career, he might even have toasted this occasion with a bottle of his finest cognac. Instead, Arnaud glanced intently at the mirror hanging above his fireplace, then dropped the copies from the notebook onto his lap.

Whatever had inspired him to consider the words in reverse, the doctor took his pen and worked backwards through the first paragraph with remarkable speed. First, he noticed prepositions and articles. Then, with enough letters deciphered, he used probability to guess at the blanks until individual words began to emerge—written from right to left.

Within an hour, Arnaud had deciphered all three pages of text, with the exception of the bird hieroglyphs. Aided by an old ornithology book, he was more or less able to identify the species from their outline. As for their meaning, the doctor could only speculate to what—or rather, to whom—each might refer.

Hoping with all his might that whatever Lise Duclos had transcribed would be useful, Arnaud stuck his pipe in his mouth, then slid the first piece of paper out from under the pile to examine the fruits of his labour:

Monday, 13 May, 14:06: [HUMMINGBIRD] ran away again at the sound of the groundskeepers approaching. This time, she noticed the hole in the fence and crawled through it. We must hide the snare close enough for it to be set off by her right leg, which—being her dominant one—should constitute seven paces from the moment she emerges into the woods. Based on her height, I make this approximately 210 cm from the fence.

Friday, 17 May, 08:33: [NIGHTJAR] returned to her usual spot today, alone. She looked hauntingly beautiful in the morning light. Side note 1: [STARLING] seems to be getting suspicious. To be monitored.

Tuesday, 21 May, 16:57: Our plan was executed successfully. [HUMMINGBIRD] ran away again and stepped on the snare. It snapped clean through the muscle—right leg. She will undoubtedly have trouble walking properly again, and I await the outcome with impatience. Side note 1: I did not see [NIGHTJAR] today.

Wednesday, 29 May, 22:33: [SPARROW] took her boat to [FINCH]'s house once again while her husband attended a choir rehearsal. Shallow, unfaithful wretches. Side note 1: I went to [HUMMINGBIRD]'s bedroom after dinner and tried reading with her but the effect was wholly unchanged. I shall try once more tomorrow.

Sunday, 2 June, 00:40: It is no use, [WOODPECKER]. [HUM-MINGBIRD] will never live up to her. I have tried every modification but she remains repulsive in comparison. I am left with no choice but to proceed with our plan.

Thursday, 6 June, 21:08: I have procured the portrait from the rancid marketplace of Mèliez, and it is a true likeness of the man. His wife must be responsible for the paintings, though between the twitching of her hands and the Slavic blanket of her accent, the woman was barely comprehensible as she sold me the portrait. Experimentation with [HUMMINGBIRD] will begin tonight. Side note 1: [STARLING] is increasingly on edge. She will attempt to leave the moment the deed is done.

Tuesday, 11 June, 02:15: The first week of experiments has been successful. Everything is proceeding to plan. [HUMMINGBIRD] is already terrified of both the man and the noise. She will know exactly what to do when the time comes.

Wednesday, 19 June, 03:02: I heard another woodpecker this evening—a male; younger, and smaller, with the uncommon habit of searching for his food at dusk. I believe he is the key, although given his reluctance to enter the gardens—which you, [WOODPECKER], have rightfully claimed as your own—I am terribly afraid of what securing the creature's proximity until October might entail. As witnessed this evening, the sound of his drilling sets [HUMMINGBIRD] off, even without the portrait. You must start to prepare yourself for what I am surely obliged to ask of you.

Arnaud barely waited to complete the final paragraph before

ringing the bell for Mrs Cadet and insisting that she bring his granddaughter to the library.

Based on the severity of the doctor's expression, no fore-words were needed for Ophélie to comprehend that the old man had discovered something significant. In silence, they moved to his desk and combed through the pages from start to finish, then turned to face one another.

Saturday, 22 June, 04:32: [WOODPECKER], the die has been cast. Your life, my dear friend, must be sacrificed in order for your competitor to take your place in the pine. Fear not—I shall make it swift and painless. No sooner will you dine on the gift I shall leave on the branch than it will all be over. And never a nobler cause there could be, for [NIGHTJAR] is depending on me to do this. It is the final catalyst, and when the time comes, it will ensure our being together.

29

Birds of a Feather

1 January; an event upon which no magnitude or mawkishness of revelry may satisfy the expectations of optimists. Nor—for those more inclined to cynicism—can a heavier-feeling date in the calendar be found.

That morning, a gentleman who identified with neither camp would greet the New Year by taking the eastern footpath through the gardens of the Institute. By the time he had reached Isabelle's monument, a layer of transpiration had begun to form under his jacket. Dropping to the ground, he welcomed the icy burn of the snow cushioning his knees.

Gaze locked on the fence ahead, the gentleman proceeded to slide the leather glove off his right hand and hold it out in front of his face. One by one, the scars across his knuckles disappeared into the chapped dimples of skin as he caressed them, and he was reminded of the bone-shattering crunch of his fist striking the wall in Kacper Smolak's attic. More displeasing still was the memory of what the gentleman had witnessed in that chest of artwork beneath the window moments before. It had taken every ounce of his strength to walk away from the scene without setting the cottage ablaze.

Steadying his breathing, 'The Watcher' extended his fingers to the grooves of the message behind the stone, then brought the white handkerchief from his pocket to his nose.

Forever waiting until we two meet again.

Head bowed, nostrils billowing, he repeated this promise so many times that the words became nothing more than vibrations of air passing through his larynx.

A minute later according to his pocket watch, the gentleman rose to his feet and rejoined the opposing path back to the Institute. Not metres on, his journey would incur an unscheduled delay when the body of a robin caused him to stop in his tracks.

The fledgling must have fallen from its nest and broken its neck on impact, 'The Watcher' conjectured, securing his glasses to inspect it. Despite the protrusion of certain bones, its overall condition was excellent. With each flaccid turn of the creature in his palm, the gentleman could only marvel at the fragile network of veins, cartilage, and organs contained within such a tiny carcass. It might be another few seasons before he came across another specimen as intact as this one—those steadfast voices reminded him—thus the gentleman slipped it into his coat pocket and continued on his way.

As noted in his head, the robin would constitute number 4,306 in the index of individual birds he had observed throughout his lifetime. The total was likely to be superior, in reality, but the gentleman had only started counting the number of winged friends that he saw at the age of nine.

Upon reflection, the day in question had been unusual in more ways than one. Tethered to the ballast of shared tutelage, the boy might have expected to spend another morning carving his initials into his desk while his classmates stammered through passages of the Aeneid. But not that day. No, on that balmy, mid-spring morning, his father had chosen to reward the boy's patience—the 'indemnity demanded of all aberrant academics'—by taking him on a hike through the mountains.

They had not been walking twenty minutes when the old man stopped, drawing his son's attention to a golden eagle soaring high above the trail.

The boy's first instinct had been to remark on how much the bird could see from up there, after which he had asked his father whether it was lost or confused, circling the sky alone in the same eternal pattern.

"Nonsense, he is picking his prey and working out the best way to catch it", had been his father's response. "When he eventually strikes, it will be so masterful that if you blink a second too long, boy, you might miss it".

Sure enough, towards the end of the afternoon, his son had glanced up again at the eagle just at the right moment; in one breath, the bird swooped down from the clouds and vanished into the trees, emerging at lightning speed with something large between its talons. Even today, the image could render him speechless.

As 'The Watcher' emerged from his thoughts and approached the pine tree beyond the orchards, the plodding of his boots through the snow gained a sudden air of reluctance.

Jolting his head from side to side, the gentleman hissed an expletive to which he rarely resorted. Impossible—that a subconscious as stalwart as his could so deceive him, leading him to a section of the gardens he had avoided for long enough to be unrecognisable. Changing course now would only add to the humiliation, the gentleman reasoned through gritted teeth. Inching towards his old seat beneath the pine tree—in the dip where the trunk seemed to have moulded itself to his frame—he slowly forced his gaze upwards. And in that one tilt of his head, the bittersweet ache of nostalgia reclaimed its victim.

Few memories could cause 'The Watcher' to grip the bark like that than the morning he had followed the echoes of drilling to that tree. It was not the first time he had observed a woodpecker from close proximity, but never had he found himself mute at the sight.

Beauty, the gentleman had later written of the encounter in his notebook; *the kind perceived solely by the awakened. In a language unheard, he called me to him. My eyes fell on the architect of such sweet sound, and in them, the creature was eternally bound.*

"Stay true, Ortus", finally emerged from the gentleman's lips as he traced a shape on the bark. "You shall not be alone there much longer".

And with this whisper, he proceeded to back away.

By the time the gentleman returned to the Institute, other members of his household had begun to stir. While a flock of professors and students descended upon the dining hall, 'The Watcher' crossed the opposing corridor without once taking his eyes off the lines in the parquet ahead of him. Another 107 balusters up the stairwell brought him to safety, from where he removed his scalpel and needle from their drawer, then placed the robin on the desk.

30

Like Crow, Like Egg

On the eve of the wedding, breakfast's saturnine silence was exacerbated by the entry of a maid. She had been sent to escort Ophélie and Manon to the bride's bedroom, for the reason that Adèle was 'sick of their procrastination' and demanded that they try their dresses on before it was too late.

Engrossed in a discussion regarding her hem, Adèle barely took notice of her sister and cousin's arrival in her doorway. Eyes unmoving from the mirror as she twirled from side to side, she eventually beckoned the ladies over, then pointed to their dresses on the bed and instructed a second maid to assist with putting them on.

Turning to face the wall, the elder twin all but retched at the satiny throttle of the material sliding over her head. Her chest tightened alongside the subsequent jerk of each ribbon to clinch the bodice in place. And from the fiery flush in her cheeks, gentle tears proceeded to emerge—so jarring to her, in sensation, that when her cousin's handkerchief appeared in her palm from behind, Manon knew not what to do with it.

Ophélie, too, kept her verbal contributions to a minimum

for the duration of the fitting. By now, she and Romain had exhausted the list of women to whom Pierre-Alexandre Perez or Nicolas Belmont might have been referring in the deciphered copies from the notebook. Even with this name, details of what had since transpired in their relationship remained wholly unclear, as did the reason behind the gentleman's continued brutality.

At this stage, the time for questions was over for Ophélie, though; while the bride-to-be gushed to her seamstress about the lavish festivities that Mr Perez's students had organised for him that evening, her cousin turned to the window and attempted to suppress the jitters in her stomach as she peered across the garden.

Several miles further south, Romain found himself visiting a site as unsavoury as they come: the slum inhabited by his father's ex-suppliers. From the surrounding stillness to the tides of graffiti heralding the entrance, this was not a neighbourhood that you would wish to stumble across after losing your way, nor one from which inquisitive outsiders lived to tell the tale.

Unfortunately for Romain, the gang was also his last chance to gain knowledge about the client referenced in his father's notebook, for these were the same associates who had helped Kacper Smolak source the *Atropa belladonna* seeds ordered to the Institute, some four years before Isabelle's murder.

Despite Romain's familiarity with the cartel, he had delayed this venture until now for two reasons: firstly, presuming they had not already vacated the area, it was unlikely that the gang would recall the details of deliveries from so long ago—let alone whether Kacper had mentioned anything about the person to whom this one had been destined. Secondly, the lifestyle that Romain had since acquired was far from compatible with their own.

As he passed the rows of grungy huts on his horse, the shivering children and narcotised women hiding inside fell silent. From both sides of the road, vindictive eyes watched him step down from the stirrups and approach the table of men playing poker before the main housing structure. Sloshing back glasses of vodka, they failed to notice Romain standing over them at first, until their leader stopped talking and glanced up at their visitor.

Identifiable by a leathery face, and a head so bald it looked as though it had never seen hair, Ivan was a man whom you would have a hard time imagining as a child. Even without knowledge of his reputation, most onlookers walked the opposite way, if for no other reason than he kept a knife strapped to his trouser leg and sported an unsightly scar across his chin that nobody dared ask about. Only two things were too sinful to warrant forgiveness for Ivan: taking the Lord's name in vain, and failing to pay him on time.

His men went to stand up as soon as they caught sight of Romain's silhouette hovering over them, but their leader waved the group down again with as much speed. Then, taking their intruder in from top to toe, he rested his boots on the table and stuck a cigarette in his mouth with an emphatic snigger.

"Well, well, well, if it isn't Kacper Smolak's boy. You've changed, kid—got all rich and proper", he began. "I'll give you this, you've got a lot of balls showing your face here dressed like that. Your father would skin you alive if he'd lived to see you become one of those posh pricks whose dirty work he did behind the scenes".

Romain brushed the snow off his shoulders and answered in the calmest manner possible: "Content yourself that I do not intend to stay long, Ivan. I have come to ask you for a small favour, then I will be on my way".

"A favour?" Ivan scoffed. "What's in it for me? Kacper never got to compensate me for his last few deliveries, you know, and I'm not the sort of man who forgets a debt, so the way I see it, you owe me that money now".

Having anticipated this argument pre-departure, Romain slowly reached into his pocket. He was not blind to the circle of men forming behind him, nor to the fact that any sign of weakness on his part would result in a physical confrontation in which he was outnumbered.

"I am aware of how transactions work", Romain replied. "All I need is for you to look at this entry in my father's notebook and tell me whether you remember anything about it. It will take no more than a minute and you will be well rewarded for your time".

With an almighty thump of his fist on the table, Ivan leapt to his feet, removing the knife from its hold in the process. "Clearly, you've been living in fairyland so long you've forgotten how things work in societies like the one you were born into. A debt is a debt, kid, so allow me to articulate this in a language that you high-and-mighty types understand: pay what's owed—plus interest for the ten long years I had to go without that money—and you get to return to whatever prim, powdered bitch you've got waiting for you at home".

Romain's voice grew stern. "You will receive that remuneration in full once I have the information I came for".

In one sweep of his fist, Ivan delivered his response by

flipping the table upside down and lunging towards him. Before the other members of his gang could react, Romain caught Ivan's arm mid-air and slammed his body against the side of a hut. Then, he lifted him off the ground with one hand around his throat.

"I may not be the boy you once knew, Ivan", Romain proceeded to mutter in their native Polish, "but never make the mistake of thinking that I have forgotten where I came from".

From behind them, the crowd lifted their weapons and surged forward, halting only at their leader's command when Romain began pressing the knife into his skin. There was a heavy silence while Ivan turned back to his aggressor, wavering between calling Romain's bluff and signalling for his men to attack. Something in the gentleman's expression must have given the gang leader reason to believe that he was more than capable of pushing the knife in, for he eventually gave the order to stand down. Only then did Romain let go.

"Listen, I'm a Christian man, so out of consideration for your dead father, there'll be no bloodshed today", Ivan raised his hands. "To answer your question, I never dealt with the client-side of Kacper's business so you're wasting your time. Now, I've fulfilled my end of the bargain, it's your turn to do the same. We are but humble people with limited resources, so you'll understand why we can't let you leave without giving us that money".

Romain tossed him a bag of coins, then strode back towards the end of the road. When he reached his horse, he unleashed his frustration by embedding Ivan's knife in a nearby table.

Had the gentleman's head not been turned, he might have noticed that from this movement, a crooked smile began to spread across the gang leader's face.

"I always knew you'd follow in your father's footsteps", Ivan called out from the crowd. "Maybe not through his lifestyle choices or livelihood, but in his ability to piss people off. You must have made an enemy of someone, kid, or why else would that guy have come around here sniffing for information about you all those years ago?"

Romain's eyes widened as he spun around to ask: "What are you talking about?"

"Seems my time is valuable after all", Ivan replied, lighting another cigarette. "Your guess for how he found us is as good as mine. Real chic type. Wouldn't have looked twice at him around your parts though, I imagine. He had a portrait of you as a boy and offered me all kinds of money if I could tell him where you went after you left Mèliez, and who you were still in contact with. Lucky for you, I didn't have those details, or by the tone of his voice, you'd already be dead. So I suppose you owe me for that, too, now that I mention it".

"Would you recognise this man if you saw his portrait?" Romain demanded, reaching into his pocket again.

Ivan shrugged. "With the right incentive. As you know, I never forget a face when money is involved".

Romain threw the gang leader another bag of coins. "You will receive the other half and more once you have confirmed his identity. Consider this my father's debt repaid, and the end of all correspondence between us".

After a nod of accord from Ivan, Romain leapt on his horse and rode back to Aixelles. When he reached his estate, he pulled out his art supplies and set about drawing Pierre-Alexandre Perez and Nicolas Belmont as accurately as he could from memory. The sun would begin disappearing by mid-afternoon, making the journey back to the cartel too dangerous. If he could finish the images in time for the wedding, however, he should have his answer from Ivan by the time Adèle and Mr Perez set off to Switzerland the following week.

Towards six o'clock, Romain completed both portraits, then prepared an envelope to be sent at first light. Now he could only pray that Ivan's recollection and integrity were as reliable as the gang leader claimed they were. As he set his charcoals down and relaxed into his chair, Ophélie, on the other hand, was donning her coat by the back door.

31

Caught

Just before Ophélie reached the bottom of the garden, she halted to glance back over her shoulder in the darkness. The air was so sharp that it cut through the wool of her hood and numbed her cheeks, but as quickly as she had turned around, the candlelight flickering in Adèle's bedroom window spurred her to face the trees and continue ahead.

The interior of the woods encapsulated all the nighttime horrors one could imagine. Had this not been a route that Ophélie knew by heart, the disorientation of advancing through a maze of gnarled, towering trunks—her path illuminated by only a half-metre radius from the lantern—would have sent her running back and forth.

All around her, the creatures to whom daylight falls blind began to crawl from their beds to reclaim the night. Between their shuffling sounds in the snowy undergrowth and the rustling tide of branches above her head, it was all Ophélie could do to force one foot down in front of the other. When she finally emerged into the moonlit clearing behind the Institute, however, she feared that the worst would be yet to come.

Tiptoeing towards the fence, Ophélie wrapped her shawl around the lantern in the event that the groundskeepers might still be on duty. Upon first glance, the only sign of movement she could detect came from the Boarding House, from which the faint echoes of an orchestra were audible. Mr Perez's party must be in full swing, Ophélie reassured herself, removing her grandfather's secateurs from her satchel.

The bottom of the fence was not easy to loosen in the obscurity. And yet, by the state of the nails holding it together here, she had not been the first to tamper with it; this must be the same section that was detached to allow Isabelle to enter the woods—once to step on the snare, and once to exit the garden on the night she was murdered. Fuelled by enough adrenaline to make her hands tremble, Ophélie eventually managed to lift three of the planks and squeeze herself through to the other side.

From here, the path was easy to remember, Mr Perez's visit during the Botany Display having commenced with a detour to show Adèle his 'charming little abode'.

By most people's standards, there was nothing little about the cottage, which was located at the end of a narrow trail through the rose gardens. Converted from a dormitory-style residence for the staff, most of its rooms sat on the ground floor and were adorned with two large windows, affording Ophélie an ample choice of entry points.

With no lamps burning anywhere inside, a quick sweep of the periphery confirmed that Mr Perez was in the Boarding House. Both doors and all of the windows had been locked in his absence except one—open half an inch at the bottom, and leading into what looked like the drawing room.

Taking a deep breath, Ophélie set down her lantern and placed both hands on the glass, sliding it up as quietly as she could. Then, lifting her legs onto the sill, she propped the lantern down on the carpet and stepped in, pulling the window shut behind her.

It took a full minute for Ophélie's eyes to adjust to the dimness inside. There was a musty odour seeping from the carpet and intermittent clunking sounds caused by the pipes beneath the floorboards. But as surrounding objects came into sharper focus, her sole cause for alarm was the apparent ordinariness of Mr Perez's quarters.

And succeeding this observation, a series of questions forced their way to the forefront of Ophélie's mind: had she been struck by madness in coming here tonight? What possible excuse could she cling to if she were found?

At the risk of feeling faint, she took a deep breath to steady her pulse, then set about searching.

First, she sifted through the contents of each drawer in Mr Perez's desk. With nothing but cards, books, and the odd gardening item inside, she moved her search to the boxes along the far wall.

Once satisfied that she had checked every cranny there, Ophélie hurried into the hallway and proceeded to apply the same methodology to each of the adjacent rooms. Within thirty minutes, she had inspected the entire ground floor with the exception of the storage cupboard opposite the entrance, which she was unable to open.

From its size, the room looked big enough to be hiding all manner of objects. More importantly, as the only one that Mr Perez had gone to the trouble of locking, Ophélie felt the hairs on the back of her neck stand on end the moment she approached it. If there was evidence to be had—Isabelle's trinkets, a lock of Madeleine's hair, love letters to the woman he had written about in his notebook—its interior was surely where she would find it.

When the clock in the hallway struck half-past seven, Ophélie revised her plan to scour the upper floor in favour of finding a tool with which to pick the lock on the storage cupboard. If she was lucky, she might have another hour or so before Mr Perez returned home, and she needed to be halfway back to Baudières by then.

Recalling her grandfather's adage that there is 'no such thing as useless knowledge', Ophélie returned to the drawing room where she had seen a small letter opener and some fishing hooks in the desk earlier. The pins in the lock should be straightforward to manipulate; this was far from the intricacy of the mechanisms with which Arnaud—whose fondness for the discipline rivalled that of Louis XVI—had regularly tested her as a child.

As Ophélie pulled back the drawer and prepared to reach inside, the plod of footsteps and the jangle of a key boomed through the cottage. Pushing the handle shut again, she grabbed a blanket from the armchair to smother the light from her lantern and ducked under the desk just in time for the front door to creak open.

Of the ensuing minute, Ophélie would remember only her mouth filling with a sour taste and her hearing heightening to the point that sound itself became painful. From the narrow gap behind the drawing room door, she held her breath and commanded every muscle to freeze while the shadow of a man entered the hallway.

After taking three steps forward, the figure, too, fell motionless. Lifting his nose, he sniffed the air with growing voracity, then slowly riveted his head towards the drawing room.

A further two steps brought him within a metre of the door, but with one foot approaching the threshold, he took out another key and turned back to the storage cupboard instead. In the darkness, Ophélie could just perceive his outline, but his inhumanly equable manner could only belong to the man she had seen in her grandfather's garden.

In vain, her eyes darted around the room to calculate the distance between the desk and salvation. Whether it was the window or the shotgun hanging above the fireplace, the risk was the same; Mr Perez would tear into the room long before Ophélie could propel herself to either. No, her only choice would be to wait until he had retired to bed, although based on his unlocking of the storage cupboard, this action might be somewhat delayed.

Having pulled the front door open, the gentleman let the hallway fill with a chilling draught and disappeared outside. When he returned, his arms were full of items which he subsequently placed in the storage cupboard, just beyond Ophélie's field of vision.

Whatever Mr Perez was doing, he repeated this course again and again, until the gaps between his comings and goings grew ominously bigger. Then finally, Ophélie picked up the scrapes of a much heavier object being dragged across the gravel path towards the cottage.

Preparing for the worst, she dug her fingers into her palms and shut her eyes. When she opened them again, the silhouette was back in the hallway holding the legs of a woman's body, which he dropped onto the floor with an insouciant thump.

Covering her mouth to stifle her gulps for air, Ophélie

231

strained to listen while Mr Perez trudged over to the cupboard and stuffed the body inside. And then there was silence; so deafening that Ophélie began to feel dizzy, anticipating the jerk of the gentleman's hand underneath the desk to pull her out. As quickly as the thought entered her head, however, he exited the cottage, without locking the storage cupboard behind him.

In the wake of his departure, Ophélie could not determine how long she waited before leaving the drawing room. The temperature must have dropped by another degree in that time, judging by the stiffness of the apparel on the coat stand. But as she edged towards the storage cupboard, her skin felt as if it were on fire.

Extending the lantern in front of her, she yanked back the handle and gasped as the bloodless face of Florence Moreau's maid lit up—skin ice-cold and covered in specks of snow. Lining the shelves behind her, the lantern glinted over an array of objects referenced in Lise Duclos' copies; a portrait of Kacper Smolak that was no doubt linked to Isabelle's murder, sketches of the gentleman's trademark symbol, and feathers set in a glass frame.

From the speed of her reaction, Ophélie's cane barely touched the ground as she marched into the drawing room and seized the shotgun from the wall to check the barrel. Two cartridges left; two chances to be heard. Turning back to the hallway, she fled into the night for a final time, ensuring that the storage cupboard was visible from the path.

The first gunshot thundered through the sky with such force that Ophélie flinched from the recoil. Readying herself to run, she crossed the rose gardens to the intersection at which the terrace of the Institute came into sight. A solitary light appeared in one of the ground-floor rooms, but the music from the Boarding House must have eclipsed the blast; three minutes later, nothing further had happened.

Realising that she would need a louder distraction, Ophélie gripped the shotgun and ran along the path until the greenhouses emerged into her line of vision. Aiming as carefully as she could this time, she steadied her breathing and pulled the trigger.

A wall of sound erupted as multiple panels of glass on the nearest greenhouse came shattering to the ground. By the time Ophélie had doubled back to return the shotgun to Mr Perez's cottage, a crowd had started to gather on the terrace.

From behind the gardens, Ophélie watched over the fence as the staff poured down both paths, waving their lanterns from side to side. Just as she had hoped, when the first group came across the half-destroyed greenhouse on the eastern side, they followed Ophélie's footprints in the snow and reassembled with the others by the rose gardens.

Once she was sure they had spotted the door to Mr Perez's cottage hanging open, Ophélie retreated into the trees and hastened her way back to Baudières.

Returning to her grandfather's garden, the ache in her legs brought her movements to a staggering halt. Finally, glancing towards the sky, Ophélie dropped to her knees.

32

The View Behind the Wall

Silence—that was the sound that met the dawn from every household in Aixelles. Some held their tongues through disbelief, others needed isolation to process their feelings, but mostly, residents averted their gaze as they passed each other in corridors for no other reason than they lacked the words to make sense of reality. Not since 'The Incident' had the villagers adopted a state of lockdown akin to this; doors closed, curtains drawn.

Mr Perez's arrest woke up the first set of neighbours towards midnight, when his voice was heard shrieking his innocence as he was thrust into a police carriage by two officers. Within minutes, rattled crowds had assembled on terraces, from where the news that the body of a maid had been found in Mr Perez's cottage was passed from estate to estate. By sunrise, their whispers had all but run dry.

Struck by the first rays of light, the Great Hall of the Institute resembled an antique painting of a ceremony frozen in time; decorations gazed glumly down on rows of chairs waiting to accommodate a hundred guests who would never come, bottles of champagne that should have inaugurated Adèle Baudin's title as Mrs Perez were deserted in their crates along with trays of half-assembled canapés, and the students were sent to the Boarding House common room by an unprecedentedly stoic Nicolas Belmont.

Alone on the right wing of Baudières, Adèle sat hunched over the edge of her bed, staring at the lacy white dress hanging in her wardrobe. Her red-raw cheeks bore the fresh stains of tears; her nightie was dotted with the splashes of vomit that she had twice been unable to suppress. If the bride could have brought herself to formulate a sentence, it would have been a sombre one indeed. As it happened, Adèle's lips had refused to utter anything other than blood-curdling lamentations from the moment she had watched her fiancé being taken away.

Downstairs, Henri Baudin lingered in the dining room from breakfast till noon. For the sixth morning in a row, the gentleman's routine had commenced with a solitary venture to the left wing, although this time, he had made it all the way to the library door before turning back. Now, accosted by the sounds of Roland consoling his wife and children from the hallway, Henri could think of nothing but the empty seats mocking him around the table. And like clockwork, his fingers reached down to retrieve the bottle of Pinot Noir nestled in his lap.

In Ophélie's bedroom, the mood was darker still. Far from feeling a sense of relief, the echoes of Adèle's moans tormented her as she glared at the ebbing flames in her fireplace.

Every few hours, Mrs Cadet would shuffle in and extend to Ophélie some manner of discourse, but her attempts were met with the same toneless mutter: 'Just listen to her. To what depths would Adèle plummet if the full extent of the man's depravity came to light?'

While the housekeeper suspected that there was more to Ophélie's indictment of Mr Perez than a history of roguish behaviour, she decided against requesting elaboration and let herself out. For now, Mrs Cadet would settle for surveying Ophélie's well-being from a distance.

A similar tactic was adopted by Romain. Having stationed himself on his terrace, the gentleman spent the coming days watching the water for signs of movement. Even in a thick coat the cold penetrated the fibres, but on the bright side, winter's throes were visibly subsiding now; from the roof of Romain's estate, receding icicles dripped into puddles, and at one point during his reflections, a young, glossy-eyed robin landed on the railing.

Of Ophélie's involvement in the arrest the gentleman was increasingly convinced, and with each scenario that he imagined, so grew his impatience to visit her. Towards the end of the week, Romain succumbed to this restlessness and took a bunch of wildflowers to Baudières, informing Ophélie that he would call on her once the initial shock had passed.

Pass, it did. It took several more days, but gradually, the villagers emerged from their estates again. Saint Valentine's celebrations might not take place as planned that year, but lunches and dinners were resumed forthwith. The name 'Mr Perez' would feature solely in the speaker's admission that they had always known the man was trouble. As for his fiancé, the subject appeared to require a more intricate level of dissection.

Had the younger Baudin twin known about Mr Perez's penchant for violence, for example? Was she his target for homicide all along? And had she resigned herself to life as a spinster? In Adèle's continued absence from public view, letters alluding to her haplessness in such terms inundated Baudières well into the second half of the month.

During one of countless endeavours to bring 'the crestfallen bride' a plate of breakfast, Ophélie would receive a note of her own. It was from Arnaud, requesting her presence 'at the earliest convenience'.

With Adèle's weight loss commanding her full attention, Ophélie could not recall her last visit to the left wing, or indeed Arnaud's most recent invitation for her to join him there. As a result, when she came to the door of the library that morning, she froze.

Dressed in his finest suit, the old man was using a cane to stand while he waited for her. The curtains on both windows were open for the first time in seven months, and in front of them, dust motes danced in the sunlight pouring into the room.

Bathed in overwhelming calmness, Ophélie felt as though her body was no longer hers to command. Only when her grandfather nodded did she step forward and slide her arm beneath his. And together, they made their way along the corridor and out towards the garden.

Somehow, nature seemed to have predicted that this would be the day of Arnaud and Ophélie's final walk. After months of gloomy skies, the snow around the footpath glistened as they retraced their old route. From a cluster of nearby trees, a family of blackbirds proceeded to grace their audience with melodious singing, and with each step, the wind softened, which Arnaud inhaled with the depth of a man who had long deprived himself of it.

When they reached the bench, the doctor slumped onto the wood with a grimace.

"Forgive me, Ophélie", he began. "We may have another month left until spring, but the roots of this old tree have grown too long. It is time that I allowed them to wither, and for the saplings beneath to flourish in my stead. A valiant effort though, if I do say so myself".

His granddaughter sat down beside him and pulled the collar of his jacket closed to protect him from the cold.

"Would you believe it, I have always found the garden to be at its most beautiful in winter. In any case, you have given me more in these past few months than I could ever thank you for, so there is nothing to forgive", Ophélie responded.

"None of that, I beg you. Ours is a relationship that requires no declarations of gratitude", Arnaud insisted.

For the next few minutes, he closed his eyes and let the breeze wash over his face. When he opened them again, the old man smirked, tilting his head towards his granddaughter to announce: "There is something I should like to know, young one. That bully your teacher wrote to me about when you were a girl—some Louis chap; what did you whisper that silenced him so brutally, the day that he teased you by the school gate?"

Ophélie smiled and stared ahead. "Louis Fabron was his name. I only met him twice, but his parents often stopped by the school. It was simple; I told him that confronting his father the next time he belittled or beat him would make him feel significantly more powerful than making fun of deformed little girls".

"Well, that settles it", Arnaud chuckled, leaning back in his seat. "You are a veritable anomaly, Ophélie. That being so, I would like to share with you a story. Are you familiar with the proverb of the fortress in the desert?"

Ophélie shook her head. "Of your extensive repertoire, it must be the only one that you kept from me over the years".

"And rightfully so—all things have their time. Let us hope my memory has not forsaken me", Arnaud paused to clear his throat. "There was once a vast walled city, hidden within an endless stretch of sand dunes. Criss-crossing medinas selling all manner of spice, cloth, and jewels adorned its interior, set on a backdrop of ornate, domed buildings and a cerulean sky.

"The fortress' population was larger than all of France—each man and woman working in harmony to create a thriving society; the farmers ensured there was an abundance of food to go around, and the bankers divvied up the money so that everyone could afford it. Those who were born in the fortress would spend their entire lives there, for all they could need was located within the city, the walls of which towered above every building.

"Now, while there was no hierarchy in the governance of the people, the only way out of the city was through an enormous steel gate, controlled by a mysterious cloaked figure. The figure would appear only when you approached with the intention of leaving, yet because of his demeanour, the inhabitants were so afraid of him that they went out of their way to avoid that section of the wall altogether. Every now and then, someone would request to walk through the gate, after which he or she would never be seen again, for it was rumoured that the payment required by the figure to open it was great enough to bankrupt any one person thenceforth.

"After centuries of prosperity, doubts began to arise among certain individuals, unsatisfied with what they had built. There had to be more; more knowledge, and more wealth, they declared, convinced that the answer lay past the walls.

Soon, the question of what they would find on the other side became the crux of incessant disputes.

"On one camp, it was believed that there was nothing but a wasteland—that the fortress was the physical limitation of all existence. On the other camp, a magnificent valley surrounded the city, boasting nature so verdant that the walls had been designed to shield it from them. As the years passed, controversy marred the atmosphere, and the inhabitants began to segregate themselves according to their convictions.

"One day, a passing boy overheard a heated clash between two of his elders, unable to agree on the subject. Frustrated with the ongoing arguments, he marched up to the cloaked figure to settle the debate once and for all, demanding to be shown the view behind the wall.

"'Be careful, child', the figure spoke, 'for the information you seek cannot be relayed once it has been learnt'. But resolved in his choice, the boy was stubborn, insisting that the gate be opened for him at once. With a nod, the cloaked figure pulled back the lever and a narrow gap appeared between the steel doors, through which the boy gladly went.

"Finally, the view came into sight and the child beamed with excitement. Armed with the definitive answer, he could now run back to put his people's minds to rest—or so he thought. When the boy turned around, the gate was sealed shut and the cloaked figure was nowhere to be seen. No matter how loudly he shouted to be let in, or how hard he pounded his fists against the steel, his words and actions would forever go unheard".

Once Arnaud had reached the end of his story, he took his granddaughter's hand and let out a sigh. "I used to despise people who lack that insatiable thirst to discover where they came from, where they are going, and why. And yet, despite a lifetime of asking questions, the truth has never rewarded my curiosity by revealing itself early. You, my dear girl, are too smart to commit my errors, though. Time is a reckless thing to waste, particularly for someone capable of doing in one day what most could not achieve in a lifetime".

Ophélie dropped her head. "And to think that your last words to me might have been a quote borrowed from François Rabelais".

"Come, none of that", Arnaud tutted, passing Ophélie his handkerchief. "There is a second and more important part to my message involving your place here in Aixelles. Now, while I appreciate that conventions exist regarding the prospects of a young woman such as yourself, I think we can both agree that you were destined for greater things than dressing up for parties and running a household, Ophélie. The world into which families like ours are born will soon be obsolete—if it isn't already. I want your word that you will do everything in your power to leave this place—that is, unless of course, you have a reason to stay".

Ophélie did her best to keep her composure and glanced down at her feet. "Beyond caring for my family, what reason do you imagine I would have for staying here?"

"The gentleman with whom you have been working to expose Mr Perez, perhaps", Arnaud replied, peering over to gauge her reaction.

With a raised eyebrow, he continued: "I may not possess your powers of perception, young one, but I am hardly blind. Something in you has changed since you met him. I look at you and I see a warmth that I am sorry to say I never once exhibited when I was married to your grandmother.

You were born to love, though, Ophélie. If you have found a person deserving of that gift—and let it be known that I trust your judgement above anyone else's—then Mr Lavarre has my approval, whatever that is worth".

Adamant to keep these words intact in her memory, Ophélie rested her head on her grandfather's shoulder, and in silence, the pair watched Dante spring through the snow.

When the old man hoisted himself to his feet again, he did so with an air of weightlessness; each step back to the library appeared to be simultaneously lighter and more taxing than before. Sliding into his bed to rest his legs, the doctor barely felt the woolly caress of the blanket being pulled over his chest, or the gentle deflation of the pillows beneath his head.

For the remainder of the morning, Ophélie stayed by Arnaud's side in the armchair while he slept. She, too, must have drifted off to sleep at some point, because when she opened her eyes again Mrs Cadet was wheeling in her trolley to serve afternoon tea.

As soon as the housekeeper entered the library, both women glanced towards Arnaud's bed and fell deathly quiet.

Lying in a state of peacefulness too still to be slumber, the old man's mouth and chest ceased to twitch. There was a tinge of paling heat left on the surface of his skin, but his grip in Ophélie's hand was lifeless now, and his face was turned to the window as if denoting that his presence was no longer with them.

It was another minute before Mrs Cadet could release the trolley and tiptoe towards Arnaud's bed. Taking note of his granddaughter's expression, the housekeeper proceeded to wrap her arm around Ophélie's shoulders, then joined her in mustering a smile.

The murky tide of grief had begun its inevitable approach. At that moment, however—staring upon the vessel that once housed the most outlandish spirit that either woman had ever known—it was impossible not to feel a sense of liberation on the old man's behalf.

Of the manner in which he had departed, Ophélie could be in no doubt; with a friendly nod to the figure by the fortress wall, the doctor had exited the gate, laughed to himself for several seconds, then closed his eyes and drank in the view.

33

Childhood Revisited

Camille waited a laudable fifteen minutes after the coroner's departure before descending on the wine cellar to break out her father-in-law's finest bottle. Almost as soon as the cork was yanked from its neck, the new mistress of Baudières flopped onto the sofa in the front room and let out a sigh. Days of paperwork lay ahead to substantiate her husband's share of the inheritance, but nothing could have dampened Camille's spirits that evening.

"Notify the other residents at once, Julien", was the heiress' ensuing order to Mr Girard, whom she had summoned from his office midway through dinner.

Behind his twitching grimace, the solicitor pictured himself throttling Camille senseless as he observed her demands for the staff to begin 'decluttering' the left wing. From the tone of her voice to the congratulatory simper on her face, the resemblance to his own mother was so chilling that he was in that moment a little boy again, staring into the eyes of a woman who—despite her churlishness—could never disappoint him. This trait, you see, was as insusceptible to culpability as the freckle etched into her upper lip.

Resolved to resign once Roland's ownership of the estate had been overseen, Mr Girard bowed and marched towards the exit.

He slipped out just in time to overhear Camille's final request to her maid: "Oh, and have Mrs Cadet arrange a carriage to the Ozanams' estate for me. I must inform them that my daughters and I shall be accepting their offer of another weekend in their townhouse in Florence after all. Thomas, too, if he behaves. I suppose that will also mean preparing an outfit for another wretched fencing match. See that it is done".

This specific instruction she gave with a grunt. If sitting through several more hours of swordplay meant avoiding both her father-in-law's funeral and the last days of Henri's company before she intended to eject him from the premises, however, the sacrifice would be worth it. Besides, as Camille stressed to her husband that evening, a change of scenery would do wonders for Adèle, what with Mr Perez's trial beginning the following week.

Having learnt the name of the prison where her fiancé was being held, the younger twin's attempts to flee the estate to visit him were becoming increasingly difficult to thwart. Prising her away from Aixelles for the weekend would not be easy, but mercifully for the residents of Baudières, Camille's persuasive clout could always be depended on in matters of urgency.

In the end, all it took was the embellishment that Adèle would be permitted to visit her fiancé upon their return to convince her to join Manon and Thomas in the carriage two days later. And with their departure, Arnaud's remaining family members were granted an evening of peace in which to prepare for his funeral.

Under Ophélie's instruction, the coffin was placed before the fireplace in her grandfather's library after dinner. Having already said her goodbyes, she retired to bed early that night, spending the ensuing hours shifting her gaze between the pages of *Jane Eyre* and the clock on her wall. Sure enough, at the stroke of midnight, the muffled clatter of furniture being tossed around Henri's bedroom finally ceased, and her uncle's door swung open.

Jaw locked in a snarl, his demeanour was that of a kamikaze warrior as he tore through the corridor in the darkness, and for a good reason; perched on his tongue was a question he had been rehearsing ever since he had learnt how to talk. There could be no ground gained by voicing it now, but given the circumstances, victory for Henri would have to come in the form of disturbing Arnaud in the afterlife.

With shallow breaths, he burst into the library and marched towards the coffin. Pangs of injustice, virulence, regret; the plates of the gentleman's armour grew heavier as his legs bridged the gap between them. And yet, when his gaze fell on his father's face, the fire blazing in his chest withered into embers.

Gone was the cavillous stare that had haunted Henri all his life. Like all those who had come before him, death had reduced the great Dr Baudin to an empty, shrivelled carcass. Indifferent or otherwise, the old man would no sooner begrudge a thought to his son now than he had done while he was living.

And in that moment, Henri's eyes were drawn to his own reflection in the mirror above him. The gentleman stared at it for so long that the light around his silhouette dimmed and distorted. Then, his forehead began to relax, and Henri's fists dropped to his sides. Tears dripping onto the wood, he proceeded to reach out his hand to his Arnaud's, and Henri whispered the three most cathartic words that a person can utter: "I forgive you".

By the time he had left the library, Henri could scarcely feel his legs beneath him. The sun would be rising in a matter of hours, but the gentleman's spirit was more invigorated than it had ever been. In that state, sleep seemed an unworthy companion. To the piano he went instead, and stretching his fingers over the ivory keys, Henri let music fill his airways until daylight's early rays slithered across the floorboards in the drawing room.

At that same moment upstairs, Ophélie awoke to the pitter-patter of Dante's paw prints atop her bed. Propping herself upright, she extended a hand and caressed the feline's head while he settled on the pillow next to her. They did not need to speak the same language for Ophélie to understand that he was grieving for his master, and she found comfort in their mutual sorrow on what would be her loneliest morning since Étienne's death.

Having given the staff leave to return home for the weekend in her aunt's absence, the corridors of Baudières had been all but evacuated overnight. Only Mrs Cadet had chosen to stay for the funeral, and it was her face that Ophélie saw next peering around the door frame to remind her that the priest would be arriving within the hour.

With a nod, she waited for the housekeeper to leave, then stood up to check the weather. Dusky above, a sea of mist collecting around the lake below; the view saturated her brain like the repetition of a song she had heard too many times, until squinting into the fog, Ophélie could almost make out the manifestation of arms reaching up to pull her under.

Crossing to the wardrobe, her memories should have been at liberty to reminisce about her grandfather as she slid the black dress over her head. With each button that she fastened, her mind was instead drawn to Isabelle and Madeleine.

Would these faces ever grant her peace if she failed to hold Mr Perez accountable for their deaths, she wondered? Had she not risked enough to expose him that she might be allowed a brief respite to mourn her grandfather's passing?

Just as Ophélie lifted her hands to her head, the silence in the corridor was pierced by the echo of leather heels click-clacking towards her bedroom. No sooner had she spun around than Henri appeared at the door, dressed so smartly that it took his niece a top-to-toe inspection of the gentleman to confirm his identity.

"The service will be beginning soon", Henri announced, his articulation so coherent as to be unrecognisable. "I thought I would accompany you to the garden, to save you making the journey alone".

"That is kind of you", Ophélie forced herself to answer as she lifted her coat off the back of the door.

"Incidentally, this was pushed through the letterbox at some point this morning", Henri added, stepping forward to hand her the parcel he had been holding. "Condolences from one of the professors at the Institute".

Ophélie reached for the item and turned it in her hands. "How strange that it should be addressed to me, and not Roland. I see no details of the sender—why do you say that it was from the Institute?"

Her uncle tilted his weight onto the door frame. "The handwriting. You may have been too young to remember, but whoever it was from, they were always sending herbal remedies to the house for Gabrielle around the time she died. Not that they helped remotely in the end. Anyway, I would recognise that penmanship in my sleep".

Ophélie glanced back down at the parcel. Given her grandfather's efforts to shield her from her mother's final weeks, she could conjure no memory of these deliveries. There was something vaguely familiar about the handwriting, though. Still, the estate had been filling up with cards ever since news of Arnaud's death had left the threshold. Reaching for her umbrella, Ophélie threw the parcel onto her bed, then took her uncle's arm.

The clouds erupted shortly after they joined an impatient-looking Roland at the bottom of the garden. Half-sleet, half-rain, it sent slabs of oozing mud tumbling down the sides of the dug-out rectangle in the grass that awaited Arnaud's coffin. And with the onset of the deluge came an unexpected, last-minute guest to the service, who was led towards them from the house by Mrs Cadet just as proceedings were commenced.

As soon as Ophélie's eyes met with Romain's over her shoulder, her face broke into a tearful smile. No words were shared between them while he took his place by the grave, but suddenly, the fact that the priest's opening sermon was drowned out by the rain did not sadden Ophélie as much. Nor did the sight of her grandfather's coffin being lowered into the ground.

In adherence to the deceased's demands for 'as little religious drivel as possible', the remainder of the service lasted only the duration of one psalm and a quote from Arnaud's favourite philosopher, which Ophélie read. It was concluded with a group of volunteers from the church arriving to cover the grave, at which point Henri suggested that the group open a bottle of cognac in his father's honour.

With no desire to return indoors, Ophélie chose to take shelter under a tree alongside Romain instead. Together, they watched Arnaud's coffin recede beneath the soil.

After a long stretch of silence, Ophélie wrung the hem of her dress out onto the grass and shook the droplets of water off her hands, finally ready to speak.

"Thank you for being here, Mr Lavarre", she began. "It means a great deal to me".

"You have no need to thank me, Miss Davenport", he answered, leaning back against the tree trunk. "I must say I am disappointed by the lack of effort made on the part of our neighbours, though. When I saw that Mr Girard had included the date and time of your grandfather's funeral in his letter, I had not expected to be the only external participant. Whatever incivility I may have heard about him from other residents, I had hoped that his medical services would at least be worth something in their eyes".

Ophélie gazed up at the rain trickling through the leaves onto her forehead. "In many ways I am glad. For the most part, their presence today would only have vexed him. There were very few people in Aixelles whom my grandfather liked, I am afraid, and he was emphatically lax in nurturing friendships with them over the years".

Romain nodded. "And what of your cousin? How has she been coping this past week?"

"Adèle will recover from this in time, and be all the stronger for it", Ophélie responded. "It is a battle she must nevertheless fight alone."

"I fear that is true for all personal hardships", Romain replied, tucking his hands into his pockets. "Extending a hand to a person in need is like dangling a rope for someone who is falling down a cliff; you can only help them once they have gripped on to it and willed themselves to make the climb, however grounded you may be at the top. Otherwise, your feet will eventually falter, and you risk joining them below".

Ophélie rested her chin on her knees and focused on the rain. In imagining herself on the allegorical precipice, she shook her head. "And sometimes, carrying the weight of others simply makes your own easier to bear".

Romain glanced aside to gather his thoughts. When he turned to face Ophélie next, there was a look in his eyes indicating that something in his disposition had changed.

In the most certain of tones, he responded: "Miss Davenport, these past weeks have taken their toll on all of us in some way. For my part, Mr Perez's arrest has forced me to question where our investigation is going, and what sacrifices it is worth.

"I have spent nearly two years plotting to clear my father's name, but ultimately, this would not make him a good man any more than an avowal from Mr Perez could bring Isabelle or Madeleine back. Perhaps the fact that the two of us know and deplore the truth is enough. Perhaps all that we can do for them is to give a regular thought to their memory, but deny their killer the power to destroy our lives as he did theirs".

Shifting herself upright again, Ophélie gazed back at him. "But could you be content with absolving Mr Perez from the blame he is due, knowing there was always more we could have done to bring about justice?"

"I am persuaded to refute whether there *is* any more we can do", Romain countered. "Public condemnation is a drop in the ocean compared with the misery with which Mr Perez must be plagued. On his deathbed, he will see them again—the people who slipped away at his command—and it shall be their arms that drag him into the darkness. No punishment could be more severe than that. If you, too, can bring yourself to draw a line in the sand, Miss Davenport, then let us wash our hands of the man, here and now".

Staring ahead at her grandfather's grave, Ophélie thought over this proposal. Accompanying each scrape of the spades, she could hear Arnaud's voice ushering her to desist from torturing herself. When the accompanying throbs in her head became unbearable, she extended a hand to Romain's and shook it. And sure enough, the instant her arm dropped back at her side, the chill enveloping Ophélie's body subsided.

Over the next few hours, Henri would take note of his niece's expression through the window each time he walked through the kitchen towards the wine cellar. He could only speculate as to what she and Romain were talking about for so long. At one point while he fetched another bottle to share with his brother, Henri thought that he saw Ophélie laughing, though, and for whatever reason, the sight caused him to smile.

It was late afternoon before Romain and Ophélie realised that the volunteers from the church had departed long ago, or that lunch had come and gone without them. They might have stayed sitting beneath that tree all evening, had it not been for Mrs Cadet scurrying down the path in a fluster around the same moment that Ophélie looked up through the branches and noticed the sky turning dark.

The housekeeper's entry came as the result of being dragooned from her bed by someone banging on the front door.

To her surprise, it was Romain's own housekeeper whom she found on the other side, imploring that he return home. The emergency that required the gentleman's assistance pertained to a window in his drawing room, which had been smashed open by a fallen branch and was letting in floods of water despite his housekeeper's attempts to block the hole in the glass.

Probably, it was just as well that Romain was pulled away when he was; he and Ophélie had barely made it back indoors when the first bolt of lightning lacerated the clouds. It was followed by a roar of thunder so deafening that the walls of Baudières shook.

By the time Romain had lifted his housekeeper onto his horse, the conditions on the road ahead of them were nothing short of biblical. From the front room, Ophélie glued herself to the window, wincing as their blurred silhouettes disappeared into the storm.

Flushed with an early fever, she eventually conceded to Mrs Cadet's demands that she have a bath to warm herself. And yet, her apprehension surrounding Romain's departure did not ease when she stepped into the tub. This niggling voice of concern continued while she dried herself before the fire in her bedroom, until it was all Ophélie could do to march down to her grandfather's library and engross herself in a book.

She was reaching for her cane when something caught her eye on the bed. In light of the day's events, it was not surprising that Ophélie had forgotten about the parcel. In consulting its contents she nevertheless foresaw a distraction, and so she tore through the packaging.

When the inklings of what lay inside became visible, her chest ceased to take in air and she let the parcel fall onto the bed. Spilling from its belly was a handful of red rose petals, scattered among the childhood drawings taken from her and Étienne's cabin. Perfectly preserved, they hid at the bottom of the pile a note on a separate piece of card, inscribed in the handwriting that her uncle had recognised from the packaging—the handwriting that, upon second inspection, Ophélie matched with the message that had been left for her on the cabin wall:

I have something of yours that I think you shall greatly want back.

Unable to feel her hands, she turned the piece of card around to find a self-portrait of a familiar-looking boy on the other side. Underneath the sketch was a number, alongside the words *G. Smolak*.

Ophélie held back a gush of vomit. Leaping from the bed, she snatched up her walking stick and hurtled towards the door.

34

The Watcher

From the far end of the corridor to the staircase, Ophélie's cries for help went unheard in the darkness. Resonating off the walls back into her ears, these hollow echoes of desperation seemed to be her conscience's way of warning her that they were alone in this fight from here onward.

The bags under Mrs Cadet's eyes that afternoon indicated that the housekeeper was already in bed on the other side of the estate. Based on the early success of Roland and Henri's drinking session, neither gentleman would be in a position to be of assistance, either. No, Ophélie's only audience now was that strangest of beasts we call the night.

Struck by the moon's rays, each passing statue came alive in shadows distorting around her as she ran, each portrait gaping down with the same ghoulish glare. Compared to the torrent of uncertainty tearing through her head, these were but the macabre phantasms that children would dream up, though, for nothing could have rendered Ophélie as delirious as the realisation that Nicolas Belmont had slipped under her radar all along.

Like the first propulsion of water through a lock, its force gave way to further questions; how and why could the professor have possessed her drawings from the cabin? Had the broken window in Romain's estate been a ruse through which Nicolas could make his way in to attack him? Romain would have returned home well over an hour ago—how much longer did he have left if Mr Belmont had been waiting for him there?

Of one thing she could be sure: that every minute represented the danger of Romain being chained up, tortured, or worse. As a result, hesitating was not an option when she reached the bottom of the stairs. With one last, unsuccessful attempt to draw the attention of Mrs Cadet and her uncles, she pulled back the door.

Lacking the protection of a coat this time, and several degrees lower in temperature, the rain greeted her like the sting of a thousand icicles plunging into her skin from the abyss above. Within minutes of joining the path around the lake, Ophélie could feel the cold, like dread, spreading through the cotton of her nightdress. Any hope of coming into contact with passers-by was crushed when her eyes scoured the fog-laden trail before her.

From the treetops to the mountains behind, the outdoor world blended into one lugubrious shade of ash-grey, and there could be no doubt that Ophélie was its sole wanderer.

One by one across the empty stretch of water, blinking lights in the windows of estates reinforced the acceptance building in her gut that nobody would be coming to her aid, yet every so often a benign eruption of lightning illuminated the path ahead. Into the mist she followed these flashes, until the gates of the Institute towered over her like gargoyles.

The padlocks wrapped around the bars of the entrance did little to bolster her courage. Habitually stationed in the driveway like a garrison, the gatekeepers were nowhere to be seen, either, nor did it appear from the eerie sight of the Institute steeped in darkness that anyone was behind its walls. Ophélie knew otherwise, though.

Scaling the length of the exterior, she followed the fence around in search of a dip in height. Twenty metres on from the main gates she found one. With the rain making the metal impossible to grip, it would be a perilous climb. Hooking her walking stick around the top of the fence, Ophélie thrust her good leg against the bars and used every muscle in her torso to pull herself up. It took an excruciating exertion of strength, but with a final push, Ophélie swung her legs over the top and thumped her body down onto the ground on the other side.

She had barely recovered from the impact before snatching up her cane and staggering down the driveway towards the entrance. By the time she started to pound on the door, a choking raspiness had seized her throat, and bruises were forming across her back.

She nearly fell to her knees in relief when Charles Moreau appeared at the threshold in his dressing-gown and slippers moments later. The professor's mouth dropped open at the sight of Ophélie drenched in a mud-soaked dress, and standing as pale as a ghost before him.

"Miss Davenport!" he cried, waving his lantern around to see if anyone was alongside her. "How on Earth did you get past the gates? And what are you doing here? Good Heavens, are you in some sort of trouble?"

Steadying herself upright against the door frame, Ophélie tried to control her panting now that she was in the presence of help. If she could have summoned the energy to throw her arms around Mr Moreau in gratitude for his being there, she would have. Instead, she timed her words between gasps for air: "Where is he?"

Struggling to make sense of her under the rumbles of thunder, Mr Moreau frowned and took a step back, weighing up what to do. With a final check that nobody was behind her, he reluctantly extended an arm to usher Ophélie out of the rain, then locked the door behind them and led her through the hallway to his study.

Placing her in the chair behind his desk, the professor poured Ophélie a glass of water and slid it across the table. "Miss Davenport, I shall need you to calm down and explain yourself. You say you are looking for someone?"

"Yes—Mr Lavarre", Ophélie blurted out, her breathing gradually returning to normal. "Please, I know you must think I have descended into utter lunacy, but Mr Belmont has him here, somewhere within these walls, Mr Moreau, I am sure of it. You have to help me find him before it is too late, I beg you".

There was an uncomfortable pause while the professor took a seat opposite her at the desk and removed his glasses. It was during this silence that Ophélie—numbed by a new wave of tension—peered around the room to take in her surroundings. Only now that her lungs could function properly did it strike her as peculiar that the ground floor of the Institute, like her own home, had been empty except Mr Moreau, or that she was being watched by rows of dead-eyed birds bearing down at her from his bookshelves.

Then, just when Ophélie felt that hair-raising alarm bell go off in her mind, the professor lent back and picked up his glasses to clean them. With a smoothness of dexterity lacking any hint of arthritis, he proceeded to remove from his pocket a white handkerchief to wipe the lenses. The sight knocked the air from Ophélie's lungs.

Lips quivering in recognition of the item, she went to scream but no sound could choke its way out. In the space of a second, the pressure in her ears built to the point that she could hear her pulse thudding like a drum within her temples, and her skin prickled under the vigour of the stare she was receiving from across the table.

With nowhere to avert her gaze than back at her host, Ophélie acquiesced, and in that one, stomach-churning look, she knew that she was staring at 'The Watcher'.

I wish I could say that her reaction was to fight, but it is naive to presume a person's instincts in the face of death. For Ophélie, the uncertainty of whether she would still be alive minutes from now caused an effect on her body similar to the waking insentience of anaesthesia.

Satisfied from her muteness that his identity—if nothing else—had been understood, the professor returned his glasses to his nose and checked his pocket watch.

"19:08", he began. "A little later than expected. No matter. Any plan must incur some room for human error".

With a sniff, he strode to the window to watch the rain, tapping his fingers gently against the sill. "I had hoped my godson's trial would already have begun by now, mind you—the result of a farcically inefficient judiciary system, at least, rather than a miscalculation on my part. Come, you must not judge my gloating, Miss Davenport; 'every bird loves to hear himself sing', do they not?"

Resisting the urge to beg for mercy, Ophélie's eyes shifted

to the door, then up to the ceiling. Her actions did not go unnoticed by the professor, who appeared to be observing her intently out of the corner of his eye.

"He is not here", were the next words to leave his mouth, spoken in a tone so spiteful that it made her flinch. "Really, you must have known that Mr Lavarre was always the problem in this equation".

Peering over his shoulder at Ophélie's face draining of colour, Mr Moreau inflicted on her the punishment of another minute of silence.

Then, with a sigh, he continued: "This was not part of the plan, Ophélie. Do you see? Everything was done as it should have been, and long did I wait for my groundwork to come to fruition. That the Smolak boy existed at all would have been nothing more than an oversight, had his fondness for you not been so apparent. But what horrified me most upon your return, Ophélie, was your own inexplicable involvement".

Swallowing to alleviate the dryness in her mouth, Ophélie dropped her gaze.

Under her breath, she insisted as assuredly as she could: "My family will come for me. Romain will come for me".

"Do not insult my intelligence, Ophélie", Mr Moreau snapped. "You, above all people, are better than that. Your aunt and cousins are in Florence on a trip to which I suggested that the Ozanamas invite them, which just leaves your uncles—far from the bright sparks your grandfather was. In any case, having witnessed Mr Lavarre spend the day in your company, I would hazard a guess that the prospect of you two eloping will not strike either gentlemen as implausible when they receive the letter I forged using your entry in my guestbook informing them so, or wake up to the sight of your bedroom vacated of all your belongings tomorrow morning.

"Of course, questions may be asked by your cousins, later, but from their sense of betrayal will come gradual acceptance. As for any others, I am confident that you dismissed your staff this weekend to give them a respite from your dreadful aunt. You will have noticed that I took the same decision upon my receipt of Mr Girard's letter. I was sure that Mrs Baudin would announce her father-in-law's death instantly, just as I suspected that Manon would switch places with you halfway through the poker tournament, and that you would so tire of receiving condolences from people who cared nothing for your grandfather that my parcel would remain unopened until this evening. You see, I know every person in this village better than they know themselves.

"Oh, and before you entertain the notion that Mr Lavarre is seconds from bounding through that door, I must inform you that I took the liberty of adding an unpleasant substance to the contents of his alcohol cabinet when I broke into his house earlier. Having learnt from the failure of my last such attempt, I was sure to increase the dose to fatal levels this time. Still, his appointment with death comes at quite a delay. I had hoped to rid us of him months ago when I handed your clumsy little cousin that shotgun during the hunting party and pointed it in Mr Lavarre's direction—but that is of no consequence. By my estimations, he will have fixed the window and be taking his evening drink as we speak. So, here we are; the end of the final chapter".

Indulging in a short interlude, the professor poured himself a glass of cognac, eyes unmoving from the window as he swirled the liquid beneath his nose. Had his back not been turned, Mr Moreau might have noticed that Ophélie's thoughts had been whirring uncontrollably over the past few minutes. Lurching forward in repugnance, her gaze shifted between the stuffed birds behind his desk and the untouched glass of water on the table as if realising something. Then, her expression went blank, and she slowly glanced up at him again.

"The nightjar", Ophélie whispered, "it was me".

"Remarkable creature", the professor replied, stroking the window pane. "An elusive, ground-nesting bird that camouflages into its background while it waits for the cloak of dusk to fall. To the unworthy masses, they pass by invisible, but not to me. I see you, Ophélie—all of you. I know what it is to question why you were cast into a world from which you derive no sense of belonging. That is why you presented yourself before my window all those years ago—why when you were sent to live with your uncle, you had but a half-life there. In solitude, you yearned for me as I did you. And then you became just like them".

"Just like them?" Ophélie croaked, timing her words to peer at the clock.

The professor shook his head. "Oh, Ophélie. How corrupted you have been. It pains me more than I can say. I believed that your gift would only strengthen while I waited for you to come of age and return to me, but I was wrong. There is no longer hope for us in this life. At last, I see our path clearly, and what must happen to rectify it".

"Allow me to prove myself", Ophélie cried as his fingers tapped the sill with increasing speed. "You want me to know that you engineered it all, and how it was done. Our investigation—everything was designed to bring me here tonight".

"That rather goes without saying", Mr Moreau muttered. "The seating plan at Mr Veaux's poker tournament? My suggestion. My godson's proposal to your cousin? The product of an engagement ring that I purchased for him. You only believed that Pierre-Alexandre was strong enough to kill because I wanted it so".

"Yes", Ophélie murmured, forcing her voice steady. "It was you moving the nurse's body that night".

"Why would I have kept her in employment all these years if not to serve a greater purpose?" Mr Moreau demanded. "And do you honestly think that my own daughter could have run away without me finding her location, or that I would be ignorant to you visiting her? Whom do you suppose wrote the letter from Florence to her nurse disclosing her address in the first place? Based on your cousin's naivety I knew that you would do anything to protect her when the time came. Your suspicion of my godson had already been sown; all I did was provide a visual aid, then refract questions regarding the gunshots or the state of the greenhouse the next morning".

As the professor said this, Ophélie's hand fell by her side, only to be met with the rough texture of wool. From what she could feel, Mr Moreau's hunting coat was draped across the back of her chair.

In recalling the last occasion she had seen it being worn—or more importantly, the contents of its right pocket—Ophélie proceeded to focus on the outline of the professor's dressing-gown. In the flickering light of his lamps, it was hard to confirm her suspicion that his respiratory condition required him to carry emergency aid on his person at all times. The bulge in his outer pocket did hint that it bore in its midst a flask and pills too, though.

With a deep breath, she added to her accolades: "You were also the person who informed my grandfather about my visits to Mèliez when I was a girl, and about my friendship with Étienne".

The professor nodded. "He had his use in the end. They both did, in fact, but it was not easy standing back and watching you leave. Such was the plan nonetheless. Such was what had to be done".

With this affirmation, Ophélie's cheeks became so hot that they burnt her hand when she went to clutch her locket. "And my mother; you supplied her with 'herbal remedies' ensuring her demise".

"She would never have understood", Mr Moreau replied, unblinking.

"But nothing was as masterful as Isabelle's disappearance", Ophélie spoke, slipping her fingers into the pocket of his coat. Once the flask inside was firmly in her hand, she elaborated: "The portrait of Kacper Smolak painted by his son was quite ingenious. You showed it to Isabelle at night, I believe, to condition her to fear the man".

"Have you ever heard of the Dutch psychologist Pieter Meulunbelt?" Mr Moreau asked, spinning around to face her. "He leveraged the prolonged stimuli of visual and aural catalysts to provoke behaviours in his patients. In one experiment, just to prove the effectiveness of his methods, he was reputed to have turned a man of the church into an assassin hell-bent on murdering his congregation. How? Through nothing but the trigger of a sound and an image".

"That was why you left me the feathers in the frame in Mr Perez's storage cupboard", Ophélie speculated. For the second time since sitting down, her eyes were drawn to the stuffed woodpecker occupying the central shelf above the desk. "It was a replica of the aural aid by which you would tap your fingers while showing Isabelle the painting".

Several seconds passed in silence, during which the professor became as rigid as the woodpecker.

Tilting his head to the side, he proceeded to hiss the words: "Much has been sacrificed in your name", then released his hands from the desk and glided over to the window.

Seizing this opportunity while his back was turned, Ophélie reached for her glass of water and used the next outbreak of thunder to discharge some of the liquid into the flask, before securing the lid and tucking it under her dress.

"You needed to 'trigger' Isabelle to run from the gardens", she continued, "and the bird's drilling was similar enough to do so. Am I correct?"

"Well, Ophélie, it is comforting to know that I was right—that a part of you, at least, has survived to adulthood and proven itself worthy", Mr Moreau muttered, keeping his eyes locked on the window. After a lengthy pause, he clenched his fists so tightly that his fingernails nearly drew blood from his palms, then slowly turned to face her. "But it will not change the outcome of tonight. In fact, it only reinforces my conviction that this cannot be delayed a moment longer. It is strange; in many ways, I envy you, Ophélie. Your beauty will forever be preserved to posterity—protected from those who would seek to destroy it".

With a final check of the clock, Ophélie gave a prolonged stint of speechlessness until the professor was forced to turn his gaze back to her. Then, loosening her body limb by limb, she began to blink for longer intervals, opening and closing her mouth sporadically.

Her apparent state of disequilibrium was greeted with a nod by Mr Moreau, and a tilt of his head towards her glass on the table—depleted in liquid from when he put it there.

Making a mental calculation, he took out his pocket watch again. "*Cerbera odollam,* otherwise referred to as *Atropa belladonna.* No doubt Florence informed you of its properties. Isabelle experienced them herself when her nurse unknowingly administered to her the medicine I had laid out that night. Rest assured that with the right dose, death can be mercifully quick. Unlike Isabelle, you are going to lose consciousness in a matter of seconds, Ophélie. But fear not, my nightjar, for the next time we see each other, it shall be on a plain far more spectacular than this prison—our home, as it was always meant to be".

Ophélie drooped down the chair and closed her eyes. Five, four, three, two, one; only the advancing plods of the professor's footsteps allowed her to gauge the distance between them. When she partially blinked again, his face was so close to hers that she could see the blood vessels branching out in the whites of his eyes.

Wrapping his arms beneath her back and legs, Mr Moreau bent down to lift her. In doing so, he failed to detect Ophélie's left hand entering the pocket of his dressing-gown to switch the flask, or the other seizing her cane from the floor.

"This is for all of them", was the last condemnation that the professor would hear her utter.

Before he could register what was happening, Ophélie rose to her feet and swung her walking stick over his head with such ferocity that her arms spasmed from the impact. While Mr Moreau clutched at his temple with gargling wails, Ophélie tore from the room, estimating that she had about a minute before the professor came to.

Remembering that the front door had been barred upon her arrival, she hurried down the hallway, rattling the handle of each room in the hopes that one would be unlocked. When that failed, Ophélie doubled back to the entrance to pick up a chair, then returned to the French windows at the far end of the corridor.

Her third attempt to break the glass left a hole big enough for her to drop the chair and continue by hand. By the time Ophélie had clawed her way out onto the terrace, the rain was falling so heavily that she could not be sure whether the liquid soaking into her sleeves was water or blood. Eyes focused on what she knew would be her only route to safety, she marched straight ahead, her leg dragging like dead weight in the mud.

A fork of lightning so close that Ophélie flinched in the aftermath soon alerted her to the silhouette of Mr Moreau entering the gardens. With only half the path to go, she clenched her cane with both hands and counted down each step out loud until the professor's private greenhouse was in sight. Gaining on her with increasing speed, he was not twenty metres behind when Ophélie flung back the door and tumbled inside.

Even in winter, the stench of rotting vegetation in the greenhouse was enough to make anyone heave. It left Ophélie in no doubt that this deterrent was intentional to prevent outsiders from coming near the specimen inside. From one row to the next, she cupped her mouth and began tipping every pot that she saw onto the ground until a thick cloud of dirt and spores had settled in the air.

She had just finished with the last table when Mr Moreau burst through the door, mouth foaming, and an enormous bruise protruding from his face.

"You ungrateful bitch!" he bellowed into the darkness. "After everything I did for you!"

Backed up against the glass, Ophélie kept perfectly still and followed the shuffling of his feet along the first row of plants. It would only take one more flash of lightning for her position to be given away, and the professor's coughs were far from violent enough to hamper his advance. Moments from being within his reach, Ophélie surrendered herself to the only remaining act in her disposition by shutting her eyes in preparation for the end.

The ensuing minute elapsed so quickly that Ophélie felt as though a foreign force had taken control of her body. First, there was a blinding explosion of light. Proceeding it came an ear-splitting boom, followed by a series of crescendoing creaks as one of the trees above the greenhouse burst into flames.

Shielding his head from the debris, Mr Moreau leapt out of the way seconds before the branches came crashing through the glass. When he turned back to face the exit, his jaw dropped, and beads of sweat formed on his forehead.

Perhaps it was the pesticide-soaked wood or the abundance of dust, but the instant that burning bark hit the ground, the greenhouse set ablaze as if someone was spewing ethanol through the roof. Within seconds, the fire had spread from the first row of tables to the door, transforming the room into a smoke-filled furnace.

With no way out now, the professor locked eyes with Ophélie and clambered towards her. Before he had taken his next step, though, another billow of fumes from behind caused him to sputter, and he fell to the ground. Plunging his hand into his dressing-gown pocket, he held back the convulsions long enough to throw two pills into his mouth. But not seconds after washing them down, the professor's movements came to an abrupt halt.

Sensing that the liquid in his flask had been tampered with, Mr Moreau examined it with a widening gape, then glanced at Ophélie with an expression of bewilderment. In one gesture, she would put an end to his speculation; inching forward until she was standing above him, she extended her arm and lifted the other flask.

Faced with this image, the professor barely flinched when the next ceiling panel caved in over his head. Letting his pillbox fall to the ground, all emotion left his face and he started to cough—so vigorously, this time, that his eyes rolled to the back of his head and hot saliva began to bubble down his chin.

Only then did Ophélie drop her arm and throw the flask into the flames behind him.

Her victory would be short-lived nevertheless; unable to keep her eyes open in the heat, she staggered to the side of the greenhouse to break the glass, but all the muscles in her body started to seize up. At this stage, the pain in her lungs was ineffable, and after a final endeavour to raise her fist, Ophélie felt herself collapsing.

She would not register the coarse soil enveloping her face when she struck the ground, or the roar of the fire ripping through the table nearest her. Floating in this semi-inanimate state, the sound of the greenhouse wall smashing faded into oblivion, as did the jolts of her body being lifted. From the darkness, Arnaud's voice emerged in her ears, and with an overwhelming aura of peace, Ophélie succumbed to the void.

35

Amends

When Ophélie opened her eyes again, pain was the only facet of consciousness she could distinguish. However much time had elapsed between her last waking memory and this one, the disorientation paled in comparison with the scorched tissue lining her lungs and throat, or the sharp throbs descending the skin on her lower arms.

Bit by bit the familiar decor of Baudières emerged from the blurriness, and Ophélie realised that she was lying in her bed. From her elbows to her wrists, thick bandages jerked her recollection of having clambered through the glass into the gardens, and from this small fragment, the rest of the image followed.

Fighting through the agony of breathing, her eyes combed the room for signs of the loved ones to whom she had returned, inciting a question to which she dreaded to consider the response: what had happened to Romain?

Having been reading in the armchair to Ophélie's left for the past hour, Adèle howled with joy when she saw her cousin's eyes open, racing to her bed with such speed that Ophélie jumped at the outburst of her voice.

"You are awake!" Adèle cried. "The doctor told us you would likely be out cold for another few days, but I knew you would pull through sooner than that".

With a wince, Ophélie's hands fumbled to grip the sheet beneath her and she hoisted herself upright, croaking: "Mr Lavarre, where is he? You must go to his estate-"

Before she could finish, her cousin interrupted her with calming shushes and propped her back against the pillow.

"There is no need, Ophélie," Adèle insisted. "His injuries are minor compared to yours. In fact, he has been by your side for the past nine days and nights, refusing to leave. Mrs Cadet and I had to send him away this morning, just to make sure that he would eat and sleep. I have never seen anyone look so worried. You can see him tomorrow when he comes back, but until then, you must try to rest".

Weightless from relief, Ophélie let her head tilt back and she gazed towards the window to gather her bearings. "Is that how long I have been lying here for—nine days?"

"Yes", Adèle murmured, placing her hand on top of her cousin's. "Do you really remember nothing from the end of that night? How you managed to get out of the greenhouse, I mean".

Ophélie glanced down at the outline of her battered limbs through the blanket. "Only the heat from the fire, and the sensation that I would never breathe again".

"Well, it is all very confusing to me, also", Adèle began, perching herself on the bed. "From what I understand, Mr Lavarre received a letter from a man named Ivan after returning home from Grand-père's funeral. If I am not mistaken, this Ivan individual had been asked to confirm, via sketches of Mr Perez and Mr Belmont, which of these men had solicited his gang for information about Mr Lavarre many years ago. Needless to say, the response in Ivan's letter was that it had been neither—that the gentleman had been older, with a more striking gaze.

"At that point, Mr Lavarre came straight to the estate and nearly broke a window to attract Mrs Cadet's attention. When he saw you missing and the note from the parcel on your bed, he rushed to the Institute to find you, following the smoke from the gardens. By some miracle, he smashed his way through the greenhouse and carried you out minutes before the fire would have reached you. Mr Moreau had already asphyxiated to death by this point. I hardly know what to make of it all, Ophélie. Word reached us in Florence two days later and we came home immediately. I suppose it is silly me asking this, but how are you feeling?"

"As though the devil has taken residence in my chest", Ophélie whispered. There was a long pause while she faced away and ran the events that Adèle had described through her brain again to make sense of them.

'Mr Moreau had already asphyxiated to death'. She had needed to hear this confirmation spoken aloud to believe that he was gone. The effect was a harmonious release that started from her toes and continued to her forehead.

Relaxing into her bed, Ophélie revelled in this acknowledgement a while longer, until the sound of sniffling alerted her attention to the unsettled conflicts that had been residing within her own home of late. Turning back to her cousin, she was met by Adèle's face brewing with an emotion Ophélie had never seen there before.

"I promised myself that I would wait, but I cannot hold it

in", Adèle gripped her cousin's hand. "Ophélie, I have been unforgivably cruel to you. How badly I behaved while Mr Perez was courting you, and how foolish I was to rebuff your attempts to protect me on the night of my engagement. And to think that I ignored you so coldly thereafter-".

"Please, Adèle, your tears and apologies are not necessary", Ophélie countered. "Looking back on these past months, I have a strange but comforting feeling that everything happened exactly as it should have. Now, what say we start afresh by you telling me where the others are. It cannot have been easy for them to receive the news of what happened".

"No indeed", Adèle smiled, wiping her face with the sleeve of her dress. "Maman hardly knew what to say when Mr Lavarre explained everything. She quit her Book Club and has kept to herself in the sitting room ever since. Now that I think of it, that might also have something to do with the fact that my father and uncle have been spending a lot of time together this week. Upon my father's order, the rest of Henri's belongings were sent for yesterday, so it seems as though he will be staying with us through spring at least".

"I see", Ophélie replied. "And my cousins?"

Kicking off her shoes, Adèle stretched out on the bed by Ophélie's side. "Well, Thomas has been scurrying in and out of your room incessantly since our return, so I am amazed you were not woken sooner. He is under the impression that showing you the fencing techniques he has been studying will assist your recovery. I have never seen him more focused on anything. Obviously, we filtered a lot of information when we told him that you were ill. As for Manon, you would not believe me if I divulged her whereabouts".

Ophélie timed her reply with a first, excruciating attempt

to clear her throat. "Try me".

"Well, as we speak, my sister is getting ready to go to lunch with Alessio Lettiere", Adèle whispered, wary that Manon's bedroom was within earshot of Ophélie's. "Do not ask me what changed in her opinion of him; we can both attest that Manon has only ever greeted Mr Lettiere with censure. He has been most supportive these past few days, though, bringing flowers and food hampers to the estate when the other villagers stayed away. Maybe that is why she took a chance on the poor soul. In any case, she will be back to check on you this afternoon, just do not tell her what I told you!"

Reminded of Adèle's own romantic predicament, Ophélie's smile faded. "Mr Perez? His trial-"

"Ended, before it even began", Adèle cut in. "Once again, we have Mr Lavarre to thank for that; he came to the prison to testify against Mr Moreau as soon as he knew that you were safe. The police proceeded to raid the Institute and discovered a stash of the professor's notebooks in an upper floor classroom. Thankfully, their team was able to decipher the most important parts using Grand-père's notes. The bird hieroglyphs were easy to attribute once the whole story was out.

"It was all there, Ophélie—the entire atrocious saga. I read the confessions about your mother, Mr Moreau's maids, then Isabelle and the farm girl—how he attempted to mould them into your image, and what he planned to do with you that night. I understand why you kept everything from us, Ophélie, but it turns my stomach to think that this was going on for so long in secret. Mr Perez has been beside himself coming to terms with it all".

"Where is the gentleman? I must speak to him", Ophélie

urged, straining to pull herself off the bed.

Her movements were halted by the sound of someone stirring from their seat in the corridor. A moment later, she glanced up to find Pierre-Alexandre Perez peeking around the door frame with his hat in his hands.

Days after being released from his cell, the lines under his eyes and the stubble on his haggard face were still those of a prisoner, but behind his unkempt exterior, there was a softness in the gentleman's expression now.

"I thought you might say that", Adèle replied, beckoning Mr Perez in. "Ophélie, I would like to introduce you to the new Head of the Institute—official as of yesterday. He has been keeping me company while I sat with you. We were not sure when you would wake up, but he insisted on staying outside so as not to startle you".

Planting a kiss on Mr Perez's cheek, Adèle left the room. At first, her departure set an uneasy tone from which Ophélie regretted requesting an audience with the gentleman so soon. Watching him shuffle towards the armchair, though, she reasoned that this would be as painless a context as any to come face-to-face with him again.

In the ensuing silence, Mr Perez stared nervously at her from across the room, searching for a way to break the tension.

"It would seem we have both been pawns in Charles' game, Miss Davenport", he began. "Personally, I am ashamed for having been so blind. My godfather was always my greatest role model—the man I respected above all others and aspired to be myself one day. I have lost more nights' sleep than I care to count wondering how he could have deceived me so, or carried out such unspeakable acts under my nose".

"Mr Perez", Ophélie interjected, "let us not speak of accountability. I am as much to blame as you are in that respect, lest you forget that it was through my doing that you found your way behind bars in the first place".

"Yes, well I can certainly see why I gave you reason to doubt me", Mr Perez muttered, dropping his eyes to the ground. "I am not a confident man by design, Miss Davenport. When your family arrived here, I admit I was drawn to you after Charles pointed you out at the Rinaldis' ball. His opinion mattered greatly to me, you see.

"Before I knew it, I was being groomed to impress you—being fed lies that you bore affection for me even when I had convinced myself otherwise. As a result, I was thrown off when my godfather backtracked months later, observing that your interests did indeed lie elsewhere. In doing so, he suggested that I consider your cousin, though, for which I am eternally grateful to him. The more I spent time with Adèle, the brighter the world became. I never had to pretend I was anyone else in her presence, and suffice to say, I fell for her instantly".

Ophélie nodded and gazed down at the bed, rolling the fold of the sheet around in her fingers. "I am sorry for not believing that your sentiments for Adèle were sincere. I did you both an injustice through my scepticism".

"If I may, Miss Davenport, I propose that we cease apologising to one another. Now is the time for making amends", Mr Perez responded, shifting forward in his seat. "Yesterday morning I sent a letter to the Lacroix family in Saint-Laurent informing them of the truth about Madeleine's death. I might not be able to bring her back, but I can, and have ensured that their farm receives the funding that it requires every year hereafter. My intention is to replicate this for each of the families of our staff whose lives my godfather took.

"Next, we come to Kacper Smolak. As well as issuing a public statement revoking his crime, I took the liberty of soliciting the opinion of Mr Lavarre, as his son, regarding how the Institute might atone for Mr Moreau's actions. His proposition was for us to lead a village-wide campaign ending the boycotting of services from the people of Mèliez. I would like to go a step further by adding, to this, the creation of an annual subsidy for Mr Smolak's village, to allow for the restoration of its homes and provision of educational opportunities for its youth. As for your mother, Miss Davenport, I am sorry to say that I find myself at a loss for restitution".

By the time it was Ophélie's turn to talk again, she was unsure of what was more surprising—the extent to which she had misjudged Mr Perez's character, or how quickly she felt herself warming to the gentleman.

"I am afraid that in my mother's case there is nothing to be done", she eventually replied, reaching for the locket around her neck. "My father's death was the predominant factor that led to hers. The two of them are together now, which is as happy a conclusion as I could hope for. What, may I ask, are your intentions for the Moreau girls?"

Flustered by this question, Mr Perez rose and crossed to the window. "Well, I am sure you can appreciate why I feel a strong familial obligation to do right by both of them. My relationship with Florence has been tumultuous in the past, due to my godfather's tremendous pressure on me to marry her. He is not the only one to be chided though—I am appalled by how I treated Florence after she rejected my proposal. My pride got the better of me, thus I went to every length to prevent this information from becoming public. In any case, I do have one idea regarding how I might personally redress the issue with Miss Moreau.

"There is an opening among my teaching staff following the departure of our venerable Nicolas Belmont, who just yesterday announced his decision to leave the 'maddening noise' of society behind for a monastic life in the mountains. Certain individuals are simply not engineered to co-exist with others, it would seem. While I wish the gentleman well in his quest for nirvana, it is my greater hope that Florence will consider accepting this position in his place. That just leaves Isabelle herself. Once again, I should be grateful for your suggestions in this matter".

Ophélie paused. "A simple, honest tribute, perhaps. Make of Isabelle's remembrance ceremony a communal service, to which the people of Mèliez and Saint-Laurent might also be welcomed. That is what I would do".

"Then it shall be done", Mr Perez declared. "Now, I should not wish to leave you on such a sombre note this morning, Miss Davenport. Before my arrest, I was one day away from marrying your cousin. I know that your judgment in all topics is of great importance to her, therefore pending your approval, I would very much like to resume our wedding arrangements and bring some much-needed merriment back to the Institute".

"Nothing would make me happier", Ophélie confirmed.

Detecting that her energy was dwindling, Mr Perez bowed his head and went to join Adèle, leaving Ophélie to fall into what would be the deepest sleep of her life.

When she awoke at midday to the clunks of Mrs Cadet's trolley being wheeled down the corridor, the morning's revelations felt so remote to her that Ophélie was forced to revisit her discussions with Adèle and Mr Perez in her head for fear that she had been dreaming.

Hit with a wave of restlessness in the process, the idea of spending another minute bed-bound while she waited for Romain to return felt unbearable. Straightening her back upon Mrs Cadet's arrival, Ophélie put on her most resilient front as she requested permission to take some fresh air in the garden before nightfall.

'Over my dead body' was the housekeeper's response while she discharged her trolley in the doorway. Before Ophélie could assert that she was feeling better, Mrs Cadet repeated the instructions she had been given by the doctor, then laid down a tray of lunch beside her patient and set about cleaning the room.

Since protesting would be futile, Ophélie turned to the bowl of soup doing its best to tempt her from the bedside table. Only then did she notice the finger-sized figurine hidden behind it.

Carved from wood, it bore an unmistakable resemblance to the ones that Ophélie had found under the sycamore tree in Mèliez when she was a girl. Her hands began to tremble as she set down the bowl and lifted the item.

A monk's robes, chubby cheeks, a cross clutched between his hands; this had to be a depiction of Friar John of the Funnels and Gobbets from *Gargantua and Pantagruel*—the final character missing from her collection.

A quick inventory of its counterparts in the drawer of her bedside table confirmed her theory, spurring Ophélie to ask: "Where did this come from?"

"Oh, that old thing", the housekeeper tutted. "Mr Lavarre

left it there for you. Hideous little creature. I did warn him that jewellery or flowers would have been a better recovery gift for you, but no—he insisted".

When Mrs Cadet turned back around, the sight of tears forming in Ophélie's eyes was enough to cause the housekeeper a guilt-induced panic attack. Scarlet blotches entered her cheeks, and she dashed over to the bed.

"Perhaps 'hideous' was the wrong word", she stammered. "All I meant was that it is an indecorous present for a gentleman with Mr Lavarre's wealth to offer a young lady, which I am sure you can appreciate. I mean, Heavens, the amount that his estate will fetch for when he comes to sell it next month should warrant nothing less than diamonds! Goodness, I fear I am not making this any better".

In her speechlessness, it took Ophélie a minute to register the latter half of Mrs Cadet's response.

Dropping her hand, she turned to verify that she had heard the housekeeper correctly: "Mr Lavarre is selling his estate?"

"Well, if the natterings of the other villagers are to be trusted. Something about leaving on a missionary ship", the housekeeper answered, conscious from the expression on Ophélie's face that she may have said too much already. "It is nothing for you to worry about, though. Eat up, and get some more sleep".

Ophélie set the figurine back down. "Mrs Cadet, I need you to prepare a boat for me first thing tomorrow morning".

"I told you", Mr Cadet countered, "you will not be well enough to leave the house for another week".

"I can assure you that I have never been more ready or more able to make this journey", Ophélie maintained, "and there is somewhere extremely important that I need to be".

36

The First Day of Spring

Spring may not have been due for another two weeks, but when Ophélie entered the garden at sunrise, she was heartened to discover that winter had already passed on. The clouds hugging the Alps were so prismatic beneath the coral explosions of light that they were indistinguishable from the mountains, and the layer of frost that had been clinging to the grass must have melted at some point while Ophélie was unconscious.

In adherence to Mrs Cadet's rules, she secured her scarf and started down the path, watching the grasshoppers bound to life beneath her feet. At the front of the estate, the family's ferryman awaited her, but there were two people whom Ophélie had wished to visit before embarking. Leaning heavily on her cane, she waited until she was standing opposite her mother and grandfather's graves, then lowered herself to her knees.

Having stationed herself at the kitchen window, Mrs Cadet supervised Ophélie's movements with a narrowing squint. Despite her best efforts, she could find no reason to order her patient back to bed; almost as quickly as Ophélie had bent down, she pushed herself to her feet and began her return, displaying no hint of infirmity. On the contrary, the warmth of her expression caused the housekeeper to clear her throat and glance away.

When Mrs Cadet's face came into focus again, it was clear to Ophélie that she had been crying. No words were exchanged between them while the housekeeper led her out to the lake, but Mrs Cadet's head remained tilted to the ground right up to the water's edge. Upon the sound of Ophélie whispering something to her from the boat, the housekeeper finally allowed herself to peer up. And lifting a shaky hand to wave, Mrs Cadet's mouth broke into a smile so profound that she felt it throughout her body.

Once the boat was far enough away, Ophélie turned to the horizon. Between the gaggle of geese soaring above her and the empty stretch of water ahead, she had never seen the lake through such an ethereal lens. In the distance, Ophélie's venture was accompanied by boats from surrounding villages, but not a door or shutter in Aixelles was stirring.

When she neared her destination, confirmation that one gentleman in the village would be awake presented itself in the form of newly built furniture strewn upon Romain's terrace. With a grateful nod to her ferryman, Ophélie disembarked onto the marina and dodged the various chairs and bowls cluttering the wood as she came to the house.

Despite the damp sheets airing on the railing and the fact that the front door was ajar, there was no sign of Romain's housekeeper when Ophélie peeked through the frosted glass panels into the hallway. After three rounds of knocking and no response from within, she pushed the door back and stepped inside.

Whatever expectations Ophélie had built for herself regarding the interior of Romain's home, the ensuing wonder on her face indicated that reality more than surpassed them.

Along the corridor for almost thirty metres, the walls were sheathed with rows of staggered paintings. Images of Ophélie reading to Étienne under the sycamore tree, the two of them playing hide-and-seek with the other village children, Romain walking unseen through the marketplace; each canvas was so rife with emotion that it imbued Ophélie's senses like a liquid, relishing in being seen by an alien set of eyes.

By the time Ophélie reached the end of the hallway, she had ceased attempting to wipe the tears off her cheeks. Detecting a cool breeze blasting in from somewhere, she pursued the flutter of the wind into the drawing room, where the waves of paintings on the walls continued like the ocean swell.

Through the simplistic composition and dramatic colours of his decor, Romain's presence was manifest everywhere Ophélie looked, even though the gentleman himself appeared not to be; atop his desk, uneven sticks of incense leaked smoke into the air in rolling, transparent threads, the ink was still wet on the quill with which Romain had answered his post, and the embers in his fireplace smouldered with the sporadic inhalations of the chimney. Then, in following the canvases past handmade music boxes and clay pots perched on shelves, Ophélie's curiosity brought her to the desk.

As she skimmed the envelopes scattered across the mahogany, the smile on her face was replaced by an ache in her chest; lying before her was a letter offering Romain a place on the next humanitarian ship leaving from Marseille.

Gripping the top of her cane, Ophélie turned to rejoin the hallway, but the faint sound of movement from the garden drew her towards the back door. Despite the tension mounting in her stomach as she approached the threshold, it was there that she would be met with the most breath-taking view of all: a bizarre, shed-like refuge, around which wooden sculptures were positioned on the grass like spectators at a theatre.

At the centre stood their creator himself. Back turned, sleeves rolled up to his elbows, he was working on a painting depicting a child looking up through the branches of a tree from the ground. When he eventually pivoted to discover Ophélie standing behind him, it was clear from the ferocity in his eyes that Romain was on the cusp of another frenetic episode, yet he would never be so perfect to her as then. Fewer examples, in fact, could you cite of one look between two people signifying everything that they felt for each other.

In the long stint of silence that followed, Romain set down his paintbrush and palette, then slowly stepped away from the canvas.

"Miss Davenport", he began, "I was just about to leave for Baudières. I have been under strict orders to rest by your cousin and housekeeper, which as you can see, I have been hopelessly unable to respect".

"Yes, I thought as much", Ophélie replied, edging closer. "I was half expecting to see the property empty after what Mrs Cadet told me. Is it true—that you are intending to sell your estate?"

Romain smiled. "It would seem that our lawyers themselves are unable to keep a secret in this village, even when their information is based on a mere enquiry. The possibility of someone purchasing my estate has been extended to me, yes, but nothing about my future here or anywhere else is certain yet".

Ophélie nodded and faced away. "When I saw your portrait in the parcel that night, I was more scared than I knew myself capable of. I thought you were dead, but as I understand it, I have you to thank for saving my life".

"You saved mine a long time ago, Miss Davenport", Romain replied, "so I believe this makes us even".

"The name on your portrait—G. Smolak", Ophélie continued. "May I ask what the former initial stands for?"

Before she had finished speaking, Romain strode forward until they were standing apart with not a metre between them. "Grzegorz, Miss Davenport—my birth name. I suppose there is no need to hide it anymore".

Glancing into his expression from that proximity, Ophélie's pulse accelerated to such a speed that she felt faint.

With a deep breath, she brought the figurine out of her pocket: "It was you, all along".

Grzegorz lowered his head and took a final step towards her. "Did I not promise in Florence Moreau's farm that I would tell you what I returned to Aixelles for, one day?"

While she formulated her next question, Ophélie kept her gaze to the ground, afraid that if she continued to look the gentleman in the eye, she would break into tears. "Will you really leave the village?"

"Well, that depends on you, Miss Davenport, and whether you wish to come with me", Grzegorz responded, lifting her chin. "Ophélie, I think you know by now that my path in life is, and always will be, wholly inseparable from your own. I would never seek to impose my interests or aspirations on you. Wherever you choose to go I will follow, if you will have me. As long as there is blood pumping through my heart, it is yours".

In all her existence, Ophélie would never know a sentiment as profound as the joy she felt in that moment. Since no words could do justice to Grzegorz's declaration—or indeed the earnestness of her own affection—she threw her arms around him and kissed him.

I cannot say how long they stayed in that embrace, for as you are aware, the passage of time often feels subjective. I am quite certain, though, that if what they say about karma is true, then Ophélie Davenport and Grzegorz Smolak were handed theirs there and then.

* * *

The Mediterranean Sea, one month later.

It is no secret that beyond the period of familial cohabitation, the number of times you will see your loved ones again drastically reduces. Parting from them for any duration becomes more difficult as a result, and it was for this reason that Ophélie and Grzegorz supplemented their spoken goodbyes with individual letters. These were dispatched on the same day that the pair boarded the missionary ship, taking with them from Aixelles only a trunk each, and Dante, Arnaud's faithful companion. Three letters, I believe, were particularly noteworthy.

The first was sent by Grzegorz to Francesca Bosco, who opened it in her nightie while heating the stove for her grandchildren's bath. There was a high-pitched clang as a set of bronze keys fell from the envelope, proceeded by a yelp so hysterical that it caused all six grandchildren to run into the kitchen at once. 'The Banshee'—or, as she would be known thereafter, the legal owner of Grzegorz Smolak's estate—thought that she might faint.

As was to be expected, the gentleman received a plethora of interest from potential buyers in the days leading to his departure. In his eyes, there had been only one person deserving of his home, though. As Mrs Bosco read these words and pulled out the deed to her new property, her hands began to shake so violently that she dropped the envelope. Extending her arm as if lifting a rock from a snake, 'The Banshee' bent down to pick it up again, scanned everything twice, then pulled her grandchildren towards her.

The following afternoon, a second letter was marched into Eduard de Corbiac's hall while he addressed the Residents' Council for the first time since 'the night of the greenhouse fire'. The room awaited its contents with bated breath as the gentleman removed from Grzegorz's envelope the blue notebook once belonging to Kacper Smolak.

Dumbstruck, he proceeded to glance up at the rows of crimson faces before him. Their combination of gasps and silence suggested that half of the villagers recalled the artefact from their personal dealings with 'The Polack', while the other half were probably able to work out what the item was based on these reactions.

The third letter with which I will leave you was an atypical one. Not only had its recipient, Étienne Sourdois, been dead for a decade, but the manner in which it was sent differed from the rest.

Months after Ophélie tossed her final farewell to him into the waves, the bottle made its way back to the shores of southern France where it was picked up by a nun walking along the beach. She was so moved by the message inside that the nun took it to the little chapel where she had grown up in Vaucluse and nailed it to the wall. It has remained there ever since, lifting the spirits of wanderers who pass before it.

For the curious or sharp of memory among you, Ophélie's letter can be found in the preface of my book. Or, at least, this is my theory regarding where that wonderful old message in the bottle came from. As for your own interpretation, like any attempt to make sense of the peculiar creatures we call humans, I leave that to you.

Printed in Great Britain
by Amazon